FROM THORNS

For Andrea,

Alie Cardet

Alison ♡

◆ FriesenPress

One Printers Way
Altona, MB R0G 0B0
Canada

www.friesenpress.com

Copyright © 2022 by Alie Cardet
First Edition — 2022

All rights reserved.

No part of this publication may be reproduced in any form, or by any means, electronic or mechanical, including photocopying, recording, or any information browsing, storage, or retrieval system, without permission in writing from FriesenPress.

ISBN
978-1-03-913864-3 (Hardcover)
978-1-03-913863-6 (Paperback)
978-1-03-913865-0 (eBook)

1. FICTION, CONTEMPORARY WOMEN

Distributed to the trade by The Ingram Book Company

For
Clyde
and
Melissa
and
Chris

It began with a gift. No, it ended with a gift. Well, I suppose it both began and ended with that gift. It's all a matter of perspective.

It was a gift intended to communicate love but instead, spoke of pain. Again, perspective. For him, it likely expressed love, but for her it reflected misery. The truth was buried in so much suffering, she didn't know how to find it. The gift led the way and opened a door. Finally, she could see some light, some truth, the possibility of freedom.

Although the truth held promise, it also revealed something frightening. Rejection and heartache were all she understood. All she was truly comfortable with. If she wanted to leave this grief behind, she would have to learn to live in a place without hurt.

Was it just a hopeless dream? Would she move from this agonizing place only to end up somewhere even worse? Was she delusional? That's essentially what he had told her—that she chased dreams and ideals and was completely out of touch with reality. Some told her she was lucky to have the life she had. But there were others who understood. And that understanding gave her hope.

She couldn't continue living a life that was destroying her. But if she didn't know the route to a better place, if she couldn't find a roadmap, then she would remain lost. Terrifying as it was

From Thorns

to take the risk, she had to try.

So, the journey began. She didn't know where it would take her. She was afraid she didn't have the strength she would need. But she was tenacious, and she would rather fight than surrender. Giving up meant death to her soul. Surely God intended for her to confront, to rise above, to be all that He created her to be, not to give in to a life of despair.

There was failure along the way. Times of wanting to give up. It was harder than she had anticipated. But once the voyage started, there was no turning back.

PART 1

CHAPTER 1

She stumbled back, tasting blood. Her father, reeking of alcohol, yanked her sweater and slapped her again, harder. She flew into the counter. He punched her. "You disgust me," he said as she sank to the floor, her vision blurring. He kicked her in the gut and the room faded.

When she awoke, Amy staggered to the bathroom and cleaned the blood from her nose and lip. Leaning into the wall, she made her way back to the kitchen, wrapped ice in a cloth, and held it gently to her eye and cheek. Hope melted with the ice. Such foolish hope.

It was too quiet. Where was he?

In her room, she lowered herself onto the bed tenderly rubbing her belly. "Hey little one, it's gonna be okay. Nothing bad can happen to you." She knew she had to leave but to go where?

When she stood, she gripped the windowsill until the room stopped spinning. She shoved as much as she could into a backpack, cramming in her ancient, worn teddy bear before zipping it closed. After carefully shouldering the bag, she pulled the quilt and pillow from her bed, intensifying the pounding in her head.

On her way past the living room, Amy saw her father in that

From Thorns

chair no one else was allowed to use, staring with that typical smug look.

Where's Mother? she wondered. Did he beat her after he finished with me? Well this time she deserved it—how could she just sit and watch?

Amy left through the backdoor. The full moon hung low in a clear sky. She paused where the dog was buried. "Goodbye, Mutt. I guess I should be grateful I'm not in there with you."

Three blocks to the park felt like three miles. She moved as quickly as she could, trying to ignore the throbbing while struggling to manage the awkward bundle of bedding.

She sank to her knees behind a cluster of bushes, pain shooting into her hip. "Ow, ow, ow!" As the pain dissipated, she folded the quilt into a makeshift sleeping bag but, suffocating in fear, she couldn't sleep.

Did he hurt my baby when he punched me? I can't go to the hospital like this. They'd call the police. They might even call *him*. Who knows where I'd end up? If the baby's not all right, I'll just die. But how can I keep it without a place to live? Without money? Maybe I should have an abortion like Tommy said. But I *want* this baby and it's *my* decision, not his.

She curled into a ball and sobbed.

Why did I think my mother would care? I'm so stupid; I should've known this would happen.

I have to find help. But where?

A church?

Not a chance.

Aunt Colleen?

No. She would call Mother.

The library to use a computer?

But then I'd have to take a bus to who knows where. No—too many people would see me.

I know there's programs for girls like me. Why didn't I pay attention in class?

After drifting into a fretful sleep, she awoke abruptly to the sound of someone yelling her name. She listened, frozen. But only the breeze whispered in the darkness.

She pushed the quilt aside and crawled out hoping to relieve the stiffening. Shivering, she rubbed her arms.

"Ow! Oh, this isn't good," she said into the night air.

After rubbing her back, gently stretching, and then walking for a bit, exhaustion pulled her back to the improvised bed.

She thought about her father. Was it my fault? Did I explain it wrong? Did I pick the wrong time?

Although she eventually floated back to sleep, pain woke her repeatedly. Each time she hoped a solution would magically appear.

It never did.

When the sun glanced over the horizon, her time was up.

This is so unfair. What am I gonna do?

I *won't* get an abortion! No one can make me!

Why didn't I bring the Advil?

Leaving the bedding behind, Amy hobbled to Tim Hortons where the washroom mirror told an ugly story.

After dropping the backpack, she gingerly pulled off her sweatshirt, rinsed her face, and held her head under the faucet. The water ran a dark, muddy red.

I probably need stitches. Yeah right, like I have time for that!

She towelled her hair with the sweatshirt before combing

From Thorns

through the knots. Ouch, ouch, ouch. Cursing, she struggled back into the damp sweatshirt.

Leaving the washroom, she collided with one of her classmates. Kate flinched. "Oh my gosh, what happened?"

"Nothing." Amy brushed past her.

Outside, pain shot through her hip as she lowered herself to the curb. Tears dribbled down her cheeks.

What now?

Kate and her friends, so pretty and perfect, emerged with their coffees. Kate broke away and walked toward Amy.

Just what I need, Amy thought. Why can't she mind her own business?

"D'ya need a doctor?"

"No, I'm fine."

Kate snorted. "It's pretty obvious you're not."

"You wouldn't understand."

"Maybe not but, like, I might be able to help."

"I'm pregnant. Happy now?"

"Who beat you up?"

Amy sighed. "What do *you* care?"

Kate's jaw clenched. "What's your problem?"

"Seriously?"

"If you can get over yourself," Kate said, "I might be able to help. Two years ago, a girl stayed with us until she had her baby. My family knows about this stuff."

Amy stared. "I'm sorry, it's just, well, you're a cheerleader and . . . I dunno" She looked away. "Sorry. So where should I go for help?"

"My house. Right now."

"Um, no, I just need information."

As if I'm going to the Raynors' house. Get real. It's probably a mansion filled with rich snobs.

"My mom will know what to do," Kate said. "If you want help, you better come with me. Do you want me to carry your backpack?"

"No, I'm good."

Amy limped to Kate's, wondering where along the way she'd lost her mind.

"Rumble! Sit!"

The dog danced in the foyer as Kate's mother approached. "No school today?"

After introductions, Kate explained why they'd come.

"It's nice to meet you," Kate's mother said. "Please call me Marge."

Amy saw gentle eyes, not hard and hateful like her own mother's.

"Would you like something to eat?" Marge asked as they moved to the living room. "I made muffins for breakfast. I think they're still warm."

The sweet scent roused Amy's hunger but she hadn't come for food. "No, thank you."

"You're hurt. Should I call the someone . . ."

"Oh no, I'm just clumsy." Amy said, feeling her face flush.

Marge nodded. "I'm kind of accident-prone myself."

"My parents won't let me stay at home anymore. Kate said you might be able to help me find somewhere to live."

"I'll look into it. Will you stay with us while I make some calls?"

"You mean for the morning?"

From Thorns

"Well, yes, for the day. And you're welcome to spend the night. We have a spare room."

Wide-eyed, Amy froze.

"I'll see what I can find out," Marge said, "but if we don't have anything organized by the end of the day, you're welcome to stay."

Amy shook her head. "I won't need to stay overnight."

Kate looked puzzled. "You might as well. You just said you can't go home—"

"It's up to you," Marge interrupted. "Just know there's a room available. Now, I'd better let the school know you girls will be taking the day off."

Amy jumped from the couch, wincing. "No! They'll call my house. My parents can't know where I am."

Marge held up both hands. "Sorry. I would never have suggested that if I knew it put you at risk. I won't tell anyone you're here."

These people were too nice. Way too nice! She would be an imbecile to trust them.

"Kate, how about you show Amy the guest room?"

The girls went down a set of stairs into a spacious room where sunlight poured through a long window above a couch. Kate opened the door to a palatial bedroom.

This had to be a mistake. Amy expected a musty room with decrepit furniture. "This is a spare room?"

"Yeah. This is where Georgia stayed until her baby was born."

"Is everything all right?" Marge asked on her way down the stairs.

"You don't know anything about me. Why would you let me stay?"

Kate laughed. "Maybe we aren't close friends, but I know you. My mom knows I wouldn't bring home a serial killer." She looked toward her mother, grinning.

With a frown, Marge suggested Kate return to school. Then, "Take a shower if you'd like, Amy, and c'mon up when you're ready. Towels are in the cupboard." Marge ushered Kate up the stairs.

Alone, Amy sank onto a loveseat. Rubbing her belly she whispered, "You better be alive in there. You and me, we're gonna look after each other."

She wondered if, maybe, just maybe, she could trust Kate and her mother. But she'd been burned too many times, so she resigned to feigning trust. She would rest in the bedroom, upright to stay awake, the door open so she could hear everything. If she had to stay the night, she would sleep in the rec room on the floor behind the couch. If they ratted her out and the cops came, they'd find an empty bedroom and she could sneak out.

CHAPTER 2

"Her face is bruised and swollen," Marge said to her husband. "Someone beat her."

"We can't rescue every hurting soul. After Georgia, we agreed no more. Please, look into shelters."

"But—"

"Listen, Marge, she's not staying with us."

Maybe I shouldn't have called Steve at work.

After a tense dinner, with Steve stony silent and eleven-year-old Jason uncharacteristically quiet, Marge retreated to the rec room. She wanted Amy to stay, even for a few days, so she could assess the girl's emotional health. A shelter would offer support, but would it be enough? She had to find a way to convince Steve.

When she heard muffled voices, Marge pressed her ear against the door of Amy's room.

Why is Kate in there? she wondered as she knocked.

"Go away, Jason."

"It's Mom."

The door flew open. "Hey Mom, what's up?"

"I thought everyone was doing homework."

"I'm just making sure Amy knows our dinners aren't normally that quiet. If she's gonna stay with us, she'll have to get used to Jason being an idiot most of the time." Kate grinned at Amy.

Amy stared blankly at Marge.

"All right." Marge backed out of the room. She found the remote under the couch and clicked on the news.

When Kate emerged, Marge followed her.

"What? You're spying on me now?"

"I need to speak with you."

"What did I do?"

In Kate's room, Marge asked about the girls' relationship.

"I already told you, she's in one of my classes."

"Okay, so she's not a friend. That's good because she won't be staying with us."

"*What?* Why not?"

"After Georgia moved out, your father and I agreed we wouldn't do that again."

"But I told her we would help. How are we helping by kicking her out? She's really scared you know."

"She'll get support at a shelter."

"No!" Kate shouted. "How are we showing love if we're not willing to look after her? She came to me and I *promised* we would help. We *can't* kick her out. Please don't make a decision without talking to me first." She shook her head. "I'm really disappointed in you."

Marge grimaced as she left the room.

Good grief. *I'm disappointed in you.* Give me a break!

She found her husband. "Our daughter wants Amy to stay."

From Thorns

"She's not in charge. And Marge, I think there's more going on here than you want to admit. You can't let your guilt spill out onto—"

"Stop! That's not fair."

Marge closed the door with a little too much force.

***

Why would they let me stay in such a beautiful room? Amy thought as she studied her surroundings. I wonder what Kate's room looks like. Do all rich kids have big rooms like this?

She ran her hand over the duvet, admiring the various shades of blue swirling into and around each other. Small white and blue pillows leaned against a white headboard. A long shallow window covered by curtains made from the same white fabric as the pillows hung above the bed. She wanted to peek through the curtains but she would have to stand on the bed and what if someone came into the room? Blue candles set on glass holders decorated the top of a white dresser, and a small desk held a lamp and a framed photo. She reached for the photo. It was old. Probably a family picture from long ago. After putting it back, she headed for the pale blue loveseat. Decorated with white cushions, it sat against a wall with a large colourful painting hanging above.

Making sure she didn't disturb the pillows as she sat, Amy's mind wandered through the day. She had fallen asleep in the morning. But exactly when? And for how long? Despite her anxious tummy, she'd devoured the sandwich Marge brought to the room. And later, when Marge said she needed more time to find additional information, Amy agreed to stay the night.

But why was it taking so long to get information? And what did Marge tell Steve? He didn't seem too happy at dinner. Was he mean like her own father?

What would happen tomorrow? How could she return to school with her face a mess?

Why bother? School's a waste of time.

Rumble, some kind of terrier mix with the cutest face, had stayed behind when Kate left. As Amy ran her hand over his head and down his back, she remembered the morning she couldn't wake Mutt, her childhood dog. Her mother cursed while digging a shallow grave. As Amy dragged the carcass across the lawn Mother growled, "Stop crying." She shoved Amy out of the way and completed the job herself. Later, her father raged, "You dug a grave? You're so stupid. All you had to do was put it in the garbage."

Amy hugged Rumble too tight and he ran to the door, scratching and whining. "Please stay," she said on her way to freeing him.

She wished someone could open a door and free her.

What happens now? Should I go upstairs to say goodnight? Or thank you?

"I think we should stay in the room," she whispered to her baby. "Oh man, I'm so scared. What's gonna happen to us?"

When her eyes grew heavy, she walked to the bottom of the stairs. Voices. She couldn't move behind the couch yet so she cozied into bed, enjoying the luxurious feel.

I'll move when everyone's asleep.

I hope the dog comes back.

From Thorns

The clock shone 6:37.

Where am I? Amy wondered.

Oh no!

It took a few moments to realize she'd made it safely through the night.

After changing out of yesterday's clothes she headed to the kitchen, dreading having to face anyone. Marge and Steve looked up from the table.

Fiddling with her fingers Amy said, "Thank you for letting me stay last night."

"You're welcome," Steve said. "We've found places that can help you. We'll talk about it this evening."

"Okay. Thank you." She turned to go. "I better get ready for school."

Back in her room, she collapsed. Why had she listened to Kate? Of course they didn't want her to stay. Anyway, she didn't want to! She reached for a pillow to muffle her sobs as a spark of fear ignited a blaze that consumed all hope falsely planted by Kate.

She dragged herself to breakfast realizing she had to go to school even though she didn't want to. Otherwise Kate would tell Marge. As she nibbled on toast, Kate stuck her head into the kitchen. "C'mon upstairs. We need to get some make-up on those bruises." While working on the cover-up, Kate invited Amy to join her and her friends for lunch.

Amy couldn't imagine anything worse. Why was Kate even willing to be seen with her? Popular kids didn't associate with students like Amy. Kate's kindness made no sense. They'd never been friends.

Thinking back, Kate wasn't mean like the others. Once, after

Amy had been bullied at her locker, Kate crossed the hall to say, "Just ignore them. They're idiots." Another time, in gym class, Kate chose Amy to be on her team before any other picks. Maybe she was one of those people who was always looking for someone to help, always looking for praise. Come to think of it, Amy had noticed her helping other students in class from time to time.

I guess I'm some kind of project, Amy decided. Oh well, for now it works in my favour.

The girls walked to school together, Kate talking non-stop.

When an opportunity to break in presented itself Amy said, "You don't have to tell me, but I'm wondering what happened to that girl you helped before. What was her name? Georgia?"

"Yeah, Georgia. Someone at the church knew her family," Kate said. "The father was going to send her away. They have a different culture and being pregnant is *really* bad. But the mother wanted her to stay. When my parents found out, they offered for her to stay with us. That way her mother could visit."

"Did she keep the baby?"

"I don't know. The family wanted privacy so we never kept in touch."

The girls walked through the gate onto the school property.

"Do you want me to go to your locker with you?" Kate asked.

"I'm fine."

When she got to class, the bullies pounced. "Wearing make-up to fit in?" "Trying out for prom queen, are we?" Amy focussed on her gait, determined not to limp, ignoring the pain along with the stupid comments.

After lunch, Kate found her outside. "Why didn't you come to the cafeteria?"

From Thorns

"I figured your friends might not be comfortable with me and I'm used to eating alone."

"Well I want you to sit with me and if someone doesn't like it, they can sit by themselves. So tomorrow we're having lunch together."

"Okay."

I can't afford to get on the bad side of Kate, Amy mused, who should worry about rejection from her friends instead of where I eat lunch.

Following dinner with the family, which was more pleasant than the previous evening's, Amy went to her room to wait for Steve.

She pulled her teddy bear from her backpack and leaned into the loveseat.

Would Steve come to get her?

Or was she supposed to go upstairs to find him?

"I don't wanna go upstairs," she whispered into the air.

"But what if he comes to get me and doesn't bring Marge?"

"I don't want to be alone with him, so I better go up."

"But I'm too nervous. I'll wait."

CHAPTER 3

"**You're** so mean!" Kate sneered.

They were several minutes into what was supposed to be a simple laying-down-the-law by the parents who paid the bills.

When Jason barged in, demanding to know why everyone was yelling, Marge asked, "Could you hear what we were saying?"

Kate scowled. "What's the matter, Mom? Worried that Amy will hear us?"

"Alright, I've had it!" Steve spat. "Jumpin' Jehoshaphat!"

Kate and Jason headed for the door. "I'm sorry, Dad," Kate said. "I know it's technically your house and you and Mom make the rules. But I really believe God would want us to help her. Shouldn't I stand my ground?"

"Yes, you should stand for what you believe," Steve said. "You should also trust your parents."

"I do trust you. But this time you're wrong."

"I can't talk about this anymore," Steve said. "I'll think about your perspective, but I won't have another discussion like tonight's. Got it?"

With slumped shoulders, Kate trudged out of the room.

Marge and Steve retreated to the living room with a glass

17

From Thorns

of wine.

When seated on the couch, Steve leaned forward resting his head in his hands. "We helped Georgia through her pregnancy. Why can't that be enough?"

Marge listened patiently to his lecture about putting family first and making decisions together.

"We need to talk about Janice," he said.

"Why?" Marge's eyes narrowed. "This has nothing to do with her!"

They twirled their wine and watched like it was the most riveting thing they'd ever seen.

"I think it's driving you," Steve said. "You've never forgiven yourself and you help everyone as penance."

"That's not fair!" Marge planted her glass on the table and started toward the stairs.

"Don't storm off."

Marge stood with her back to Steve.

He sighed. "Amy should stay with us for a few days. *Only* because Kate's young and idealistic and we need to give her time to figure out that we can't move every stray into our home."

"So I don't count at all." Marge stomped up the stairs ignoring Steve's plea for her to return.

The next day, Marge asked Amy to stay until they could organize a plan. After accepting the invitation, Amy sequestered herself to the lower level. Concerned, Marge went to Amy's bedroom and poked her head through the doorway. She caught a glimpse of Amy shoving her teddy bear behind her back.

"Would you rather go to a shelter than stay with us?"

"Oh no, I'm really grateful you're letting me stay for a while.

It's just, well, I don't have any money so I don't know how I can pay rent."

"My goodness, we don't want payment."

Amy looked at the floor. "My mother said I should pay. If my parents wanted rent then I should definitely pay you."

Marge cupped her hand under Amy's chin and lifted gently. Amy jerked back with terror in her eyes.

Marge stiffened. "I'm sorry."

"I'm so sorry," Amy sputtered, "really, I'm sorry, I don't know why I reacted like that. You're such a nice person. I don't know what happened."

Marge attempted a smile. "I just want to assure you that we don't want payment. Okay?"

"Okay."

"Do you want to come upstairs and help me set the table?"

"I don't know how to do that in a proper way but I'd like to learn."

Poor girl, Marge thought. What's her story?

Amy agreed to see the family doctor. Marge booked an appointment for herself immediately afterwards.

At Marge's appointment, when Dr. Hawk learned she only wanted information about Amy, he reminded her about patient confidentiality.

"But she's withdrawn. I can help better if I have some details."

"The baby has a healthy heartbeat." Dr. Hawk stood and walked to the door.

"What about her injuries?"

The doctor raised his eyebrows and stared.

"I know, I know, patient confidentiality. I'm only asking so

From Thorns

I can provide the care she needs."

"I discussed, with my patient, the nature of her injuries and suggested she involve the authorities. She wasn't willing and, because she's sixteen years of age, it's her call. Now don't ask me anything else. And don't book an appointment following any more of Amy's."

"Sixteen? She can decide that at sixteen?"

"That's right. She doesn't need anyone's permission to withhold personal information, to notify parents, to decide where she lives, or whether she even attends school."

Marge shook her head. "I had no idea." She stared out the window for a few moments. "She's not asking about abortion, is she?"

Dr. Hawk opened the door and motioned for Marge to leave.

"How am I supposed to help her if I don't know what's going on?"

"Give her time. She'll open up but she has to feel safe and that might take longer than you'd like."

In the car, Marge asked Amy about her appointment.

"Dr. Hawk says I'm fine. He heard the baby's heartbeat. And I have to do an ultrasound. Do you know what that's like?"

Surprised at Amy's willingness to talk, Marge used the drive home to answer questions, reassure, and hopefully build some trust.

"It's going really well, don't you think?"

"I wasn't expecting it to go badly; I just didn't want to get into this again." Steve shrugged. "You want her to stay, Kate's not giving an inch, Jason likes her. She's polite and quiet. And I'm at work during the day so it doesn't affect me much. This isn't what I wanted, but I can't find a good reason to make her leave."

Marge threw her arms around Steve's neck. "Thank you." She pulled away. "Amy needs our help more than Georgia. How can I make you see it?"

"Give me some time. For now, let's tell her she can stay for the month. To give me room in case I change my mind."

CHAPTER 4

Amy felt like a burden. She worried her parents would show up. She stressed over being different. At the same time, she enjoyed the comfortable bedroom, the delicious meals, and the opportunity to watch a typical family interact. Assuming this family *was* typical . . .

One evening, Jason barged through the front door with a bloody nose yelling for someone to bring him a tissue so he could get back outside and pound the life out of the kid who had hit him.

Amy darted from the couch into her room, hid behind the door, and listened.

No yelling. Just soft voices.

She slid to the floor and released her breath.

What happened? Did they drag him upstairs for the belt? But he'd be crying, wouldn't he? Why was it so quiet?

The front door slammed, and laughter ensued. Marge and Steve were laughing!

Later, when Jason came in they asked if he and his friend had sorted things out. It took all night for Amy's initial panic to dissipate.

Jason and Kate squabbled over all kinds of things. Occasionally Steve yelled something like 'fer the lovapete you two, cut it out!' Nobody ever got hit.

Steve had a lot of funny expressions. Although he was nothing like her father, Amy felt an underlying fear. Thankfully he was at work during the day. But she overheard him talking to Marge and she knew he didn't want her to stay.

Marge and Steve talked without anger or screaming. They hugged and laughed and went for walks together.

Kate's friendly demeanour continued. She gave no signals of superiority or disapproval. Amy wondered when that would change.

There were hardly any quiet times with the constant interaction among family members. They even yelled requests and shouted answers from different rooms. On school mornings, Jason was often missing some important piece of homework despite having been told to get it ready the night before and despite having assured everyone that he had. Sometimes he couldn't find socks or his favourite shirt. And it seemed he never remembered to take his lunch without a reminder. Kate spun a different kind of chaos. Problems with her curling iron, clothes that didn't coordinate properly, and lost mascara. She was vocal about every issue.

At dinner, Kate and Jason commented on food items they didn't like. Marge repeatedly offered to let either of them prepare the meal, but she never got angry. Steve always thanked her like it was something special she had done. And Steve always said a prayer before they ate.

Amy worked at engaging, hoping her intense anxiety didn't show. If only she could come across as normal maybe she'd be

From Thorns

allowed to stay longer.

She had to get money for rent though. Maybe Marge didn't care, but Steve would.

Kate refused to drop the subject of lunch so Amy joined her and her friends.

"Kate's the head cheerleader y'know," one of the snarly girls told Amy.

"I know."

"That's the *only* reason we let you sit with us."

The girls talked about fashion, shopping, movies, parties, and the popular boys. Nothing Amy could relate to. She was glad they ignored her, although Kate continually tried to drag her into conversations.

The bullies created new harassments. "Do you seriously believe sitting at that table makes everyone think you're cool?" It was amazing how bullies could always come up with something to throw at their victims. A change in circumstance just forced them to think.

Before long, classmates began to whisper and point which gave the bullies more ammunition. "How stupid do you have to be to get pregnant?" "Ever heard of birth control?" Amy knew this was coming but, barely showing, she hadn't expected it to start so soon.

When Kate noticed the bullying, she announced her intention to report it. Amy begged her not to get involved, and she wondered if Kate was the source of the gossip.

After school, since Kate and Jason generally had activities, Amy returned to the house on her own. Marge greeted her with a snack and a desire to chat followed by instruction to go to her room to do homework. Amy complied. Marge didn't need to know that weak students don't do homework.

The time dragged. She wondered what Marge was doing, so one afternoon she took a risk and went exploring. Marge invited her to help prepare the meal. From then on, Amy joined Marge for dinner preparation.

While they worked together, Marge told funny stories. She asked questions too but never pried. She showed interest when Amy talked as if she actually cared. So different from where Amy came from. Her mother was usually in the dark kitchen with a glass of scotch beside her ashtray, cigarette smoke rising, spewing remarks like "Are you home already?"

With Marge, Amy learned she enjoyed working with food but she felt uncomfortable asking so many questions. "I'm sorry for always needing help. I never cooked before."

"Helping is part of working together. We're a team. And I'm having fun."

Really? Amy wondered. I'm sure she's just trying to be nice. It won't be long before she comes up with an excuse to get rid of me.

One afternoon when mixing cookie dough, Amy measured out too much sugar and poured it into the batter.

"Oops, we better double the recipe," Marge said.

"I'm so stupid," Amy said when the error was explained.

Marge put her arm around Amy's shoulder. "It was a simple mistake anyone could make."

"You're going to get sick of having me here making mistakes."

"Love is patient," Marge said.

What?

The family constantly said, "I love you," when someone left

From Thorns

the house, at bedtime, or when a favour was done.

One night when Amy was on her way to her room, Marge said, "I love you to the moon and back."

Jason called, "I love you to Uranus and back," followed by a crash and uproarious laughter. Peering into the kitchen, Amy saw him lying on the floor beside his toppled chair.

While swallowing a laugh she said to Marge, "Thank you. You're so kind."

"Love is kind."

Although Marge was a little weird, it didn't matter. She treated Amy nicely.

A stranger travelling in a foreign land, Amy wished she could just relax and trust. But she remained on guard, worried she might be ushered out at the next mistake or more likely, at the whim of Steve's mood.

CHAPTER 5

Amy slammed into the wall. "Ow! What the..."

"I told you to get an abortion. Did ya think I wouldn't notice?"

She pulled away. "Leave me alone!"

Tommy grabbed her arm and yanked so his face was inches from hers. "If ya have this kid I want custody. And I'll get it 'cause I got a job, pays good money, I can afford a kid. Can you?"

It took seconds for dread to seep from her pores.

"I talked to your father."

"*What?*"

"He said he'll help me go after you. He doesn't want you banging on his door looking for help. He said you're stupid to think you can take care of a baby. Abortion is so obvious; any idiot could figure it out. I guess you're lower than the average idiot."

Amy turned to run. He grabbed her arm again, twisted it, and pulled her back, his gritted teeth bared. "I'm not foolin' around. Do what you're told."

When he released her she ran home, ignoring Marge's "Hello" as she pounded down the stairs to her room where she

From Thorns

curled into a ball under the covers with her teddy bear, whom she had named 'Bear.'

She heard Marge's voice. "What happened?"

Through sobs Amy said, "I have to get an abortion."

"What did you say?"

Amy pulled the covers off her face. "Tommy," she released a wail, "Tommy told me he's been talking to my father and they're gonna get custody of my baby." She resumed sobbing.

"Tommy? The baby's father?"

Amy nodded.

"Give me a break!" Marge said. "There's no way. Try to calm down. We'll talk with Steve after dinner."

For the rest of the afternoon Amy fretted. What if...? What if...? What if...?

At dinner while Jason yattered on, Kate leaned into Amy and asked, "What's wrong?"

"Tell ya later."

Following the meal, Amy joined Steve and Marge in the living room. Steve assured her that no court would grant custody to a birth father when the mother is properly caring for her child. "Anyway, he's a high school student. He couldn't possibly support himself and a child."

"He's graduating. I guess he's already got a job," Amy said. "What if he really does have enough money?"

"He won't get custody," Steve said. "He's just trying to scare you. Does he have some kind of relationship with your dad?"

"No. But sometimes my father is at the school fence. I never told you because I thought you might make me talk to him. But I can't. Please don't force me."

Steve and Marge looked at each other.

From the stairs Kate said, "*What?* Why didn't you tell me?"

"Please Kate," Steve said. "We need to figure this out. Go do your homework."

"Fine." Kate stomped up the stairs and slammed her door.

Amy massaged her neck. "Every time I leave the school my stomach is in knots. I don't want to see him but I always look for him. I can't help it. One time we locked eyes and he smirked like he always does. I can't tell you how scary he is." Amy shivered. "I guess he talked to Tommy."

Steve stood. "Okay, we need to get on top of this."

"You have a home and support so no one's going to take the baby," Marge said. "Steve and I will figure out what to do about Tommy and your father."

After going to her room Amy heard faint arguing. She mounted the stairs slowly, avoiding the creaks.

"First, you didn't talk to me before offering our home to a newborn along with the teenage mother," Steve said. "And secondly, after the birth they're going to a shelter. I've already found the right place."

"How *could* you?" Marge said.

"She'll be fine. There's good support. If the father is up to anything more than just scaring her, which I doubt, they'll help her deal with it."

"I know he won't get custody but what if he's allowed weekend visits? Maybe, just maybe, she's going to need more than an institution to help with all this."

"Marge, I'm getting to the end of my rope. You know full well that shelters provide excellent care."

Amy returned to her room.

She says I can stay; he says I can't. What if Marge is right and

From Thorns

Tommy gets weekends?

Amy rubbed her belly. "It's okay, Little One. I'll make sure you're safe. Tommy can take his abortion and shove it! And when Steve kicks us out, I'll be ready. I'm gonna do my own research and *I'll* decide which shelter we go to. I'll quit school and get a job and get my own place."

A knock on the door interrupted her thinking.

"C'mon in."

"Why didn't you talk to me about Tommy and your father instead of going to Mom and Dad?" Kate demanded.

Amy stared.

"I thought we were friends. Why don't you tell me this stuff?"

"I was in my room crying after school and your mom knocked on the door." Amy shrugged. "So I told her what happened."

"Typical Mom." Kate shook her head, lips pressed together. "Never minds her own business. But why didn't you tell me your dad is at the fence sometimes?"

"I didn't want anyone to know," Amy said.

"Okay, I understand. I just hope you know you can talk to me about anything."

"Thanks."

How am I gonna make sure I tell Kate enough that she won't get mad but not enough that she'll tell her friends everything?

She barely slept. Memories of her father: his drunken anger, the beatings he had delivered to both her and her mother, his reaction when he learned of her pregnancy, the look on his face every time she'd seen him at the school. She knew he wanted to hurt her. Did he really want to help Tommy get custody? How did he even know Tommy? Or were the two of them trying to figure out how to get rid of the baby? Would they kidnap her and drag her off to someone who would perform an abortion against her will? Would they beat her to kill the life she carried?

In the morning Amy feigned illness.

When Kate and Jason were gone, she confessed to Marge her suspicion that her father and Tommy would gang up and make sure they killed the baby. "Maybe they'll kill me too. One stone, two birds. I'm not going back to school. And I know Steve doesn't want me to stay. I don't blame him, but I need a plan. Will you help me figure something out?"

"Of course Steve wants you to stay."

Why won't she be honest? Amy wondered feeling annoyed.

"Hi John, thanks for coming," Marge said upon opening the door. "How are Jane and the kids?"

"All good. We'll have to get together soon."

The officer listened to Amy's version and promised to visit both Tommy and her father. "If you have anymore trouble, get in touch with me."

"With the nicer weather, I walk every afternoon," Marge said. "So from now on I can meet you after school."

Um, no.

"There's no point in going to school," Amy said. "I don't get anything out of it. Ever."

"It's important you finish the year well and also show that miserable, irresponsible boy that he can't intimidate you. Hold your head high, trust the police, the school staff, and us. And carry this whistle. If you feel afraid, blow it. I'll be waiting down the block when you leave the school."

I guess down the block isn't too bad, Amy thought.

From Thorns

Two days later, she returned to school wondering if ignoring the threat made sense, knowing she couldn't trust anyone, yet wanting to take a shot at having the upper hand.

Tommy continued to lurk and sneer. She made sure she was never alone and always maintained a high alert consciousness. After a full week she felt like maybe she would come out the winner. A welcome new experience.

CHAPTER 6

Amy lay awake listening to the rain beat against the house.
"Good morning, Little One."

The smell of bacon called her to the kitchen.

Steve motioned toward the stove. "Grab a plate and help yourself." Then, "Fer the lovapete Jason, stop feeding Rumble from the table. *How many times do I have to tell you?*"

Kate announced that everyone should thank her for the basket of unburned biscuits. "Typical Mom. She answered the phone and then wandered off to chat without setting the timer."

Sunday mornings were always the same. A big breakfast and church. On Amy's first weekend Marge had invited her to come along. Because she didn't want disapproval, Amy agreed. Thus far attendance hadn't been too painful.

Following breakfast and a chaotic time of getting ready, everyone piled into the van.

"Wait, I forgot my bible."

Marge released an exaggerated sigh. "Oh Jason, you'll have to do without it this morning."

"I don't have my offering. I put it in my pocket. What happened to it?"

From Thorns

"I always tell ya," Steve said, "don't leave important things to chance. That's why belts are sold with pants."

Marge shook her head, Kate rolled her eyes, and Jason said, "They don't sell pants with belts. Ya have to buy them separately."

The people at the church were friendly, especially the minister. He said funny things and people often laughed when he gave his talk.

Today he spoke about love. How God loves people. How He wants people to love Him back. How people are supposed to love each other.

Amy's mother had occasionally mentioned God, to point out how evil Amy was and how much God despised girls like her. As a child she had wanted to please this disapproving God, but she always failed. The idea of a loving God made as much sense as Superman coming to the rescue. Maybe people with easy lives could believe the fairy tale.

She struggled to suppress the brewing anger and bolted to her room when they got home. Her anger intensified, pushing reason off-balance.

Then came a knock at the door. "Yes?" Amy said through gritted teeth.

"Can I get you something to eat?"

"No, thank you."

"Are you okay? You don't sound good."

Amy threw the door open. "Leave me alone!"

Shock spread across Marge's face. The conversation upstairs stopped.

Dread instantly consumed the rage. "I'm so sorry."

"It's okay. You need some time on your own." Marge turned to go.

"No, please don't go. Please let me explain." Words poured from Amy's mouth like water from a broken faucet. "My parents told me I was evil and God hated me and everyone treated me like I was bad and I believed it and when I got punished it was God showing me how much he despised me so when I heard the minister talking about love this morning it was confusing and I felt mixed up." She sucked in a breath. "And when you knocked on my door I was thinking about it all and I didn't mean to yell at you. I'm so sorry."

Amy stared at the floor. All those years with her parents, she never gave up hope. And God was missing in action. If there really was a God, there were two alternatives: He was cruel and took pleasure in watching others suffer, or He hated Amy.

"You have been lied to," Marge said. "God does *not* hate you."

They sat on the edge of the bed in silence.

"It's important to be honest. And it's all right to get angry. I know your reaction wasn't directed at me personally." Marge took Amy's hand. "Are you all right?"

"Why are you so nice to me? I know it's not okay to lose my temper."

Marge sighed. "I guess it's up to me to show you that it's okay to be yourself. For now, I'm asking you to *try* to believe that I'm not upset. I'm actually glad to see you let your walls down and speak freely."

"Can you forgive me?" Amy said.

"Love forgives."

Marge kept coming up with new ones.

She stood. "I'm going to make lunch. Why don't you and

From Thorns

Baby rest." On her way past the bed, she looked toward the pillow where Teddy Bear's ear poked out from behind. She reached for him while saying, "He looks like he's been a good friend over the years. And he looks well-loved." The bear was worn, missing all its fur in most areas. Marge placed him gently on top of the pillow before she left.

Great, Amy thought, now she knows about Bear. She must think I'm a big baby.

And what will she tell everyone about my outburst? How will they react?

When Amy opened her door after a restless nap, Jason and Kate leapt from the television. Jason hopped onto the bed and started bouncing.

"Wow, you really yelled at Mom," Kate said. "What were you fighting about?" Before Amy could answer Kate shouted, "Cut it out Jason! Do you want the baby to be born right now? How old are you anyway? Geez!" She turned back to Amy. "C'mon, tell us what happened."

"I was confused about something the minister said and I got upset when your mom asked me about it."

"Well you should have talked to me, *not Mom*. She has a way of saying the wrong thing. So next time you have something you need to talk about remember—talk to Kate, not Marge. That is, if she doesn't barge in and force you to answer her questions."

Why did Kate always find fault with her mother? Sure Marge could be annoying, but she was a thousand times better than Amy's own mother. And why wasn't Kate angry about Amy's outburst? She never yelled like that. What was everyone hiding?

Amy excused herself and went into the bathroom. She leaned

into the counter and concentrated on breathing. There's no way she could face Marge.

But she couldn't spend the rest of her life in the bathroom either.

She took a deep breath and slowly emptied her lungs. Time to face whatever waited upstairs.

Marge looked up from her book. "I made a sandwich for you. Grab a seat. Let's chat."

Uh-oh.

When Amy returned with her sandwich Marge said, "I got some more maternity clothes from the church. They were ready for donation so they're being donated to you."

"That's really nice of them. Thank you." Whether she needed clothes or not, Amy didn't want anything more, especially not now right after her outburst!

"Are you feeling a little better after a rest?"

"Yes," Amy lied. "I still don't know how you can forgive me."

"Maybe *you* need to forgive *me* for barging in when you needed alone time."

Huh?

"Let's put it behind us," Marge continued. "I want to tell you about my sister, Janice. She got pregnant when she was only fifteen. She was afraid to tell our dad. Now, as an adult, I know he would have helped but at the time we both thought he would blow up. She found someone who claimed to be a doctor who would do an abortion at his house. I didn't want her to, but she was desperate and I didn't have any other solution."

Marge sighed while wringing her hands. "Janice died. She didn't stop bleeding, and we didn't tell Dad until it was too late. I was pretty mad at God for a long time. Look, I'm not

From Thorns

comparing that situation with how you were treated. I just want you to know that I don't think badly of you for being angry at God. I've been there too."

Her eyes are glassy. Is she crying? What am I supposed to say?

"I admire your passion," Marge continued. "I respect you for wrestling with your thoughts and feelings and for being honest. You're a very intelligent girl."

Intelligent? Respected? Admired? Amy forced a smile and said, "Thank you for being so nice."

From the corner of her eye, she saw Steve watching. He did *not* look happy.

CHAPTER 7

Marge reflected on what she had learned through her school contacts.

The consensus painted Amy as a loner. It seemed she didn't participate in anything outside of the curriculum. Sometimes she was seen with a boy, never one of good repute. Prior to her pregnancy, Amy had worn skimpy clothing and heavy makeup. During breaks she went off school property to smoke.

The office staff speculated about her parents. It was believed they were close to forty when Amy was born. Supposedly a boy died in infancy beforehand. Rumour had it, the father blamed his wife for killing their son and when Amy was born female he wanted nothing to do with her.

Neither parent had shown up for high school events. Apparently they weren't involved at the elementary level either. Amy had had a good start but somewhere along the way her aptitude slipped and continued a downward trend. According to a retired elementary teacher who volunteered in the office, teachers had suspected a learning disability. Her parents were informed but they never followed up and the school didn't have funding for testing.

From Thorns

"Gossip is rarely accurate," Steve said when Marge relayed the information. "You should know better."

"I don't know how you expect me to find *factual* information." Marge believed every bit of what she'd been told.

Despite Steve's holier-than-thou response, his interactions with Amy changed. It was that very evening when he started helping her with schoolwork.

If only I could learn enough to sketch a clear picture, Marge thought. At least she's not dressing inappropriately anymore. And I've never smelled cigarettes.

"I wanna tell you something," Amy said to Marge a few days after the post-church outburst.

They settled in the rec room. Amy hugged a cushion.

"You know my parents weren't nice to me, right?"

"I gathered," Marge said.

"Father killed our dog."

"You mean he had the dog put down because it was old or sick?"

"No," Amy said. "I think he was mad and kicked it to death. He kicked the dog a lot."

Marge felt her eyes grow wide.

"Father was mean to all of us. Me, Mother, the dog. I promise I'll never hurt Rumble."

"Of course you wouldn't!" Marge squeezed Amy's hand. "Why do you call them Mother and Father?"

"Father said it showed respect."

Marge nodded.

"So you don't think I'm a bad person for telling you about the dog?"

"Of course not!"

"I wanna tell you something else but I'm scared you'll hate me."

"I promise I won't hate you."

"Okay." Amy looked at her hands. "Father told me I had it good compared to him. He said his father was a piece of work. He said I better not complain or he'd give it to me worse, the way he got it. Aunt Colleen told me my grandfather got sent to a religious boarding school for boys after his mother died and his father remarried. The sisters got to stay home but Grandfather needed discipline, so he got sent away.

"The people who ran the school were called brothers, and they treated the boys bad. Grandfather ran away six times and every time he went back home. His father locked him in a closet until the brothers came and took him back. Then he got punished. Aunt Colleen wouldn't tell me what happened but I heard her and Mother talking about it once. They tied him spread eagle to the bed and beat and sodomized him. There's more, but that's the worst of it."

Amy stared into Marge's eyes. "The brothers believed in God. They taught about God at the school. I don't understand how God is loving if that's how the people who believe in Him treat other people."

Marge dropped her head into her hands. "I'm going to make some tea. Regular or peppermint?"

In the kitchen Marge swallowed hard, suppressing tears. Could it get any worse?

Amy stood when the tea came down the stairs. With a quivering lip she said, "I'm sorry. I shouldn't say such awful things."

As Marge placed the tea on a table she said, "You have nothing to be sorry for. I'm sad to hear what happened to your

From Thorns

grandfather. I guarantee, the treatment he received was *not* condoned by God."

"It was a Christian school," Amy said.

"Just because a place calls itself Christian doesn't mean it practices what it preaches. There's *no way* God had anything to do with that behaviour."

"But how can it be Christian if God's not part of it?"

"Like I said before, just because a place calls itself Christian doesn't mean it truly is."

"Okay... but God can do anything, right?"

"Yes, He can," Marge said, "but He doesn't usually interfere."

"Why? If I had power, I would have sent a lightning bolt through those brothers. God sat back and watched."

"God gives everyone freedom, although sometimes I wonder why. God tells us to treat each other with love. But He doesn't force us. We choose to love or to hate. We choose good or evil."

"So how can a *loving* God watch innocent people get hurt because of someone *else's* choice?" Amy said.

"If he intervened to prevent the bad stuff, choice is dead and we're nothing more than robots. I told you about my sister. God could have prevented her from getting pregnant. But when she did, He could have sent a competent doctor. Even if the doctor *was* incompetent, God could have made the guy's hands work properly. When the surgery was botched, God could have healed my sister Himself.

"The bottom line—Janice was responsible for getting pregnant and deciding to hide it. I was responsible for going along with her plan. After the procedure when she didn't heal, I went against every ounce of common sense and said nothing. Why? Because I didn't want to get in trouble. So I hoped it would all work out. When it didn't, suddenly it was God's fault.

"We want Him to leave us alone to live as we please but show up and fix everything when life goes off the rails.

"Different from my sister, your grandfather didn't do anything to bring on abusive treatment. But the horrible outcomes in both cases were because of somebody's choice. God's never going to take away our freedom to choose."

"It's so sad that you'll never get to see your sister again."

"Oh, I'll see her again. In heaven."

"Heaven? Seriously?" Amy said. Then with a reddening face, "I'm sorry. It's just, well, I'm not so sure about heaven." She looked into Marge's eyes. "But I should believe."

Marge smiled as she shook her head. "There are no *shoulds*. I love that you're honest."

Really? Amy wondered. Or will you go away and judge me? Or tell Steve and then he'll kick me out.

CHAPTER 8

"Whose birthday is it?" Amy asked as the girls came through the door to Happy Birthday balloons.

"Yours! Duh... I didn't say anything at school 'cause we wanted to surprise you."

"How did you know?" Amy asked.

"Ohhh Mom has her ways." Kate watched for a few seconds. "Smile girl, we're gonna celebrate your birthday. We've got some presents and Mom's making a cake. It's gonna be fun."

Amy cupped her hands over her mouth. "I've never had a birthday party."

"Seriously?"

She shook her head as she wiped her eyes with a shirtsleeve.

"Well you're gonna have one today. We each got you a present which means you'll have to look happy about Jason's dumb gift. Can you pull that off?" Kate crossed her arms. "I can't believe you never celebrated your birthday."

The front door flew open. "I'm *so* sorry. I wanted to be here when you girls got home." Marge held a bouquet of pink lilies. "I bumped into Barbara and we got chatting and I lost track of time. Happy birthday, Amy! Come take the flowers."

Alie Cardet

"How did you know it was my birthday?"

"I probably shouldn't tell," Marge said, with an impish grin. "I don't want to get anyone in trouble..."

Kate shook her head. "Let's hear it." Looking at Amy she said, "We better sit. This could take a while."

"I volunteer at the school. The reason you've never seen me is because Kate made it clear that it's not cool to have your mom hanging around." Marge frowned. "She never felt that way when she was younger."

"Back to the story," Kate said.

"So I asked my friend, Sue, who works in the office. She said I'd have to ask you but I didn't know you well enough—"

"Speed it up, Mom."

"Fine! In the end I managed to get the date from Sue. But she really shouldn't have told me so please tell anyone."

Kate smirked. "Good detective work. I know who to come to if I ever have a mystery to solve."

"I hope it's okay that I asked about your birthday," Marge said. "Kate volunteers at a math tutoring session. I told Sue that you went for help and Kate thought it was close to your birthday and she wanted to do a little something," Marge shrugged. "Sue didn't ask any questions."

Kate rolled her eyes. "She wears her naivety with pride." She pushed off the couch and headed toward the kitchen.

Marge frowned. "Of course she knows you live with us *now*, but I didn't say anything until I knew you would be safe. It turns out you're old enough to make your own decisions about where you live. And anyway, Sue's not going to tell anyone."

From the kitchen Kate called, "You know what? This is her first birthday celebration."

From Thorns

Marge slowly turned her head to look at Amy. "You never celebrated your birthday with your parents? Or with friends?"

"We didn't celebrate anyone's birthday."

"Well then, it's high time you had a party. I suggest you get at your homework."

"I've got a snack organized for both of us," Kate called. "Don't worry Mom, we won't ruin our appetites." She stepped back into the living room and stared at her mother. "What are you planning for tonight? I don't see any food in here."

"Don't you worry. I've got it all under control. Now I don't want to see either of you again until I call you for dinner. And don't eat too much. I don't want you ruining your appetites."

Kate sighed as she walked toward the stairs. "Didn't I just say that? She never listens to me."

Amy wasn't listening to anyone. Would her churning gut permit the onslaught of food?

The aroma of freshly baked bread called the girls to dinner.

Amy eyed the *Happy 17th Birthday* banner on the wall and the fancy napkins on the table. The knots in her stomach tightened.

Steve came through the patio door with steaks and potatoes.

"Where's Jason?" Marge said. "I called him a few minutes ago."

"Jason. Hurry up!" Steve yelled.

The sound of feet pounding on the stairs preceded Jason flying into his chair. "C'mon everyone, sit down! I'm starving."

"I'm not too hungry," Amy said.

"Well save room for cake."

"If Amy doesn't have to eat everything, then I don't want vegetables."

"Fer the lovapete Jason, stop arguing. Eat everything on your plate or no dessert."

Jason's mood soured, which made for a quieter than usual dinner, which raised Amy's anxiety even higher.

When the cake appeared, Jason's mood righted. On his knees leaning over the table he said, "What did you wish for?" after the candles were extinguished.

"Cut it out," Kate said. "You know the wish has to be kept secret. Now sit down!"

Marge placed three beautifully wrapped boxes on the table.

"You shouldn't have bought gifts. Flowers, balloons, a fancy dinner..."

Kate grinned. "You better open them before you say anything. It's not like we know you well so it was a total crapshoot."

"It was no such thing!" Marge said. "Each of us picked out something we thought you'd like. This one's from Jason."

Amy unwrapped slowly, her hands shaking. "My very own basketball! Thank you. Now I won't have to use yours."

"Mine next," Kate said. "I couldn't get you a basketball because Jason beat me to it. Sooorrry." The box held a gift certificate to a Day Spa. Kate slipped her arm around Amy's shoulders. "You don't know what it's for, do you?"

"Good grief! I can't believe you didn't put a note in there explaining."

"Relax Mom, we're having fun. Right Amy?" Kate delivered a gentle elbow jab to Amy's ribs. "I'm taking you to my hairdresser. You've got amazing highlights and a gorgeous natural wave, but you need some style."

When Amy didn't react Kate said, "So... do you like it?"

"I love it. Thank you." Amy wondered if she could put the appointment off until summer. There's no way she could go to

From Thorns

school with some new style. The bullying would be merciless.

"This is fun," Steve said.

Jason grinned. "It'd be more fun if I got a gift too."

"Oh Jason!" both parents said in unison.

Amy pulled sandals from the last box.

Kate twisted in her chair. "Those are the ones I want! I hope you picked up an extra pair for me."

Steve's eyes narrowed. "Is it *your* birthday?"

"Sorry." She draped her arm around Amy's shoulder. "Those are really in this year."

"You can have them," Amy said.

"Don't you worry. I'll get my own pair." Kate looked at her mother. "Well done, Mom. You didn't even ask me for help. I'm impressed."

After another round of thank-yous, Marge shooed everyone from the kitchen reminding Kate and Jason that the routine of kids cleaning up would resume tomorrow. As Amy turned to go, Marge caught her arm. "Did you have fun?"

"You shouldn't be doing so much. I'm not even paying rent." If only Marge could know how uncomfortable Amy felt. And scared. Kate wouldn't condone this much longer. Amy wanted to stay under the radar and a party in her honour escalated her into that zone.

Marge took her by the shoulders. "Love delights in giving and celebrates the happiness of others."

Since Amy didn't have a clue what Marge was talking about, she continued. "Kate doesn't even have those sandals and now I have a pair. That's crazy. She's your daughter. She deserves them, not me."

"Deserves?" Marge said with raised eyebrows. "As a member

of this family Kate's been blessed over the years. But what has she done to *deserve* anything? You were born into a family that didn't celebrate your birthday. Did you deserve that? Absolutely not!"

Marge pulled Amy into a hug. "You meet a need for me that no one else does. Are you listening? *You* meet a need for *me*. Until you moved in, preparing dinner was a lonely endeavour. But now I have company in the kitchen and I love it. I'm thinking about teaching a cooking course, all thanks to you."

Kate's voice broke in. "Hey Amy, bring up another piece of cake. It'll help our concentration."

"Is that okay?" Amy asked, grateful for the interruption.

"Absolutely. At your age the calories don't seem to matter."

Later, after Amy climbed into bed and pulled the duvet tightly around herself and Bear, tension released.

"I'm gonna do a birthday party for you every year," she whispered to her baby. "And I'll buy you the best presents. You'll have your real mother and you won't feel afraid. I'll read you stories and I'll make sure you have friends to play with and I'll teach you to cook.

"I'm sorry for thinking about getting rent money from . . .

"I woulda been doing it for you so they wouldn't kick us out. But I could've got an infection so I didn't. Because I was looking after you. See, I'm already a good mother.

"Do you think Kate or Jason resent me? They should. When do you think they'll tell Marge they don't want me around anymore?

"We don't want to go to a shelter, do we?

"When they make us leave, I'll quit school and figure out how to get enough money so we can get a place. I'm already

From Thorns

looking for a job. I'll do whatever I have to.

"And I'll make sure Tommy doesn't get close to you. *Ever*.

"We'll be okay. You'll see."

CHAPTER 9

A scream fractured the silence.
Marge bolted out of bed. The clock read 2:46 a.m.
"Did I hear something?" Steve muttered, his eyes half-open.
"One of the kids must have had a nightmare. I'll attend to it."
Both Jason and Kate stood in their doorways.
"It's okay, Amy must've had a bad dream. Go back to bed."
They didn't move.
"Now!"
Did someone break into the house? Her father? Tommy? Is she miscarrying?
The bedside lamp lit a vacant room.
Marge knocked on the bathroom door. "Are you all right?"
When the door opened, Amy pressed her fingers to her quivering lip. "I'm sorry. In my nightmare I screamed. Did I scream out loud?"
"Don't worry about it. I'm just glad you're okay."
"It was a dream about my father."
Marge tensed. "Would you like to talk about it?"
"It's the middle of the night."
"I feel like sitting up," Marge said. "So we can chat, or I can

From Thorns

go read by myself."

They cozied onto the couch, each wrapping in an afghan.

"Wait," Marge said in a tone that suggested she'd just found a cost-effective way to generate wind energy. "Should we make some hot cocoa?"

Amy nodded.

"My father was chasing me with an axe. His eyes bulged out of his head. He kept swinging at me and I dodged with only inches to spare. I kept running and every time I looked back he was closer. Finally the axe hit and my arm hung by a thread, pouring blood. It felt so real." She pulled her knees up to her chest and wrapped her arms around them.

"Did your father ever threaten you with an axe?" Marge asked.

"He chased me once, but I got away." Amy looked at Marge who had her hands over her mouth. "I never told you stuff that happened because I didn't want you to think badly of me."

"I *certainly* wouldn't think badly of you. When a parent is abusive it's never the child's fault."

"My father always said it was my fault when he hit me or whatever."

Marge could feel heat moving into her face. "The only person responsible for your father's behaviour is your father."

"But my mother agreed with him."

Moving toward the couch, hot cocoa in hand, Marge said, "Well she was wrong." She took a moment to calm her mounting anger. "Look, I don't know your parents. All I'm trying to say is—there's never an acceptable reason for a parent to react with violence."

Amy wrapped her hands around the warm mug. "They were disciplining me."

Marge shook her head. "What happened on the night you left home?"

Amy looked like she was going to speak, but then looked away.

"Don't feel pressured to tell me anything you're not comfortable with."

"I'm afraid you'll think I'm stupid and you'll realize I deserved exactly what I got. And then you'll tell me to leave."

"You've gotten to know me. Do you really think I would react that way?"

Marge waited through the silence.

"I told my mother I was pregnant. I thought she might be happy to have a grandchild. I even thought she might decide to leave Father and we could live together with the baby.

"Instead, she spit in my face and called me a slut and yelled other stuff which I don't blame her. I'm sure you would yell at Kate if she gave you that kind of news. Anyway, Mother called out to Father. He was so mad when he came into the room that he couldn't control himself. He punched and slapped me. I smashed into the cupboards and fell on the floor. Then I think he kicked me but I sort of passed out. I don't remember anything else."

Marge clasped her hands against her chest. "Oh Amy, it breaks my heart to know you were treated like that. You needed love and support, not to be beaten and thrown out. Your father should be in jail."

"They didn't exactly make me leave. I ran away."

"Good decision."

Amy twisted the corner of the afghan around a finger. "Would it be all right if I went back to bed?"

What all went on in that home? Marge wondered. It was early summer and getting hot, but Amy still dressed in long

From Thorns

pants and long-sleeved shirts. She had noticed the occasional scar but nothing that should necessitate completely covering arms and legs. Was Amy cutting?

Marge decided to look for counselling. For herself. So she could learn to navigate these unfamiliar waters.

Three hours later when the alarm woke them, she told Steve about her 3:00 a.m. conference.

"If I ever meet that SOB—"

"Calm down! We want to help Amy, not take justice into our own hands."

"Speak for yourself." Steve strangled his pillow and threw it back onto the bed before heading into the bathroom.

A couple of days later, after school and while eating banana bread with Marge, Amy casually said, "I felt something weird today. Twice. A sort of twitch in my belly. Could it be the baby?"

Marge clapped her hands. "Yes, it probably is. That's wonderful!"

During dinner preparation Amy was so excited it reminded Marge of the fizz from a soda can when opened after being shaken.

"I think I know how we should rearrange the room to fit in a crib," Amy said.

"Baby could use a cradle for a while, if you'd like. Then nothing has to be moved."

"Do you think we can find a used cradle? I don't want to buy a cradle and then a crib too."

"My friend, Donna, already offered her cradle. She's saving it for her own grandchild."

"What if I break it?"

Marge laughed. "It won't get damaged, but if it did Steve can fix anything. Don't worry."

When Kate arrived home Amy flew to her, words bubbling forth.

"Cool," Kate said. "Let me feel it, okay?"

"When it starts to kick, for sure."

The girls overtook the dinner conversation. Marge broke in occasionally, telling fun stories from Jason's and Kate's early years.

As the evening settled Marge felt joy wrap itself around her body like a warm towel after a shower.

The following day, Amy came through the door at noon looking like her world had imploded.

"What's wrong?" Marge asked.

As Amy rattled off a list of guaranteed failures coming her way, Marge led her to the living room. "What happened?"

Amy paced. "I don't know how to be a mother. I don't know what babies need. I don't have a job." Pausing to look at Marge she said, "Do I have to breastfeed?" Back to pacing.

"I'm not smart enough to get good grades. I'll never make enough money if I can even find a place that would hire me. I don't have a home." She paused and turned toward Marge again. "I won't be here after the baby comes." More pacing.

"I want to love my child but I don't know what that even means. Will I treat it like my parents treated me?"

"Okay, stop!" Marge said. "You may not know some official definition of the word but I can assure you, you know *how* to love. You will *not* treat your child in a cruel way because that's not who you are. And when you finish school, you'll find work and you'll succeed at whatever you take on because you're interesting

From Thorns

and intelligent and creative.

"When I was pregnant with Kate, I had many of the same fears. I didn't have a mother so my friends helped. And I'm going to help you. We're all looking forward to meeting the little one. We want you and the baby to stay here with us."

With a sigh Amy plopped onto the couch. "I know Steve doesn't want that. Probably Jason and Kate don't either."

Marge ignored that comment. "You don't give yourself enough credit. You have a maturity beyond other girls your age. Kate confided that she respects you more than anyone else she knows."

"*She* respects *me*? She's the one with high grades who's going to university. The one everyone wants to be friends with. She's good at sports, she's a cheerleader, she's on committees at school. Why would she respect me?"

"Maybe you should ask her."

After a few moments of silence Amy said, "I'm feeling better. I guess I should go back to school."

She doesn't look like she's feeling better, Marge thought.

When she shared details of the afternoon conversation with Steve, he said, "I already told you I don't want that. I care for her too and I'm glad she decided to stay with us through the pregnancy. But a crying baby? Jason and Kate need to grow up in a normal home environment."

Marge stood and excused herself.

"Suffrin' Hannah, you can't go stomping off every time I have a different point of view."

"I need to be by myself right now. Do you mind?" Marge said sarcastically.

"Fine!"

He's glad she decided to stay, Marge fumed. What a crock. If it wasn't for Kate's badgering, he would have moved her to a shelter on day one. How many times has he gotten to the end of his rope and drawn a line in the sand? At least he didn't bring up Janice.

The following day, Amy's spirit remained low. No smile, no chatting, not interested in meal preparation. She sat at the dinner table under a dark cloud and picked at her food. Jason's normal monopolization of conversation vanished. Marge and Steve talked about their respective days.

Following dinner Kate asked her mother, "Do you know what happened?"

"No. Let's give her some time."

A couple of days later Kate wandered into the kitchen. "Amy takes off at lunch instead of sitting with the girls. Has she told you anything yet?"

"She's probably worrying. Imagine how you would feel in her shoes."

Kate frowned. "When I asked, she just said she wasn't hungry. I thought she talked to you about stuff."

"She's not eating her lunch?" Marge said. "The baby needs nourishment."

"How's she acting when you guys work on dinner?"

"She hasn't helped the past few days."

"So she won't talk to you and she won't talk to me." Kate stomped down the stairs. Her loud voice held no compassion when she demanded, "What's wrong?"

Marge couldn't hear Amy's reply.

From Thorns

"Something's *obviously* wrong," Kate said, even louder.

After a period of silence, Kate stomped back up the stairs and slammed a door.

CHAPTER 10

Amy couldn't find the energy to care about anything. She tried to believe the things Marge told her: that she was interesting, creative, and intelligent, that she knew how to love, and that she would be a good mother.

She wanted to believe she could stay after the baby was born. What really happened to Georgia? Kate said she didn't want an ongoing relationship with the family, but was that true?

Why wouldn't Marge be honest about Steve's wishes?

Amy descended into a cavern of despair where she ruminated.

I'll never make a good mother.

I'll never get a decent job.

We'll probably end up living on the street.

Tommy will probably get custody.

Or they'll take my baby and put it in foster care.

What's the use in even trying to keep it?

Why didn't I get an abortion?

She kept to herself. She continued to eat with the family, because she knew they expected her to, and she tried to show interest but it exhausted her.

From Thorns

After a few days of considering all the potential negative outcomes, her deficiencies, and certain failure, she resigned. She might as well stay with the Raynors as long as possible.

Then she remembered Kate's angry outburst. On top of that, Amy had ignored her and her friends. How would she get back on the right side of Kate?

What about Marge, Steve, and Jason? Were they all fed up? What would happen now?

As the sun rose after a night of restless sleep, Amy heard the faint sound of voices. She made her way to the kitchen. "May I join you?"

"Of course."

As she reached for the coffee pot, she noticed Marge and Steve exchange the same questioning look.

"I want to apologize for being so grumpy this past week. I've been worrying a lot and I guess I felt afraid to trust anyone, including you. I know that was totally unfair and I'm sorry."

"Hey, it's okay," Marge said. "You've got a lot on your plate."

"You're so nice to me just like always, but I know I behaved horribly."

"No need to worry," Steve said.

Huh? That's not like Steve.

Amy continued, "I'll apologize to Kate and Jason too."

While Marge walked Steve to the door, Amy breathed a sigh of relief.

As she topped up her mug, she recognized how easily she'd initiated the conversation. It felt good but it also left her terrified. In the universe she came from, her feelings were irrelevant and if she had behaved the way she did this past week . . .

She shuddered.

It seemed she could now express herself with some confidence but when everything got resolved, fear dug in its claws. If only she could feel comfortable in this new world. If only she could learn to dance instead of always darting.

Jason wandered into the kitchen and slumped into his chair. Kate leaned against the wall, eyes down.

Amy wondered what they were doing up so early.

"Okay, they're ready to talk," Marge said.

Oh no! She dragged them from bed. Why couldn't she leave it alone? I had a plan...

Amy took a deep breath. "I'm sorry for how I've been acting."

Jason stared. Kate looked intently at her nails.

"I've been so worried about the baby..." Amy paused stuck for words.

Kate straightened. "Geez Mom, why didn't you tell me there was something wrong with the baby? I would have tried to help." Looking at Amy she said, "Is everything okay now?"

Amy looked at Marge.

"It took some time," Marge said, "but she got answers and she's feeling better."

"While I was worrying," Amy said, "I know I shut down and didn't even try to explain. I should have told you Kate. You too Jason. I hope you'll forgive me."

"Of *course* we forgive you. Right, Jason?"

"Uh-huh. What was wrong with the baby?"

Marge looked at her watch. "There'll be plenty of time to talk after school. If you can get yourself organized Kate, you can talk to Amy on your way."

From Thorns

"I'll hurry."

Amy yawned. "I'm gonna take a little nap before we leave. Can you wake me?"

On her way to her room Amy heard, "Mom, is she okay?"

"Yes, I think she is but she's fighting battles we can't understand. There might be more hard times ahead and she'll need support. Do you think you can handle it?"

"Definitely. I feel bad for jumping to a negative conclusion. It won't happen again. But you might need to work on Jason. I don't think he can be as mature as me."

Amy slept soundly through the morning. When she made her way upstairs, Marge explained it was her fault she wasn't wakened for school.

Amy didn't care.

After school, when Kate wandered into the kitchen where Amy munched on cookies, she said, "Hey, leave some for the rest of us. I know you're feeding that baby but . . ."

Amy swept her hand toward the plate, her mouth too full to speak.

Kate took a cookie. "I hear Mom blabbed some of my opinions about you—not that I really care in this case. But honestly, she needs to learn to mind her own business. Anyway, she told you I respect you more than my other friends, right?"

Amy nodded.

"She told me that you didn't believe her. Well it's true. My friends are great but they complain about stuff that's totally insignificant compared to what you're going through. Everyone's always worried about what colour they should put in their hair or if it's time to redo their nails. You don't complain about anything.

"And I'm sorry for not trusting you last week. I thought you were mad at us and I didn't understand. So I kind of reacted unfairly."

"I don't blame you for being ticked."

"I wasn't ticked." Kate shrugged. "But I guess it looked like it. Sorry."

Amy took the plate from the table and held it to Kate. "They're good, eh? I guess I shouldn't say that since I made them."

"Yeah, they're fantastic! You're rivalling Mom.

"And speaking of Mom, she made me leave this morning without waking you. Said you needed more sleep."

"Yeah, she told me."

"Okay good, because I didn't want you to blame me. I'm gonna do homework now and I think some more cookies will help me focus." Kate grinned.

As she wandered off, plate of cookies in hand, Amy wondered why apologies kept coming her way when she was clearly the one in the wrong.

CHAPTER 11

The end of the school year brought welcome relief. A break from the bullies. Escape from the nonsense conversations at lunch. And Amy hoped she would never see Tommy again.

While Amy delivered job applications, Kate returned to the hardware store she had worked at the previous summer. After her first shift, she arrived home with good news. "They're hiring and I recommended you and they want to interview you. It's for stocking shelves so there be might some night shifts. Do you wanna go for it?" Amy was offered the position at the end of the interview.

"Thank you so much, Kate! I would never have gotten a job on my own."

Kate frowned. "Of course you would. But it'll be fun working at the same place." Her face morphed into a grin. "Now, let's go for cheesecake to celebrate."

Amy couldn't understand the friendship she had with Kate. It was great, but why was Kate interested? Or willing?

While the girls worked, Jason holidayed with his parents. Not entirely sure why Marge and Steve would trust her, even with Kate around, it was fun living without any adults.

When Amy started paying room and board, a waterfall of relief flooded her soul. And she finally had enough money to get a cell phone with the cheapest plan she could find. No more having to borrow Kate's.

One evening after work, Amy burst into Kate's room and shoved her laptop onto the desk. "Look!"

The email read, "I'm not going away."

"Oh no," Kate said, "what're ya gonna do?"

"I don't know."

"Dad," Kate yelled from her room. She grabbed Amy's hand and led her across the hall into her father's study.

Amy explained how she had tried to avoid Tommy at school. Sometimes he harassed her when she was alone in the yard or if he saw her walking in the hallways. "But I just walked away pretending I didn't hear him. Sometimes he shoved mean notes into my locker." She shrugged. "But he never touched me again so I told myself to ignore him."

"To start with," Steve said, "let's get your email address changed. And I think it's time to involve the police. I have a friend I can call—"

"We already talked to them. I don't wanna do that again. Tommy won't be able to figure out my new email."

She didn't change her email address for several weeks until she realized he wasn't going to stop. Throughout the summer she kept watch, always looking over her shoulder and around corners but she never spotted him.

She hoped he had no idea how much he scared her.

From Thorns

At the end of summer, she asked Steve for a meeting. "I know you haven't always been keen on having me stay with you, and I'm pretty sure you don't want a baby underfoot, so I've done some research and I've found the shelter I'd like to go to. Will you please help me move?"

Steve smiled. "True, I've struggled at times but Marge and I have decided we'd like you to stay on, unless you'd *rather* move to the shelter."

"No, I would rather stay with you. Are you sure you want a crying baby in the house?"

"You and Baby will have your own space downstairs. I know we'll all face challenges but we're willing if you are."

"I don't want to be here unless everyone's good with it. And if I'm going to have to move, I'd rather go before the baby comes."

"Marge!" Steve yelled. When she came into the room, he asked her to explain everything and then left. Marge reiterated what Steve had already said.

Amy found Kate. "Did you know your parents want me to stay after the baby's born?"

"Of course they want you to stay. If they didn't, *I'd* go with *you*."

Amy laughed and pulled Kate into a hug. "I know your dad didn't want me to stay. Do you know why he changed his mind?"

"I guess he came around. Don't worry."

She worried anyway. But in the end she decided to stay until asked to leave. Having the support meant a lot. And now that she paid some rent, she felt less guilt about occupying space and had less fear of potentially being tossed.

Amy could have done without returning to school in September. Her size provided plenty of material for chatter. But she didn't have to watch for Tommy. Thank goodness he'd graduated.

A few weeks in, Amy felt a dribble down her leg. Was her bladder giving out? Or was she about to have a baby? By the time she got home, the dribble had gained volume.

Marge clapped her hands. "Your water broke! Get your bag!"

At the hospital, they walked the halls hoping to accelerate labour. This provided plenty of talk time. Amy relived the pregnancy, revisited many of the challenges she tackled during the previous six months, and discussed the upcoming school year with potential options for completing it.

Marge offered assurances where needed.

"Can I ask you something?" Amy said.

"Anything."

"You mentioned your parents had died. Is that why your mom wasn't around to help when you had Kate and Jason?"

"That's right. My mother died when I was only thirteen. A horrible form of cancer destroyed her body from the inside out. It was heart-wrenching to watch her suffer before death swept the agony away.

"Dad passed away ten years ago. Heart attack."

"Do you think you would have told your mom about your sister's pregnancy if she was alive?"

"I don't know. My dad was a gentle soul. If we couldn't tell him, I doubt we would have told Mom."

Marge had a hard life when she was young but somehow she'd found happiness. Could Amy hope for the same?

Thankfully labour was short, and the pain was manageable. Baby Jessica weighed in at seven pounds, had an

From Thorns

excellent APGAR score, healthy bloodwork, and there were no complications.

Steve brought a carload of excitement to visit. "You're so lucky," Kate said. "I want a baby." Steve's reaction sent both girls into cascades of laughter.

Jason remained glued to the side of the bassinette.

"When's she gonna wake up?"

"Her blankets are too tight. She can't move."

"Can I unwrap her hand?"

Finally Amy knew what love felt like. Jessica Margaret Peterson—a most amazing miracle. There just might be a good God after all.

The hospital discharged mother and baby the following day with detailed instruction on feeding schedules, issues to watch for, and a follow-up appointment with a pediatrician.

At home everyone wanted to hold Jessie and work on eliciting that first smile. Breastfeeding was fascinating to Kate and gross to Jason. Amy was grateful it worked. Only Marge offered to help with diaper changes.

A day after returning home, Jessie's skin and eyes showed some yellowing. The hospital had included this in the list of things to watch for.

"Don't worry," Marge said. "Both of my babies had jaundice and they outgrew it."

Marge offered to take some middle-of-the-night shifts, but Amy wanted to handle it on her own. Jessie didn't fuss and drifted back to sleep as she finished nursing.

Even during the day Jessie slept well and seldom cried. With each new day she slept more soundly, and Amy had to wake her for feedings which Jessie half slept through.

During the fifth night Amy woke the house screaming.

The sound of feet pounding on the stairs preceded a frantic Marge bursting through the bedroom door with Kate on her heels.

"I can't wake her. She's dead!"

Marge rushed past Amy to the crib. "She's warm. Let's get her to the hospital."

Kate stood to the side, crying. Steve held his arm around her shoulder. "C'mon, Mom and Amy need to go. Let's get you back to bed."

"Are you kidding?" Kate said before calling to Amy who was running up the stairs, "I'll be praying."

Amy held her lethargic daughter, refusing to use the car seat.

The emergency department took them immediately and ordered an ambulance to transport Jessie and Amy to the nearest Children's Hospital. Marge followed in her car.

Jessie was taken to the neonatal intensive care unit.

A young nurse met with Amy and Marge. "Jessie's bilirubin is very high. Did you notice her skin and eyes yellowing?"

"It didn't seem too bad," Amy sputtered through tears.

"Often parents don't see it getting worse because it's gradual. Have you had a pediatric appointment?"

"It's today."

"Ahh, I see," the nurse said. "Well now we're going to put her under what we call phototherapy lights. They'll help break up the bilirubin in her blood and get her feeling better."

"Will she be okay?"

"Most babies recover just fine. You did the right thing

From Thorns

bringing her in."

Amy stopped crying. "Most? What's the worst that could happen?"

"It's rare but severe jaundice can result in deafness, brain damage, or cerebral palsy. But it's very uncommon. We're going to watch Jessie closely and do our best to ensure she's okay."

Amy and Marge wailed in unison.

"This is all my fault," Marge snivelled. "I should have known."

The nurse put her hand on Marge's arm. "No. When you live with a newborn it's hard to see the subtle changes. It's not anyone's fault."

Marge fell into a chair sobbing with her hands over her face. "Oh God, oh God, oh God . . ."

Amy joined her.

When the crying eased, they looked each other up and down and laughed.

"I've never gone out in my pajamas before," Marge said.

Their laughter morphed back to wailing.

Jessie slept in a tiny plastic bed under the ultraviolet lights. Amy pumped breast milk which was fed by a feeding tube inserted through Jessie's nose. She looked like a science experiment. Amy stood over the little bed, tears falling on the plastic covering while she tried holding Jessie's tiny hand. Only exhaustion stopped her tears and then only for brief periods.

An unhappy-looking nurse told her to get a grip. "Loads of the babies here have little chance of making it out of the NICU. You're lucky your baby's only problem is bilirubin and a feeding tube. And stop holding her hand—you're getting in the way of the lights."

If Amy had a gun . . .

She sat at Jessie's bedside day and night. She rarely slept, always waking in a panic. Every minute her hands weren't otherwise occupied, one of them rested beside Jessie. "Please God, if you're real make her get better." Amy was afraid to eat or visit the washroom unless Marge was present.

Time passed slowly, so very slowly.

On the second day Jessie vomited at three of her feedings and an intravenous tube was inserted to keep her hydrated and nourished.

When Marge arrived Amy flew at her, bawling. "She won't stop vomiting. I think she's gonna die."

Marge brought a nurse over.

"I already told you Jessie isn't going to die. Try to relax."

"She never told me," Amy growled.

Those two days housed the 2,880 most frightening minutes of Amy's life.

On the third day hope arrived. Jessie's bilirubin dropped to a safe level and Amy was permitted to hold her for half an hour. "I promise to take better care of you," Amy said, as her tears dribbled onto Jessie.

After five days Jessie was released from the hospital. A *welcome* banner greeted the car as it pulled into the driveway. Kate presented Jessie with a blanket she had crocheted, a beautiful dark pink.

"When did you learn to crochet?" Marge asked.

"Melissa showed me. We made it together."

Amy sat beside the crib, awake through the night and sleeping during the day when Marge or Kate could take over.

Two weeks ushered in normalcy. Jessie slept only as much as

From Thorns

a newborn should. She cried and fussed which left Amy ecstatic.

A surprise shower at the church was rearranged and heaps of gifts arrived at the house including some new jeans and tops and luxurious bath products. "They thought a huge shower at the church would be too much after what you've been through," Kate said as she helped unwrap.

"They should have just cancelled. They didn't have to do all this."

"Oh, but they wanted to," Marge said. "Everyone prayed for you and Jess. I mean *everyone.*"

When Amy resumed academics, the school agreed to her working from home with a few conditions. This allowed her to experience Jessie's first smile, first laugh, and the day she discovered her hands and feet. The love Amy felt was beyond anything she could have imagined.

Although never far away, Marge was different. Humility replaced the forcefulness and overbearing confidence she had imposed when Jessie first came home.

At times Amy ran out of patience and those moments scared her. There was no excuse for irritation—she was lucky her baby was alive. Was she like her own mother? Would her impatience explode into something terrifying that would destroy this young life?

She kept the fear to herself so no one would take Jessie away.

CHAPTER 12

As the nights grew longer and the temperature fell, autumn gave way to the festive season. Decorations went up December 1st, decadent baking began, Jason and Kate laughed more, complained less, and even got along with each other—most of the time. Amy had seen mall decorations and houses adorned with lights but she never imagined a home could completely transform.

One afternoon while working on shortbread with Marge Amy casually said, "Since Christmas means nothing to a three-month-old there's no need to buy anything for me or Jess."

Marge dropped the parchment paper and turned to face her. "Try to imagine how we would feel on Christmas morning if we were exchanging gifts amongst one another and had nothing for you or Jessie."

"I couldn't stand receiving presents without being able to give back." Summer earnings net of board payments had accumulated in a bank account, but Amy wanted to save that for emergencies.

"Kate buys small, fun things. I give Jason money—let me give you the same amount I give him."

From Thorns

"Absolutely not!"

When Marge looked away Amy said, "I'll buy a small gift for everyone like Kate and Jason do. I have enough funds if I keep it small."

"I don't want to force you to spend your money," Marge said.

It sure feels like you're forcing me, Amy thought.

"Now that I've thought about it," she said, "I definitely want to participate. But please keep it small for me and Jess."

She planned a shopping excursion with Kate. Silliness and laughter accompanied them until Amy looked at her watch. "Oh no, we gotta go. I told your mom I'd be home when Jess woke up."

"Relax. Mom loves it when she gets Jessie to herself which is not often enough by the way. Let's not ruin her fun."

"Would you mind calling to check?"

"Hi Mom, sorry we're late. Amy's worried. I knew you'd say that. See you later."

"She wants us to take our time." Kate grinned. "Let's get some cheesecake."

When friends came to visit most brought something for the baby. After Amy's first protest Marge assured her that people enjoyed bringing gifts. "They're actually jealous that I'm the first to have a grandchild."

Amy's mother had complained on the rare occasions when she felt compelled to send a gift. "Why would I want to shop for that? Do they think I can just poop out money?" There were times Amy had been told to go to her room to find something that could be wrapped and given away. "I know your aunt brings you things. You think you're hiding it from me, but I know. You don't need all that stuff; go find something I can use. And don't bring junk that's broken or torn."

Oh, Amy knew better than to believe all visitors wanted to bring gifts.

And why did Marge refer to Jessie as her grandchild?

Christmas Eve embraced the tradition of attending a candlelight service followed by a ham dinner. The family showered Amy with accolades for her delicious black forest cake. After Jessie was tucked in and while Marge cleaned up, they played Catan on the living room floor.

"The game is meant for four people," Marge said, "so I won't participate tonight. But tomorrow night, Amy and Kate, you two will look after cleaning the kitchen."

"Oh great," Kate muttered. "What about Jason?"

"I've got a job for him too."

The game ended with Jason complaining, "I shoulda won."

Kate scowled. "If ya played fair you mighta won."

When a verbal battle erupted Steve spat, "Well isn't this a lovely Christmas Eve."

Marge came into the room with wrapped boxes which righted the mood. Everyone received a pair of matching Santa pyjamas with instructions to show up at the tree wearing them. "Family photo before gifts," she warned. Jessie would wake in her new reindeer sleeper.

Too early in the morning, Jason pounded on Amy's door. "Ho-ho-ho, Merry Christmas!" After rubbing Jessie's back until she returned to sleep, Amy joined Jason by the tree.

"No opening presents until the coffee's made and your mother and I have a cup in hand," Steve said.

Marge added, "And the family photo is done."

From Thorns

Jason grinned. "Ho-ho-ho."

The gifts overflowed from under the tree the way fresh snow spilled over banks, encroaching on driveways and roads. Along the edge of the tree a stocking sat ready for each person, except for Jason's which already rested on his crossed legs.

Marge respected Amy's request and kept her gifts small. Later in the day, Amy overheard Kate asking, "Is something wrong? Why didn't you buy her very much?" But Amy felt like royalty to have received so many gifts. And more, she enjoyed the expressions of happiness as each person opened what she gave them.

When she retreated to her room for the night a carousel of special moments revolved in her mind. Although Marge had described what the day would be like it was only words until Amy lived it. She drifted off to sleep wondering if this represented a typical Christmas for most families.

CHAPTER 13

The new year ushered in Amy's final semester. Organized and focused she achieved a respectable GPA. And when it was behind her stress released like smoke billowing after water is poured over hot coals.

"See. I told you!" Marge smirked. "I hope you now believe you're intelligent and capable!"

What Amy believed was that Jessie was a powerful motivator.

When Steve and Marge asked for a meeting she expected a deadline for moving out. But instead they asked her to consider a college program. "Thank you, but no," she told them. Achieving independence was far more important than attaining a diploma.

"I need to talk to you about something else though. Tommy's got my new email and lately he's been sending messages. I know he's just bullying, but—"

"That bas—"

"Steve," Marge yelled. "Cursing won't help!"

"How long has this been going on?" Steve demanded.

"Through the semester but I don't wanna talk to the police. That'll just make him mad and it'll get worse. What should I do?"

Steve wrote a reply from his own email account.

77

From Thorns

> I will not tolerate harassment of anyone living under my roof. Leave Amy alone or you will face unpleasant consequences.

When he shared the email with the rest of the household he said, "If anyone sees Tommy or hears from him, I expect you to tell me."

That's the last time I tell Steve anything, Amy thought. I don't need him making things worse.

The hunt for work had started before the semester ended, without results. Amy asked the pastor, "Do you know if anyone who attends the church is hiring?"

"There might be something in the office. Should I pass your name along to the administrator, Sheila?"

Working in a church was likely inappropriate since Amy remained skeptical about God. The flame of anger wasn't burning as bright but it wasn't extinguished either. However, if the pastor was offering...

"Thank you! Yes!"

She turned to Marge. "Can you look after Jessie until I get something arranged?"

"Yup," Marge said. "I would have liked to keep her full-time but I understand the benefits of daycare environments."

"I would rather she stay with you than go anywhere else. Are you sure?"

"Absolutely!" Marge said.

"I've got some conditions. First, if it's too much you have to tell me. Promise?"

"I promise."

"Second, you have to let me pay you."

"Oh no, I can't do that. She's my granddaughter. I would never let Kate pay me."

"I insist," Amy said. "I get money from the government and I'll have a pay cheque. Either you let me pay you or I look for a daycare."

"My goodness, when did you become such a tough negotiator?"

"And you can't use the money to buy stuff for Jessie."

Marge smiled. "So we've got a deal?"

They shook on it.

"Fer the lovapete Marge, you should have talked to me before committing to childcare."

They really need to work on volume, Amy mused.

"I'm feeling lonely. Amy used to help with dinner but she doesn't have time anymore. I thought about teaching a cooking course but the ones I'm interested in are only offered in the evening and I'm not up to that. Looking after Jessie is the perfect solution. It'll be fun dragging her around with me. She takes a long nap every afternoon so I'll have plenty of time to myself."

Steve sighed. "I know there's no point in arguing with you. Just promise you won't drive yourself into the ground. If it becomes too much, I'll help you figure out what to do."

"I promise."

Why didn't she tell Steve I had the same concern? Amy wondered. He probably thinks I'm totally selfish. Geez!

Amy resolved to keep watch. She would intervene before Marge got tired. And she would be ready with childcare alternatives when the time came.

From Thorns

After a short interview Amy was offered a part-time position of three days a week.

Stress coursed through her veins on the first morning. But everyone was friendly, the work was straightforward, and questions were welcomed. Although she missed her baby girl, she enjoyed the work environment and she savoured the opportunity to build independence.

She continued to apply for other part-time positions and within a month a pharmacy hired her as a cashier.

"I'm going to have to work some evening shifts," Amy said. "You'll have to do the whole bedtime routine. It might be too much."

Marge laughed. "You won't find any childcare that goes into the evening. After 5:00 it's on the family."

Amy blushed. "Of course." She massaged her temples. "I better keep looking. I won't work at the drug store. I have to be able to move Jess when you get tired."

Marge frowned. "What makes you think I'm going to get tired? Jessie's easy. I won't get tired. Now stop worrying and enjoy the new job."

"Please talk to Steve to make sure he's okay with this."

"All right, I'll talk to Steve, but I guarantee it's all good."

Hopefully Marge will tell Steve about this conversation, Amy thought, so he'll know I'm not taking advantage.

In quiet moments, she reflected on how sixteen months had transformed her life. The fence of fear was slowly breaking away.

For the first time she felt like, maybe, just maybe, she mattered. Maybe she had some worth. Some value. She trusted cautiously.

She wasn't evil—the Raynors liked her. Other people did

too. She wasn't stupid—she'd completed high school with better marks than she thought possible. She wasn't a loser—she had two jobs. She knew how to cook, garden, and look after an infant.

Her parents were wrong!

But every time she made an error, their voices charged at her. Always accusing, always demeaning, only destructive.

CHAPTER 14

The church launched into fall programming with an introductory event toward the end of August. Amy volunteered for a pre-teen evening program, hoping to get a glimpse of what would be available for Jessie some day. Adventure Club required one evening per week, no preparation, and Jessie would be ready for bed before Amy had to leave.

On opening night, she followed the sound of voices into the kitchen. Someone called, "Hey Amy, how are ya? C'mere. I'll show you what we're doing."

Her stress ebbed.

"We're starting with ice cream sundaes. Toppings have to go on the tables."

While delivering the second set of bowls, Amy called to a guy snacking on jellybeans, "Hey, I put those out for the kids not you."

He grinned, grabbed a few more, and walked off.

Back in the kitchen Amy said to the room, "There's some moron out there eating what I'm putting on the table."

"Tall, good-looking?"

"I guess," Amy replied.

"He's here for university. He's gonna be trouble. I don't know who let him into our program."

The following evening all the leaders met. He sauntered in, sat at the head of the table, and pontificated his ideas for improving the program.

If I have to work with him I'm quitting, Amy decided.

Thankfully the youth pastor arrived and the rest of the meeting ran smoothly.

When people started to leave, the annoying university student dropped into the seat beside her. "Hey, I think we got off on the wrong foot. I'm Matt, and you are . . ."

"Amy." She stood and gathered her material.

"Sorry about the jellybeans yesterday."

"It's okay," Amy said on her way to the door.

Two days later Matt came into the office. "Hi again," he said with a big, goofy smile. "I didn't know you worked here."

"Do you need something?"

"I've got a meeting with the pastor. Maybe we can grab a coffee on your break?"

"I don't have time for a break today."

As if I want to waste time with him. He needs to back off.

At the next Club meeting, Matt approached Amy again. "Whatever I did to you, I'm sorry." He walked off without waiting for a reply.

When the meeting, ended Amy caught up with him. "Look, I'm sorry. I got the impression that you don't take anything seriously and I reacted."

Matt shrugged, "When I'm nervous I talk too much and rub

From Thorns

people the wrong way."

"Do you have time for coffee?" Amy said.

What am I doing? she asked herself. *I don't have time and I don't even like him.*

"You don't have to rescue me," Matt said.

Sympathy took control. "I'd really like to if you have time."

A silly grin spread across his face.

Amy felt dwarfed beside his six-foot frame as they walked to the café.

When seated with their drinks, Matt's mouth went into high gear.

She studied his chiselled features encompassed in a square face. Wisps of dark brown hair teased his forehead and defined temples bracketed bright, turquoise eyes. When he turned his head she could see a pierced ear, but no earring.

He's hot, she concluded. Too bad he's such a jerk. I guess that's why he doesn't have a girlfriend. At least I hope he doesn't, otherwise I pity her.

He had recently moved to attend the same university as Kate and was enrolled in a master's program. He talked about family, friends, and interests. Aside from mentioning Jessie and her jobs, Amy revealed little. Matt didn't give her much time to speak which suited her just fine.

His father and Pastor Mike were friends so the choice of church was easy.

"Why the youth program?" Amy asked.

"I have a brother with dyslexia so he has trouble reading and the teasing was bad over the years. I got involved in the program back home to keep an eye on him—make sure the kids were treating him right. Since I enjoy working with kids that age, and because it's a good way to meet people, here I am," Matt said with an exaggerated smile.

When Amy felt tired and suggested they wrap up, she was shocked to see two hours had passed.

He insisted on driving her home. He called his very old car a bucket-of-bolts while assuring her it was safe.

What would he expect for this favour?

But when they pulled into the driveway he said, "Good night. See ya next week." And then he drove off.

Marge was waiting. "Is everything all right?"

"Yes."

"Did the meeting go well?"

"Yes."

"Do you need to talk?"

"No."

Amy ran her thoughts and feelings past Rumble. Maybe she'd have coffee with Matt again. Trust of men hadn't suddenly descended from the stars, but just as Steve was different from her own father, Matt seemed different from the boys she had known. One on one he wasn't so bad.

After making eye contact at the next club event, Amy walked toward Matt. He turned and left the room.

I should've known. He's as despicable as the rest of them.

When the meeting ended, Matt approached her. "Can we talk for a few minutes?"

What the . . .?

"Okay," Amy said with a tone of confusion mixed with annoyance.

From Thorns

Matt didn't waste time on small talk. "I'd like to be friends but I'm not looking for a relationship. Just wanna make sure we're on the same page."

He had clearly flirted the last time. Pretty annoying and two-faced but she appreciated the honesty.

"Perfect. Friendship's all I want."

In fact, she didn't want anything and she didn't need this nonsense.

On Sunday Matt greeted her in the church foyer. She'd never seen such dumbfounded expressions on either Marge or Steve. Nor could she remember heat moving from her neck through her entire face with such speed. Kate and Jason were already inside, thank goodness.

After she fumbled through introductions, Matt asked to sit with her during the service while she stood like a statue, incapable of thought.

"Of course," Marge said. "We'll find Amy after the service."

"I can drive her home if you'd like."

Amy found her voice. "Matt and I will sit with you and I'll drive home with you afterwards."

On their way into the sanctuary, Matt said, "Where did your daughter get to? I was looking forward to meeting her."

"Kate took her to the nursery."

"Maybe I'll meet her after service then?"

"Today's not the best." Amy wasn't about to introduce Jessie to someone she barely knew who was clearly off-balance. And what had she done or said to make him think he should sit with her? Was he some kind of stalker?

Thankfully Marge said nothing during the drive home or at

lunch. But when Amy began clearing the table Marge whispered, "We have something to chat about don't we?"

Why couldn't she leave it? Amy had her own thoughts and emotions to deal with. She didn't need questions. "He's the reason I was late getting home on Thursday. But neither of us wants more than friendship."

"Well, he seems like a nice young man. I hope you'll bring him around sometime."

Fat chance!

"Hi. I wanted to catch you before we started." Matt sat perched on a desk in the foyer when Amy arrived for the next club meeting. "I need to apologize for pouncing on you Sunday."

"Don't worry about it. Let's head in." She walked past him.

Matt's apology ebbed and flowed throughout the evening.

When parents arrived for pick up, Amy found Matt shrugging into his coat. She touched his arm. Whoa, he did *not* look happy.

"I'm sorry for being abrupt," she said.

"I feel like an idiot. Intruding into your space on Sunday and asking to meet your daughter when you don't even know me."

After an awkward silence he said, "Let's go for another coffee. I wanna talk to you about something."

"Sure." Amy felt sorry for him. She'd never met anyone this strange.

They chatted about the kids they worked with and laughed at some of the antics. Matt asked a few personal questions, always careful to point out he wasn't prying.

"I should get going," Amy said when the conversation slowed.

"Before you go, I need to tell you something."

Here we go.

From Thorns

"When you told me you had a child I sort of freaked. Cards on the table—I originally asked you to go for coffee because you're so pretty." He shrugged looking sheepish. "Shallow, I know."

"Okay." What did he expect her to say?

Matt sighed. "Look, I'd like to spend some time with you, get to know you, you get to know me, and, well, maybe..."

Amy suppressed a grin at the sweat developing on his brow.

"Okay, this is awkward," Matt said. "D'ya wanna hang out sometime? Friends?"

"Sure."

Having the upper hand felt great.

CHAPTER 15

Matt suggested taking in the last of the greenery before autumn painted a new scene. Amy brought Jessie—if he didn't like it he wouldn't suggest hanging out again.

Matt confessed to being a little too deep and serious for most people. "I have a learning disability which makes it hard for me to read people so I don't do well in social situations. I've never had a relationship that lasted."

Amy breathed, "Uh-huh."

He described his background and his early struggles both in and out of school.

"I had a hard time in school too," Amy said. "And I didn't have a lot of friends."

He glanced at her. "I didn't like *any* of the stuff they tried to teach me. I didn't like the teachers, I didn't like the kids, and none of them liked me. It was pretty bad.

"I'm doing okay now, obviously, if I got into a master's program. But I still struggle because I can't read social cues or body language. I can't read between the lines. I can't read facial expressions. I work at it. I've tried to learn strategies to counteract my misperceptions, but it's really hard."

From Thorns

Matt talked on and on without asking Amy anything about herself or how she was managing the information dump.

In the parking lot he turned to look at her. "I'm interested in you. I'm nervous that you have a kid. I like that you're responsible. Honestly, I'm confused. I'd like to hang out but I don't want to lead you on."

After she got home Amy told Marge, "He seems nice and he wants to get to know me and I sorta like him, although I don't know why. He's kinda weird."

"Weird?"

She summarized the afternoon conversation. "And he talked non-stop. I barely had a chance to say anything."

"He sounds intense," Marge said. "But he's willing to be honest, which is a rare trait. Take it a step at a time."

Sunday morning, standing with her friends, Kate stopped mid-sentence when she saw Amy walk past with Matt.

Back at home, she dragged Amy to her bedroom and demanded details. She knew everything about boys and relationships and offered a lot of advice. "You have to give Matt a chance. Sure he's different, but he's honest and he's real and he's *so* good looking!"

"Thanks for the help," Amy said. She walked to the door and then turned to look at Kate again. "Can I talk to you about something else?"

"Sure."

"I see Tommy sometimes."

"By choice?"

"He comes to the pharmacy to buy stuff. He never says anything, just looks at me in a way that makes my skin crawl.

But I know I'm safe at work and I never see him anywhere else. I don't want your parents to know because your dad might get worked up and do something to make the situation worse. Do you think I should do something? Or tell someone?"

"No. Tommy just wants to scare you. Don't say anything to Matt. Or my parents."

After continual texting, daily telephone chats, one more coffee date, and with Marge's and Kate's encouragement, Amy invited Matt to Jessie's birthday celebration.

He, Steve, and Jason played basketball on the driveway. When Amy and Jess trespassed onto the basketball court, Matt jumped out of the game, took Jess by the waist, held her above his head, and attempted airplane sounds as he lowered her to the grass. It looked like he enjoyed kids. Was it an act?

Amy took Jessie's hands and redirected her unsteady feet toward the other side of the lawn, but she pulled away and began a fast crawl toward the driveway. After a few unsuccessful attempts, Amy had to take her inside to find a distraction.

When the basketball finished, Matt and Steve sat on the couch and appeared to converse easily, even laughing sometimes.

"Hey, do you guys wanna watch the baseball game with me?" Jason asked.

"Leave the adults to relax," Steve responded.

"Baseball's relaxing," Jason argued.

"We just want to chat for a while. Please go watch it on your own."

Jason shuffled off muttering something about his dad having too much authority.

When Marge called Steve to the kitchen, Kate inserted

From Thorns

herself onto the couch.

"Is it okay that I talked to Matt?" she whispered to Amy afterward.

"Why wouldn't it be?"

Kate shrugged. "Some girls get jealous if another girl talks to their boyfriend."

"Well I'm not like that. And he's *not* my boyfriend!"

"Really? He sure looks like your boyfriend. Hey, let me take Jess downstairs so you're free to be with him." Kate winked. "If you can drag him away from Dad."

During dinner, Jason engaged Matt in a sports-related discussion. Kate drew Matt into a university program conversation. Steve and Marge asked questions whenever they could break in. There wasn't a quiet moment.

Matt spoke with confidence. Was he at all tentative?

Following the meal, Amy brought the cake to the highchair and Marge blew out the candle before a tiny hand grabbed the flame. Jessie dropped her face directly onto the top of the cake and came up licking icing. Everyone laughed except for Jason. "Don't cut my piece from there. I don't want drool on my icing!"

While Steve and Matt cleaned up the dinner mess, Amy peppered Marge with questions. Did she like him? Did she think Steve liked him? Did Marge think he liked Jessie or was he pretending? Should she continue spending time with him or not?

"Do you like him?" Marge asked.

"I like him a lot. But I shouldn't feel this way about a friend."

"Oh, I suspect you're more than a friend to Matt."

"But he said—"

"Let's wait and see how things go."

What would Matt expect from a girlfriend? Amy wondered.

After tucking Jessie in, Amy stood by the crib rubbing her back. Time had flown quickly just like the birds do when they move south to escape the cold winters. If one doesn't grab the opportunity to look up, the moment passes and the birds are gone. How many moments of Jessie's first year had Amy missed?

Kate appeared at the door. "I need you to come upstairs."

As they approached Kate's bedroom Amy could hear Marge and Steve arguing.

"Shh," Kate said. "Listen."

Steve's voice. "She's not ready for this. She's too young. She's only developing some confidence now. She's learning to raise a child. C'mon. This isn't right."

"Well I think it's time for her to have something good happen. And Matt's such a nice boy."

"Matt's not thinking with his head! He's no more ready to be a father than Amy is to be a mother. She doesn't have a choice, but he does."

"Looks like he's choosing Amy and all that goes with her," Marge said. "Why can't you be happy for her?"

"Because I see her slamming into a mountain of disappointment if they keep this up."

"You need to lighten up Steve. She's going to make her own decisions and she'll need our support."

Kate shut her bedroom door. "Just because you have a child doesn't mean you have to give up everything else. Don't pay any attention if they decide to *have a talk* with you which they probably will. They're old. They don't understand what it's like today.

From Thorns

I can tell that Matt's crazy for you so promise you won't listen to them. If you have questions talk to *me*, not Mom or Dad."

Different from previous boys, Matt showed interest in more than just her body. They took walks, watched movies, and discussed ways of making Adventure Club better for the kids.

Amy painted a partial picture of her childhood home. Matt's eyes grew large as his face turned red. He bent at the waist, leaned on his thighs, and breathed deeply. When he stood again, he pulled her into his arms.

"I'm sorry I upset you," Amy said.

"You didn't upset me. I'm horrified at how you've been treated."

For a few days he looked at her differently. It was subtle but she could see it. And then their interactions returned to normal.

She asked how he felt about Jessie.

"Like I told you before, I wasn't keen on the idea but I'm falling in love with you and to be honest, Jessie too. My parents told me it was a bad idea laying out all sorts of reasons. Steve took me aside to tell me I was getting in over my head. But they don't get to decide about us. I've thought about it a lot. I've prayed about it and talked to my friends. I wanna be with you."

He's falling in love? He feels the same as me!

Although Steve *said* they were moving too fast, he seemed to like Matt. Amy heard them discuss many topics with ease and Steve happily accepted his help when something needed to be fixed.

Marge said Matt was unique, that many his age just wanted to have fun and not be bothered with anything serious. According to Marge he was just what Amy needed.

Amy laughed. "I'm glad somebody knows what I need."

There were times when fear consumed her.

"I can't do this. I don't have time. I have a child to care for."

"Am I getting in the way?" Matt asked.

"Sometimes, yes."

"I'm glad you told me. What do you need?"

In fact, she didn't need anything. They only spent time alone in the evening while Jessie slept. Amy was just afraid. Afraid of being used. Afraid of falling for him only to be dumped. Afraid Steve's disapproval would result in her being ousted. And mostly afraid she would do something stupid and he would see her as a loser.

"Why are you so understanding?" Amy asked.

"I dunno," Matt said. "It's what my parents are like. I think it's pretty normal."

Normal? He should meet *my* parents.

Kate checked in frequently. Amy's fear stole most of their conversation. "I don't think I should keep seeing him. He's too good for me."

"No, he's not," Kate insisted.

"He's so good-looking. What would he want with me?"

Kate dragged her to a mirror. "You get that you're beautiful, right?"

"He's too smart for me."

"No! He's! Not!"

Amy believed she should end the relationship. Instead she continued moving forward, enjoying the bond but believing it would end, trusting Matt but questioning everything, and drowning in apprehension when she was alone.

Although the dark cloud of insecurity and anxiety hung over

From Thorns

her, she and Matt found much sunshine. They continued to discuss movies, take Jessie to play structures, and walk Rumble. And they laughed. A lot.

"Man, you have an amazing sense of humour," Matt said.

Amy wondered where it came from. There certainly wasn't any humour in her childhood home.

She asked Marge about it.

"As you grow and learn to believe in yourself your true character will emerge. Your sense of humour and your ability to make people laugh is a part of who you are. You have many wonderful characteristics and I'm watching you blossom. I think Matt may be part of the reason." Marge winked.

While Amy felt mixed up about most aspects of this relationship, touch was something she understood. Touch from her father meant pain. Touch from previous boyfriends screamed of selfish gratification. But when Matt's hand moved gently across her back and his arm wrapped around her waist, when he pulled her close, when their bodies touched and she melted into his full embrace, she felt a tingling and warmth spread throughout her body until the heat consumed her.

And then she remembered the scars beneath her clothes and a cold fear replaced the warmth. Other boys didn't care about disfigurement as long as they got what they wanted. Matt would care. And he deserved better. But, being in love, she pushed those thoughts away.

Three months of spending loads of time together delivered diminished fear and a degree of confidence. Amy hoped, with time, she could learn to believe the things Kate and Marge said. Maybe then she could sweep away all of her insecurity.

With Christmas came reflection. Less than two years ago, Amy had been living with her parents, a young girl who believed she was good for nothing. She had conceived a child with a boy who cared nothing for her. He, along with her parents, had thrown her aside like trash.

Now she had a beautiful, healthy child and enjoyed a relationship with a good man. Sometimes she wondered if it was all a dream. Other times she felt her past was just a horrible nightmare.

After Matt returned from holiday time spent with his family, he and Amy joined a group of friends for a New Year's Eve event. When the ball dropped Matt took her in his arms, stared into her eyes with a look she hadn't seen before, and kissed her, lingering, consuming.

Did he love her as much as she loved him? It was different from the love she had for Jessie which kept her grounded. What she felt for Matt sent her to another universe.

The next morning when Amy replaced the calendar on her wall, she tried to imagine what the coming year might have in store, with no idea of the disaster about to unfold.

CHAPTER 16

"There's a young man at the door," Steve called. "He wants to talk to you."

"Who is it?" Amy asked as she ascended the stairs.

"Don't know."

When she got to the foyer, Amy froze. "Tommy? What do you want?"

"I wanna see my daughter."

"*Why?*"

"Because she's my kid and I have rights."

"You told me to get an abortion!"

"I hired a lawyer."

Steve moved in. "I'm Amy's dad." As he started to close the door he said, "We'll be in touch."

Tommy blocked the doorway. "You can't shut me out. I'm the father."

"I *said* we'll be in touch."

"Fine. But if you think I'll go away, you're wrong."

When the door closed, screaming filled the air. "No! No! No!" Amy looked at Steve, her eyes pleading. "I thought you said he couldn't do this!"

Steve called his lawyer.

The outcome of the legal consultation was, provided Tommy was a reasonable sort-of person, he had rights.

"He threatened me," Amy said, "and he attacked me at school. We had to call the police."

"Is there a police report?"

Amy looked at Steve. "I doubt it," he said. "A friend from the department came by to talk to Amy. He visited Tommy; said we shouldn't have any more trouble." He looked to Amy. "You never signed anything?"

"No." Amy paused. "But he also sent harassing emails."

"Do you still have them?"

"No."

"What about text messages or social media?"

"I only got a phone recently—he doesn't know the number. And I'm not on Facebook or anything."

The lawyer looked to Steve. "Can you find out if the police have any record of the school incident?"

Amy wished Tommy had raped or beaten her. If only there were hospital records. She hoped there was a police report, something, anything, that would cause the court to consider him unfit.

Her despair consumed her. She couldn't eat. She barely slept. She took time off work. She met with the pastor for counselling and the doctor for medication.

She tried to end her relationship with Matt but he begged her not to. "Love doesn't walk away when the going gets tough."

But she couldn't talk to him. She couldn't talk to anyone.

While Jessie napped, Amy crawled into bed with Bear and

From Thorns

sobbed. She pleaded with God. She schemed. But nothing changed.

"How're ya doing?" Kate asked from time to time.

Amy just shook her head wondering how Kate could ask such a stupid question.

Marge's repeated encouragements, "It will all work out," "We'll stand with you through this," "We won't let anything bad happen to Jessie," got absorbed into the walls, ignored by Amy.

Her life was a ship off course sailing toward a sea of anguish.

During the legal process Tommy cooperated. No criminal record, no indication of addictions or abusive behaviours. He agreed to supervised visitation and began making support payments.

Although his contributions helped with costs, Amy didn't want his money and she didn't want to sign the mutual agreement for supervised visitation. She wanted to take it to court to buy time. But her lawyer advised, "If the father sees you cooperating it'll go better for you. And it's best for the child if the parents can get along."

The only glimmer in the midst of total darkness was the long waitlist for the access centre where visitation would begin. Where Tommy would be supervised. Hopefully he would show his true colours and this whole mess could be swept away.

The fight drained out of her and acceptance filled the void.

She called Matt on Valentine's Day. "I've been withdrawn for too long. I'm sorry."

"I understand—you've been trapped in a nightmare. When can I see you?"

Twenty-four hours in a day wasn't enough. So Matt brought his schoolwork to the house and found whatever quiet space was available to study. Although Amy busied herself with chores, she invaded his space frequently. The excitement experienced before Christmas reignited.

"I love you."

"I love you, too."

"I love you more than all the cinnamon hearts in the world."

Winter's frigid air didn't deter them from exploring new activities. Matt taught Amy how to skate and she agreed to try snowboarding.

Thankfully Jessie hadn't developed a shyness. She was as comfortable with Matt as she had been before Tommy messed everything up.

Jason and Matt reconnected as though no time had passed. They enjoyed watching hockey on television and they attended some of the local games together. Steve drew Matt back into household projects.

Matt stayed for dinner most evenings.

"Are you sure you're okay with him being here so much?" Amy asked.

"We love having him here!" Marge said.

"I should contribute more for groceries."

"Relax. If we start to run short on funds, I'll be sure to let you know."

And the subject of Tommy got packed away in a small container never to be discussed. When Amy was alone she unpacked it, but to no useful end. She would have to wait through the next few months. By then she hoped Tommy might have lost interest.

Before long Matt's thinking chose a direction. "I only have another year in school and I've got some income and you're working. Let's get married this summer."

From Thorns

Marge confessed to overhearing these discussions. "I think you should wait. Next summer you'll have known each other for less than a year. And you're going to have to deal with Tommy which could get messy. You need more time together before making such a big commitment."

Amy and Matt considered Marge's thoughts and decided she didn't understand the depth of their love.

A mere two months passed before Amy received an invitation to bring Jessie into the supervised access centre for orientation.

"They said it would take around six months. This isn't fair!"

The centre was designed to make any child feel comfortable and Jessie took to the effervescent supervisor, Nathalie. Following the tour Nathalie looked at Jessie, "We have a nice room filled with cool toys. Want me to show you?"

After being assured that Mommy would wait in the hall, Jessie took Nathalie's hand and happily walked off.

"Why couldn't she have a shy streak?" Amy moaned. "She should be nervous around strangers."

"That might have prolonged the process," Marge agreed. "But on the other hand, her outgoing nature will make it easier at the first visitation. We want it to be easy for Jessie, right?"

Amy stared at the floor.

After a brief playtime, Nathalie and a smiling Jessie emerged from the room. "Let's have one more visit before we invite Dad in."

"*What*? Jessie needs more time!" Amy protested.

When Jessie started to whimper, Nathalie invited Amy into the playroom.

"She's an outgoing child. Happy. Confident. You're obviously a great mom. I understand your fear, but you'll have to find a way to keep the anxiety from Jessie. The process has to move forward and you are a key part of its success."

"I don't *want* it to succeed," Amy blurted.

"For Jessie's sake we need to make the transition as smooth as possible."

When they got home, she pulled the phone from her pocket and sprinted to her room.

"C'mon, c'mon, answer."

"Hi gorgeous."

She burst into tears at the sound of Matt's voice. "Tommy gets to be with Jess soon, probably in a couple of weeks, and I have to act happy about it for Jessie's sake except Jessie needs to *never* see him and she doesn't need me putting on a smile as though any of this is okay and—"

"Whoa, slow down, breathe," Matt said.

"I can't handle this," Amy blubbered.

"We'll get through it together."

But Amy withdrew and grew sullen.

Matt begged her to let him help. "I can't change the situation but I can support you, listen when you need to cry, offer hugs to lift your spirits."

"I'm sorry, I need to be alone right now."

"You can't push Matt away," Marge said. "Involving him shows trust and he's earned that."

Angry, Amy retreated from Marge. How dare she push her nose into this! Couldn't she see that Amy was doing her best? She didn't even have enough energy for Jessie right now. Matt would have to wait!

From Thorns

After Amy's and Jessie's next trip to the access centre, the counsellor scheduled Tommy's first visitation.

During that visit Amy waited in the parking lot, trying to take comfort in knowing her daughter wasn't alone with that monster.

Jessie appeared happy afterwards and Nathalie confirmed it went well. "Tommy seems like a good dad. I won't have to supervise much longer."

No more denial—Tommy's in.

His motivation, unknown.

CHAPTER 17

"I'm sorry for pushing you aside," Amy said when Matt answered the phone. "I love you so much, but this situation is taking everything I have. Please give me time."

"Of course!"

After a couple of days of depression, Amy regained composure and set her mind in charge. She had often heard Steve say, 'your feelings are your warning system, but you make decisions with your head.' It was time for her head to create a recipe to control this disaster, and it didn't take long to form a plan.

Before moving forward Amy reviewed her idea with Kate, and then Marge, and then Steve. With everyone's approval, she took a deep breath and dialled.

"Hello."

"Hi Tommy. It's Amy."

"Wha'd'ya want?"

"Jessie had a good time at your first visit. Not that we had a conversation, obviously, but I could tell. I thought you'd want to know."

"Why are you calling?"

"I want us to be friends. I really liked you in high school

From Thorns

and I'd like to get to know you more. I mean, we're both Jessie's parents."

Silence.

"It's up to you of course."

Amy looked at Marge who mouthed, "You're doing well."

"I'm kinda surprised to hear from you," Tommy said, "but… okay."

They agreed to meet at a coffee shop. Amy selected the one closest to home.

She arrived first and chose a table. As she watched Tommy walk toward her, she cringed. The scent of his aftershave filled the space around them. It was a fragrance she had once loved, but now it made her sick.

The conversation centred around Jessie, but Tommy took airtime to brag about his accomplishments and possessions. He even owned a house. Amy feigned interest. He didn't ask much about her world which was just as well. She hadn't planned to share more than absolutely necessary to keep the game going.

As the conversation wound down, Amy asked if they could go out again. Tommy agreed.

Success! She had fooled him into believing she cared. She had controlled her fear and masked her hatred.

The way clouds dissipate after a storm, Amy's fear dissolved. A seed of hope led to growing confidence that she would be able to gain Tommy's trust. And with that she felt certain he would soon be comfortable telling her anything she wanted to know.

She called Matt.

"Why didn't you tell me you were planning this? I would have been at the coffee shop ready to jump in if anything went wrong. And I'm not sure this is a good plan."

But he didn't have any other suggestions.

They agreed to meet the following evening.

Holding hands, they strolled through a park enjoying the sweet scent of budding blossoms. Their conversation wound around work events, church happenings, Matt's courses, papers, tests, and marks. No mention of Tommy. As the sun rolled toward the horizon, the breeze turned chilly.

Back home they snuggled into the couch. Amy thanked him for accepting her decisions.

Matt shifted away from her. "I don't like it but it's not my call." Amy looked down. "This is hard on me," he continued. "You've withdrawn and shut me out more than once. I get it—you're in a horrible situation. But I'm your boyfriend and I should be a person you trust. It feels like you don't want me involved."

"I'm sorry." Amy drew her legs up and wrapped her arms around them. Looking away she said, "I'll try to do better."

She called Rumble to come join them. He provided the momentum to turn the sour air into something more palatable and their conversation turned to lighter topics.

When it was time for Matt to leave, Amy thought things had returned to normal, until he pulled her into a hug. Where had the passion gone?

A few days later on her birthday, she chose to spend time with her new family, quietly, without any fanfare. Matt didn't call. Had he forgotten the date? Or was he so annoyed that he didn't want any involvement? But as the week progressed they resumed daily chats. Neither mentioned Tommy.

On the weekend Matt joined the family for dinner. Before the

From Thorns

meal he split his time between Jessie and Jason, much to their glee. Steve had to intervene occasionally to keep the activity level under control. "Jumpin' Judas! You guys need to get outside. When's this rain gonna stop?"

The dinner conversation was jovial as always. Kate joined the group to eat but excused herself as soon as dessert was done. Her world now revolved around university activities and new friends.

After settling Jessie into bed Amy returned to the living room to find Steve and Matt drinking coffee and talking. Matt was clearly comfortable with everyone except her. Oh he pretended all was well, but she felt the undercurrent.

She wandered into the kitchen where Jason sat at the table doing homework. He looked up and grinned. "I'm glad Matt came over tonight."

"I'm glad too," Amy replied. "But it hasn't been long since he was last here. It's not like this was some kind of reunion."

Jason dropped his head and stared at his homework.

I've got enough stress without guilt from you, she thought.

She joined Marge at the sink. "Would you like me to take over the dishes?"

Marge glanced toward Jason, "I need to supervise. Grab a towel." She lowered her voice to a whisper. "It was good to have Matt join us."

Amy changed the subject.

During the following week, the tension settled. After a few good conversations Matt returned to the habit of visiting every day. The only thing standing between them, Amy thought, was how Matt felt left out of her plan to protect Jessie.

"I'm sorry I didn't talk to you about spending time with

Tommy. It's only to fool him into telling me everything I need to know." She suddenly realized she had discussed the idea with Kate and Marge and Steve. Why not Matt?

"It's okay. You're living in a disaster. I've never walked in your shoes and I need to be more understanding. Anyway, it's all sorted out now."

"Thanks Matt. I'm gonna meet Tommy again tomorrow. But only to keep the charade going. I hate him!"

"I hate that you'll be with him, but I get it and I'm glad you told me. Please call when it's over."

It had been two weeks since their first meeting. Tommy was waiting when she stepped off the bus. As they walked to a Mexican restaurant, Amy felt her anxiety dissipating.

While perusing the menu Amy said, "I've never tried Mexican. What do you suggest?" Tommy helped her make a selection.

"How was your time with Jessie on Saturday?" She had hoped to play it cool, to say nothing, to wait for Tommy to bring it up. But her need-to-know won the inner tug of war.

Tommy's face lit up. "It was good. She kept me moving. I guess it was the same when Nathalie was with us but I had her for longer this time. She tired me out."

"What did you do with her?"

A frown replaced the smile. "Is this an interrogation?"

"Of course not! I'm just interested."

"Okay. Let's talk about something else."

As they ate Tommy spoke of his expertise in carpentry and how he applied the skill at his new house. He talked proudly about his construction knowledge which would enable him to

From Thorns

complete the renovations on his own.

Amy found herself asking questions with some interest. She remembered him as a boy of few words which he certainly wasn't anymore. And he had some impressive accomplishments.

If only she could say the same about herself.

Tommy beamed when Amy thanked him for helping her make such a great selection from the menu.

While they waited for the cheque he asked, "Why did Steve say he was your dad?"

"When I left home they let me live with them and I ended up staying. You know how much I hated my own parents and they've been really good to me and Jess, so I just think of them as my family."

Tommy's eyebrows arched. "I don't get it. Even if you want to think of Steve as your dad, why would he think of you as his kid? They have their own kids. Doesn't make sense."

"I know. But Marge told me they've adopted me. It sounds weird but I kind of like that they want to think of me that way."

"Okay, whatever."

He looked toward the waitress who was serving another table. "If she wants a tip she better get moving." He shook his head as he turned back.

"Another thing I've wondered—why did you call her Jessie?"

"When I was a kid, I always wished my name was Jessica."

"Hmm." He shrugged. "Makes sense."

They chatted about trivia until the waitress arrived with the bill.

After paying Tommy walked Amy to the bus stop. He reached into a bag he'd carried all evening and retrieved a gift for Jessie. A cute summer dress that would fit perfectly.

A third get-together was arranged.

Back in her room, Amy reflected on the evening. Tommy had helped her order a meal without belittling her lack of experience. And he'd accomplished a lot, owning a house already. But he didn't want to talk about his time with Jessie. Yet he brought a gift.

Maybe he'd changed. He was still in high school when he told her to abort. Now, with a job and money maybe he regretted all that.

The next day she called Matt. He listened but was vague in his responses.

"Do you think I'm on the wrong page?" Amy asked.

"I'm afraid he's playing you."

"Okay, so if he is what am I supposed to do? Don't I have to continue getting to know him for Jessie's sake?"

Matt sighed, "I suppose."

"Will there ever be a time I can give him the benefit of the doubt? Or do you want me to see him as a monster, and nothing but a monster, forever?"

"I don't care about Tommy and I don't care how you see him. I care about you and Jessie and I don't want him to con you into believing anything other than the truth."

"Well there it is," Amy said. "You'll never see him in a good light. But I need to try. He's the father of my child. He has visitation rights and he could get joint custody. I need to know him so I can protect my daughter. And if there's good in him then I won't have to worry as much."

"Don't be so naïve. You've had two meetings with him. It's not hard for someone to conceal their true colours for a few

From Thorns

hours every couple of weeks."

"I have to go," Amy growled.

"Fine."

What if Tommy *is* playing a game? How can I know? Does it even matter? Actually, I'm playing the game trying to get him to trust me. That's what I need to tell Matt. If he could understand then he wouldn't be so upset. But he should believe me even if he doesn't get it. Why can't he be like he was before Tommy barged into my life?

An hour later the phone rang.

"I'm sorry," Matt said.

"I need support not opposition."

"I know." Matt paused. "I'm biased and I suppose I'm not really open to the possibility of Tommy being a decent person. I keep thinking about how he showed up on your doorstep. But I'll try harder to put my prejudice aside."

More of these difficult conversations led Amy to question the wisdom of speaking with him about anything related to Tommy.

CHAPTER 18

The evening before their next outing, Tommy called to ask Amy if he could pick her up at the house. He wasn't comfortable facing Steve so he asked that she wait outside.

Before he arrived Amy wrestled with confusion. Was Matt right? Was she missing something? Or was Tommy sincere and Matt just jealous? How was she supposed to figure it all out? She would have to pay close attention this evening.

Tommy took her to his favourite hamburger spot. They giggled when they had to reposition themselves to avoid wearing a variety of condiments. They laughed as Amy recounted some of Jessie's antics.

Humour had been a part of their early relationship. Maybe that's why laughter came easily now. And clearly Tommy was growing more comfortable which was Amy's entire goal.

Following their meal, Tommy said he needed to talk about something serious and he wanted to go somewhere private.

Amy certainly did not want privacy. But she didn't want to upset him either. "Okay. Where are we going?"

He drove to a spot on the river where he liked to fish. While they walked, a warm breeze offered some relief from the summer

From Thorns

heat and kept the bugs away. The path was crowded with people, allowing Amy to relax.

"I never really wanted you to get an abortion," Tommy said. "I was a kid in high school with no way to support a family and I was scared. Abortion seemed like the only way."

"Really?" Amy wanted to believe him.

"Yeah. And I threatened you to try to make you think. I mean, I didn't know how you were going to do it. I knew your parents wouldn't help. And I didn't have money."

"Did you really talk to my father?"

Tommy shook his head. "I don't know why I said that."

They walked in silence for a bit.

"Anyway," Tommy continued, "eventually I found out you were staying with Kate's family." He stopped walking and stared at her. "I couldn't believe it. You weren't exactly friends."

"Kate approached me. Said her mother could help. I didn't have any other option."

"And they just told you to move in?"

"Not exactly. But one thing led to another."

"Bizarre." Tommy resumed walking. "And I don't understand why they're letting you stay. Or why they say you're one of the family. Are you sure you can trust them?"

"They've been really nice to me. I haven't found any reason *not* to trust them. In the beginning I kept thinking something would go wrong, but it never did." Amy looked at her watch. "Even though they're nice I can't take advantage. They look after Jessie a lot and I know they like me home before they go to bed."

"Well anyway, I just wanted you to know that I'm proud of you for going through with it and I feel bad for letting you down."

At home, she invited Rumble to join her for a chat. By the

time she felt sleepy the situation made sense—Tommy was no longer the irresponsible boy she had known in high school. And maybe he wasn't even irresponsible back then. Maybe *she* was irresponsible for thinking she could handle the pregnancy and raise a child. She got lucky with the Raynors but what if they hadn't taken her in?

Tommy had a good job and, although he was only three years older than her, he already owned a car and a house. It seemed he just wanted the chance to love his daughter. Amy reasoned that her initial hatred made sense under the circumstance of Tommy's intrusion back into her life. She now understood it was the only thing he could do.

But his threatening emails and visits to the pharmacy? How did those pieces fit into the puzzle?

The next day she enthusiastically shared her thoughts.

Marge suggested that Amy hadn't given it enough time, that she shouldn't offer this kind of trust so easily, that more interaction was needed before she could reliably draw conclusions. "Don't forget how he's treated you. And how he's disrupted your life. My gosh, his behaviour sent you into a depression."

"I know. But now I have more information and it turns out he's actually glad I went through with it and had Jessie."

Marge rolled her eyes. "Don't believe his words! Look at his actions and believe that."

"What else was he supposed to do? He knew he couldn't afford to take care of me and a child so he suggested abortion. Now that he's got his life together, he just wants a fair chance."

"A fair chance," Marge muttered while shaking her head. "If that's what he wanted he shouldn't have shown up on our

From Thorns

doorstep threatening legal action. And he didn't *suggest* abortion. He threatened you. Said he would take Jessie away if you didn't abort, followed by some nasty emails."

Amy agreed to think about it more but she felt irritated.

That evening, she called Matt. His reaction was much the same as Marge's.

"Why is everyone assuming the worst?" Amy demanded. "People change. I've changed a lot. What makes you think Tommy can't change?"

"I love your optimism and I hope you're right," Matt said. "I just don't want to see you get hurt. Remember, he has a goal and he'll play you to get what he wants. I don't think you can afford to trust him."

Amy remained silent.

"How about I join you the next time you meet?" Matt suggested. "If I can get to know Tommy, I'll be able to put my fears to rest and support you better through all of this."

Again, Amy said nothing.

"Y'know, I think Tommy and I *should* get to know each other."

"I'll think about it," Amy said. "I gotta go."

Of course she couldn't introduce Matt to Tommy. That would make Tommy shut down and refuse to spend any more time with her. Why would Matt even suggest such a thing?

A restless night afforded time for thinking. She woke up angry.

Why do people think I'm too stupid to figure this out for myself? Matt's got his own ulterior motives. Maybe he should look inside himself instead of telling me how to figure out Tommy. He said he would try to be more positive but I'm not seeing that.

When she called to confront him, he asked if it was time to end their relationship. Her stomach did a somersault. "Of course not. But I feel like the rope in a tug of war. I want to keep Jess safe so I'm getting to know Tommy. And I also want to please you but I can't seem to do anything right."

Matt sighed. "I'm sorry. This is a tense situation and I feel like I'm on the outside. I need to be involved. I need you to talk to me. And trust me."

"I *do* trust you but I'm the one who has to make decisions for Jessie, and getting advice from everyone is confusing. I'm not spending time with him because I *want* to. It's only for Jessie's protection."

Why can't Matt see he's wrong? Amy wondered. And Marge is no better. She doesn't know anything about Tommy. She hasn't spent time with him. Everyone was happy for me to go out with him to learn more, but now that I have no one will accept what I've learned.

I don't want any more favours, Amy decided. It's time for me to arrange childcare somewhere else. What about evening shifts? I'll talk to my supervisor. Maybe I can switch to working days, the days I'm not at the church. But that will mean less income.

I need to figure this out.

The following day she asked Marge to leave the situation alone. She promised to bring concerns forward if anything came up.

When Steve came home Amy sat on the stairs where she could hear everything. Sure enough, Marge jumped straight into it.

"How can I make Amy see what a big mistake this is? They've only gone out three times. He walked out of her life when she

From Thorns

needed his help and then waltzed back in without a care for the people affected. She needs to talk with some girls her own age. Girls who have come from good families. If only Kate wasn't so darn busy."

"She's a sensible girl. I'm sure she'll figure it out. Stop worrying."

Smiling, Amy returned to her room.

CHAPTER 19

A week later Tommy suggested a tour of his house. They stopped to get Chinese take-out on the way. The house was near her childhood home which caused her to feel so uneasy it upset her stomach.

Inside, Tommy asked her to ignore the current state of things—it would soon look totally different. He poured a glass of wine for each of them. It had been a while for her and back then it was only for zoning out and forgetting.

They ate at a small table in the corner of the kitchen. Amy picked at her food with her gut refusing to loosen its knots. About ten minutes in Tommy asked, "Don't you like Chinese?"

"Oh no, I really like it but my stomach's a bit upset."

"Do you want to lie down?"

Amy shook her head. "I'll be fine. The wine is helping."

Tommy added more to her glass.

When they finished eating he put the leftovers in the fridge. "I'll take that for lunch tomorrow. Ready to see the house?"

As they toured, he explained that housing prices were depressed in the area but didn't go low enough for him to afford anything other than a total fixer-upper. The main floor of the

From Thorns

two-bedroom bungalow revealed ripped carpet, missing baseboards, broken light fixtures, and a need for extensive cleaning. Tommy stopped to articulate all the changes he planned to make in each room. Amy wondered at some of his ideas. But then, what did she know? "Are you really going to be able to fix this place all on your own?" she asked.

Tommy's brow furrowed. "Are you saying you don't think I can do it?"

"I just think it might be too much work for one person."

"Why?"

Amy shrugged. "It's a lot, that's all."

"Yeah, it's a lot of work but I know what I'm doing, and I'll get it done on my own." He continued down the hall.

Poor guy. He thought I was criticizing.

"The basement isn't finished," Tommy said. He described his plans for that level as he poured more wine and then directed Amy to the couch. "I got this furniture second-hand. Obviously I want nicer, but for now—"

"It's great!" Amy said. She enjoyed being in a house owned by someone of her generation and to be sharing a bottle of wine.

When the evening drew to an end they agreed to spend time at the house again the following week. Tommy drove her home.

When she called Matt she downplayed her time with Tommy, not mentioning they went to his house. She also didn't mention the plan to return next week.

"What did you do together? Where did you go?"

"We just hung out at a park for awhile." She felt guilty about lying to Matt. But she knew he wouldn't be okay with her spending time at Tommy's house.

She enjoyed the first official day of summer in Tommy's backyard under a clear evening sky and wrapped in a pleasantly warm temperature. In her bare feet, the green grass felt lush. Amy wondered aloud why someone would have let the gardens deteriorate while keeping the grass healthy.

Tommy explained that the yard was a disaster when he took possession of the house the previous fall. He had immediately seeded and nurtured the lawn to perfection. He went on to describe the patio and rock garden he planned to put in.

"I like red and yellow flowers mixed together, dahlias especially," Amy said. "Marge taught me how to plant and care for them."

"Yeah, well I know a lot about flowers too and I already know what I'm gonna plant."

Does he think I wanna take over? she wondered. I need to be more careful of his feelings.

Tommy barbequed burgers. They ate while sitting on a blanket on the lawn and reminisced about their third date with the messy hamburgers. Amy felt distracted by the smell of his cologne. She loved it when they were together in high school, she hated it when they first met up a few weeks back, and now she found herself feeling drawn to it.

They looked back on their high school history, laughing at or lambasting several of their teachers. Tommy remembered fellow students he hated. Amy's memories didn't include hatred except for her parents, but she'd certainly experienced dislike and resentment. She supposed Tommy wasn't treated any better than she had been. Because he was a grade ahead, their paths hadn't connected until recesses or after school. And they'd never

From Thorns

talked about anything serious except for how much Amy hated going home.

After the sun disappeared behind the broken fence, Tommy asked if she would like to come over the following evening, but Amy had a shift scheduled at the pharmacy.

"I also have to think about Jessie. I'm leaving her with Marge too often. I tried to find childcare but it's really expensive and they don't cover evenings and Marge doesn't want a teen coming in to babysit."

Tommy shrugged. "Bring her with you."

When tucked into bed Amy relived the evening. She felt something new. Attraction.

Though not tall or handsome like Matt, Tommy was attractive in his own way. She remembered their high school relationship and her feelings when they were together. The memories were cloaked in excitement.

Tommy had a good sense of humour. There hadn't been much talk outside of jokes but she never needed more. Laughter and love provided brief interludes of pleasure. She hadn't fit in with any community of girls, she hated going home to face her mother, and when her father got home . . .

Amy shivered.

She had felt special with Tommy. Back then he was the only good thing in her life. She wondered if she'd filled the same kind of void for him.

Their relationship ended when she got pregnant. But now she knew that was only because he couldn't afford a baby. Today he wanted involvement which is what she had hoped for in the first place.

She ended her relationship with Matt.

He didn't argue.

She felt torn afterwards. Matt was a good person. He fit in well with the family and she knew he loved her. But lately he wasn't as nice as Tommy.

He was the biological father and no one could love a child more than the birth parents. Nothing could be better for Jessie than to have her parents together. She imagined providing a good family dynamic for Jess where she would experience the kind of love that Amy, herself, had never known.

When she discussed her thoughts with Rumble he didn't offer a single objection. He wasn't able to remind her that she had grown up with her biological parents.

CHAPTER 20

"What's going on around here? Since when did we become a daycare, or should I say night-care?"

"Relax!" Marge snapped. "I tried to talk to you about this and you waved me off. *It'll all be fine. She knows what she's doing.* That's what you said and now here we are."

"What are you talking about?"

"I knew things were going wrong, that Amy was making a big mistake, but you wouldn't listen."

Steve shook his head. "I'm talking about Jessie! Amy *will* figure it out. Meanwhile Jessie is our task most evenings."

"Oh, that's good." Marge walked to the other side of the room. With her jaw set she turned to look at her husband. "Jessie isn't *our* task. I don't see *you* doing a thing. And it's not *most* evenings. It's *some* evenings."

"Great. Now we're arguing over someone else's kid."

"I can't believe you just said that. We committed to this together."

Steve threw his hands up in the air and brought them down on top of his head. He sighed audibly and then spoke softly. "I'm not saying I want Amy and Jessie out of our lives. I just don't think it's fair for *you*—yes *you*—to spend so much time attending to Jessie after I get home from work. You're not young anymore. I just thought Amy was working too many evening shifts. That we could ask her to cut back."

"If only." Marge shook her head. "I don't know what else to do. She's way too close to Tommy and if I tell her I don't want to look after Jessie on the evenings she's with him, what will happen? She's fragile and she needs us. I don't want to be the reason she runs off with that creep."

"I thought she was just getting to know him as protection for Jessie."

Marge stared at him, her mouth agape. "You're kidding, right? Matt's out of the picture and Tommy's in."

"Oh no."

"Oh yes."

Marge left Steve in the living room while she made tea.

What's wrong with that man? How could he not have noticed that Matt's disappeared? I've even told him but clearly he wasn't listening. Typical.

Steve wandered into the kitchen. "I think we better invite Tommy over. It sounds like Amy's made some bad decisions and she needs some redirection."

"Do ya think?" Marge shot back. Then she sighed. "I'm sorry. Yes, it's worth a try. I'll ask her to invite him."

What did Tommy want with Jessie and Amy? Marge wondered. *From the one conversation where Amy confessed Tommy's impatience it didn't sound like he had any genuine interest in either one of them.*

CHAPTER 21

When she saw the easiness between father and daughter, the tension Amy didn't even know she was carrying emptied from her like a sink full of water swirling down the drain.

"We've been invited to a family dinner. Everyone wants to meet you and get to know you," Amy said with excitement.

"Not a good idea. I'm sure they all hate me for stealing Jessie."

"Please," Amy begged.

"I don't like their influence on you. No make-up. And your clothes! You used to look hot."

Amy felt her cheeks redden. "Do you find me unattractive?"

"Of course not. But I wish you dressed like you used to and I know the only reason for the change is *them*."

"You're right; I care what they think. Also the pregnancy changed my perspective on everything. But I'll try to do better. I'm glad you told me."

"Thanks," Tommy said as he pulled her into a hug.

"I still want you to meet them."

Amy persisted and eventually Tommy gave in.

Barbequed chicken, corn on the cob, cucumber salad, potato salad, and homemade corn bread. Marge refused Amy's help. "We want to make Tommy comfortable so you need to stay with him."

Out on the deck, Jason joined the group for dinner with sports-related questions. Tommy wasn't interested in sports and didn't show any interest in Jason, who excused himself after the main course.

"How did you get interested in carpentry?" Steve asked.

"The father of a friend from school is a carpenter and he taught me."

"Are you a dedicated carpenter at work?"

"No. I have other construction skills so I do lots of different things."

"What does a typical day look like?"

Steve had no end of questions. Although Tommy answered, he shifted in his seat and appeared to avoid eye contact. Amy wanted to help him relax but didn't know how. They stayed on the deck until the mosquitos joined the gathering.

When they moved inside, Jason reappeared. "How did you know we were about to have dessert?" Steve asked with a wink. "I thought you were doing homework."

"I'm feeling faint," Jason said as he dropped his head onto his forearm. "I need sugar real quick." He took his dessert and disappeared.

The adults settled in the living room. "It's unusual for someone your age to be able to afford a house. Well done!" Steve said around a mouthful of cheesecake.

When Tommy spoke about the renovations Steve became

From Thorns

animated and offered to help.

With eyebrows arched Marge said, "The reason my kitchen hasn't been updated is Steve won't let anyone else do the job. And I'm not going to let him start something that will take years to complete."

Steve looked at Tommy with an expression Amy hadn't seen before. Marge groaned, "Oh no," as Steve wondered aloud whether Tommy would be interested in lending a hand on a kitchen reno.

Following coffee, Amy took Tommy downstairs to show him where she and Jessie lived. Jason turned off the T.V. and headed toward the staircase.

"You don't have to leave," Amy said.

"It's okay. My show's over."

Amy shrugged. She gave Tommy a tour of the lower level. As she walked toward the couch Tommy stopped her and motioned toward her bedroom. "Let's sit in there. We'll have more privacy."

"That went really well," Amy said. "I can tell they like you."

"Didn't you notice how Marge reacted when Steve suggested I help with their kitchen work?"

Amy thought for a moment and then she laughed. "Marge wasn't saying 'oh no' regarding your involvement. She just doesn't want Steve to start something that will take forever to finish."

"I think you're being pretty naïve. All Steve's questions about my job and the house . . ."

"They're interested," Amy said, "and they want to get to know you."

"Get real! They were just digging for information so they can talk about it later and figure out how to convince you to stop seeing me. Don't forget how Marge reacted a while back when you told her you wanted to spend more time with me."

Amy wished she hadn't shared that detail. Had she poisoned his mind against the family? "I just think we need to spend more time with them so we can all relax and let our barriers down. They're good people. Look how much they've done for me."

"I'm busy for the next few days," Tommy said. "Do you want to bring Jess over to my place on Thursday?"

I guess he's not comfortable talking about this just yet, Amy reasoned.

"Sure. What time will you pick us up?"

"I won't be able to pick you up. Too busy at work. But I told you how to get there by bus. It won't take long for you to come back here for Jessie and then make your way to my place. I'll put a key under the front mat so you can let yourself in. I'll get groceries on my way back tonight so you can start cooking before I get home."

Through the summer, Tommy devoted more time to renovating such that he could barely make time for Amy or Jessie. Had the novelty of having a daughter worn off? Had he lost interest in Amy? She asked if she had done something wrong.

"What do you mean?" Tommy said.

"You don't have much time for me or Jess anymore."

"That's not true. We spend lots of time together."

"Sure we're all at the house, but you work. When I first started coming over we hung out together and talked."

He breathed an exaggerated sigh. "This is the season I can work outside. Do you want a nice house or not?"

"I'm sorry." Amy felt sweat bead on her forehead. "I was just

From Thorns

worried you might be avoiding me 'cause I did something wrong."

She didn't know anything about houses, construction, or renovation. Why had she said anything? The voices from her past whispered, *stupid girl, always in the way.*

Tommy took her face in his hands and kissed her bottom lip. "It's okay. I'm not upset." When he drew close the scent of his aftershave flooded her senses.

"I'm really sorry. You've got enough on your mind without my stupid issues." She searched his eyes but couldn't discern emotion.

"Stop worrying. You said you were sorry." He smiled. "Now I've gotta get back to work."

"Of course. Thank you for working so hard. For caring about Jessie and making the house nice for her."

Why am I feeling scared? she wondered. He didn't yell or anything.

"It's not just for Jessie. I'm doing this for all of us." Tommy turned back to his work. Without looking up he said, "You better go find her."

Amy was already on her way.

He's doing this for all of us. Including me!

She brought Jessie back to the work area. "Look what Daddy's doing."

Tommy didn't look away from his project.

"Maybe we should have dinner again with the family. Steve asked me to ask you."

Tommy dropped his tool and stood. "I told you," he said, his eyes darkening, "I'm not going through that again. Now leave me to do my work."

CHAPTER 22

Marge felt Amy withdrawing. It had taken so long for her to come out of her shell, to show some happiness, some confidence. And now it was being replaced by the sadness she moved in with. Marge could also smell fear. She had to do something. So, she baked a red velvet cake loaded with cream cheese icing and invited Amy to have a piece with her.

After a few minutes of small talk Marge dove in. "You and Tommy are spending a lot of time together. Things going well?"

Amy put her fork down and stared at her hands.

Marge reached across the table and placed her hand on Amy's. "I know I haven't been totally supportive in the past, but I enjoyed the evening we spent with you and Tommy. Steve and I are anxious to get to know him."

Amy leaned back in her chair. "I'm confused sometimes and I don't know what to do. I like being with Tommy. Jess has fun when he plays with her. Yet he's so busy that he can't give her much time anymore. But I know he loves her. And I know it would be good for her to have a complete family. And Tommy's house is perfect. He has a great yard and we could get a swing set and put in a sandbox and invite friends over to play when she's

From Thorns

old enough. But there are things I don't know how to handle."

Marge tried to keep the horror she felt off her face. How on earth could Amy be thinking about living together as a family? Were they talking about marriage?

Through repeated sighs, Amy explained that Tommy didn't have patience for her questions. He didn't like her ideas. Sometimes he laughed at her suggestions, sometimes he told her he already had a plan, and sometimes he just ignored her. But the thing she was having the most trouble with—he wouldn't tell her what he wanted and then he criticized her choices. "Like yesterday, I asked Tommy what he wanted for supper. He told me to decide so I made pork chops, but he didn't enjoy it because I had made another pork dish last time I went over. I should have known he wouldn't want pork again that soon. I guess that's not a great example. But there are lots of other instances. Anyway, I don't know how to figure out what he needs. How do you know what Steve wants?"

She thinks it's her fault he didn't like the pork, Marge fumed. I'd like to wring his scrawny neck.

She took a deep breath and slowly let it out. "Steve doesn't expect me to read his mind." She suggested that Amy wasn't doing anything wrong. That Tommy was finally losing his ability to keep up the charade. That Amy was now seeing the real person. That she should prepare for it to get worse.

"Oh," Amy said.

Marge caught herself. "I'm sorry. That might have been too harsh. It's just that I don't have to guess at what Steve wants because he tells me. Of course all relationships have issues. But Tommy's being unfair to expect you to read his mind since that's impossible. And he shouldn't be impatient or belittle your ideas. You have *great* ideas. I've experienced them. So I'm not sure how to advise except to say he's not being fair. I hope you know I'm saying this out of love."

"Tommy's working hard. Anyone in that situation would lose patience. And it's his house after all. That's probably why he doesn't appreciate my ideas. Maybe he feels like I'm trying to take over. I know you liked Matt but Tommy's Jessie's father."

Amy stood and took her plate to the dishwasher. On her way through the door she said, "Look, I know you want to help but you don't know him."

Marge continued to sit at the table, her head heavy in her hands. What had she done? The tirade. The truth. Amy needed to hear it, to face reality, but she obviously wasn't ready.

Have I pushed her further away?

CHAPTER 23

Marge answered the phone.

"Hi, it's Leigh. You free for lunch?"

At the café Leigh said, "I need to talk to you about something personal. Is everything alright at home?"

Marge frowned. "Yes, why?"

"It's Amy. She's not herself. I thought you might be able to shed some light."

Marge sighed. "I've let her see that I'm not supportive of her relationship with Tommy and she's shut me out."

"Tommy?"

"Jessie's biological father."

Leigh frowned. "She's seeing him? We knew he had shown up and caused trouble. But Amy told us it was sorted."

Marge shook her head. "You knew she broke up with Matt, right?"

"She didn't tell us, but we suspected," Leigh said. "What's Tommy's last name?"

"Jeers."

Leigh scrubbed her hand across her forehead. When she looked up Marge said, "What? You're scaring me."

"Look, I don't really know anything. It's just, well, Tommy's Aunt Linda and I are in the same book club. You know how people like to talk. Anyway, I've only heard a one-sided story. Who knows what the truth is? I'm sorry I reacted."

"Oh no, you're not getting off with that."

Leigh didn't say anything.

"Talk to me. Please."

"He's an only child," Leigh said. "His father walked out when he was young. According to Linda, her brother left because Tommy's mother, Janis, is crazy. Supposedly she never let Tommy out of her sight. Except for school. And she only worked during the hours he was in school if she worked at all. She came from money and her parents attended to her every whim—she didn't have to work."

"Continue," Marge said.

Leigh stared at her hands and sighed. "Janis had no friends and didn't let Tommy have any either. So it was just the two of them. All the time. Linda tried to stay in touch but Janis shut her out completely. Look, I don't know if any of this is true. She told us quite a while back. And it was *her* brother who left the marriage so of course she would take his side.

"What's happening?" Leigh abruptly said. "All the colour has drained from your face."

"Tommy told Amy his parents are dead."

"Oh." Leigh paused. "Well maybe they are. Like I said Linda told us some time ago."

"You don't believe that any more than I do." Marge stared into her lap shaking her head. "It's even worse than I thought," she muttered.

"I've tried to be supportive. We had him over for a meal. We

From Thorns

worked hard at conversation. Steve found ways to relate. And that's the last we saw of him. Worst of all, I'm watching Amy sink back into fear and depression. What am I supposed to do?"

"I've never walked in your shoes," Leigh said. "Maybe it's time to let go."

"I *can't*," Marge said. When people at adjacent tables stared, she lowered her voice. "I've invested too much. We made a commitment. She's become a part of our family. And anyway, she doesn't have anyone else. She needs us now more than ever."

"I know how much you care about her and Jessie. The thing is, you can lead a horse to water . . ." Leigh cocked her head to one side and shrugged. "Perhaps you've done all you can for her. You need to start processing that. Maybe the situation will turn around; maybe it won't. But it's not in your control and I don't want to see you devastated if she walks out."

"I need to see her through to a positive outcome. Being able to support Amy has helped me let go of past mistakes. Sort of." Marge's shoulders slumped forward as she pressed her fist against her mouth. "And it's not just about that. I grew to love Amy. And Jessie—I think of her as my own granddaughter. We've seen Amy through so much. It's all for nothing if she ends up no better off than when we took her in."

Leigh moved her chair closer and put her arm around Marge's shoulder. "I'm so sorry."

As Marge dabbed a tissue to her eyes Leigh gently said, "I have to go—my break is over."

Marge straightened. "No, you can't leave yet. I need to know everything. Linda *must* have had thoughts about what happened. What else did she say?"

Leigh sighed. "It's gossip."

"Put yourself in my shoes," Marge said.

"Okay. Fine. But you have to keep it in perspective."

Leigh focussed on her tightly clasped hands. "Linda's brother, Bruce, suspected sexual abuse. He's a gentle guy who couldn't handle confrontation so he moved away, married someone else, has a whole new family. Supposedly Tommy's mother got him to sign away parental rights in exchange for dropping child support." Leigh rolled her eyes. "Can you imagine a father agreeing to that?"

"Why would he surmise sexual abuse?" Marge asked.

"I don't know. The only other thing Linda said was that she occasionally bumped into Tommy and Janis when he was young, when Bruce was still in the picture. Janis was weird in her interactions with Tommy. Manipulative in a sick sort of way. Whatever that means."

"Do you still see Linda at book club?" Marge asked.

"Yes."

"Please ask her what else she knows."

"I'm not waiting until book club!" Leigh looked at her watch. "I really have to go."

CHAPTER 24

Amy found a way to have more time with Tommy—she offered to prepare dinners every day.

Tommy became less defensive and more patient in their interactions. He offered to pick up ingredients on the days Amy took a bus. He let her borrow his car if her menu required additional items. When she worked late he would sometimes order take-out.

Following a few discussions with Rumble she understood the reason for Tommy's earlier withdrawal. She had been putting too much pressure on him while not doing enough to look after him.

For a while Tommy relaxed. He spent more time with Jess. Sometimes he sat with Amy over a glass of wine.

However, it didn't take long before impatience and intolerance wove back into his reactions. Her suggestions continued to draw his scorn. He laughed when she recommended a deck layout. He firmly said, "No," when she proposed adding a vegetable garden. He rolled his eyes at her hints of effective paint colours. But she had observed his inability to coordinate colour so why wouldn't he want her help?

Did he think she was criticizing?

On evenings Amy couldn't go to the house, he accused her of making excuses.

A late meeting at the church drew responses like, "They don't pay you enough to attend meetings. You think you're important. That your opinions matter. But they don't. Tell them you can't attend."

When she was too tired after a late shift to fetch Jessie, take her to Tommy's, and then prepare a meal, he said things like, "I'm tired every day. But I come home and continue working. If you wanted to, you'd figure it out."

Was he right? Was she selfishly neglecting his needs?

When he began finding fault with her parenting, Amy wondered how he could possibly think he'd spent enough time with Jessie to be able to give advice. And then she reasoned, he probably came from a good home like the Raynors' and he could see what she was doing wrong.

She wasn't about to confide in Marge. And university kept Kate too busy. So Amy talked to Rumble but found this to be less helpful than in the past.

She tried to do more for Tommy but her energy wasn't sufficient to fulfill all of his expectations. She tried to be more considerate but couldn't seem to get it right. She thought about ending the relationship. But Tommy was Jessie's father. And Amy loved the idea of being a family in Tommy's house. She certainly didn't want to prove Marge right so she rationalized that it would get better with time, when the demands of house renovations lessened, when Tommy knew her more and realized she was doing her best.

From Thorns

Summer rolled into fall.

"Marge wants to do a birthday bash for Jessie," Amy said.

"She's our kid," Tommy growled. "*We* should plan her birthday *not* Marge," He suggested the three of them visit a zoo or take in a kids' movie.

As though a two-year-old would sit still through a movie.

"I agree, we should do the birthday celebration at your place," Amy said. "But Marge looks after Jessie when I work and I don't pay much for rent or childcare. I feel like I owe her."

"Yeah, well they obviously don't like me so why should I spend time with them? Why would you even ask me to?"

Amy shrugged. "Jess loves Marge so much and they all love her, so the family has to be part of it this year." She paused. "You don't have to come but I think Jessie would like it if we were all together."

Tommy leaned forward, his face inches from hers. "So you would go ahead and have a birthday party without me."

"Of course not." Amy felt a knot tightening in her stomach. "I'll let Marge throw a party with her family and then we'll do our own thing with Jessie. But I wish we could do it all together. Just for this year. Never again."

"Fine. But this is the last time. And I won't allow any other people to come. I mean it."

She didn't want other people to come either and now she could blame it on Tommy. Perfect.

Amy spent the morning preparing food and hanging balloons. It was like old times. Busy, chaotic, loud. She had forgotten how much fun she had with the family.

Just before the scheduled time for Jessie's arrival, Marge

pulled Amy aside. "I was hoping we would have had some time together in the kitchen without anyone else around. I'm really disappointed."

"Let's plan an evening next week. Just you and me."

"I'm going to hold you to that." Marge sighed. "I miss you and Jessie." Then she straightened. "But I'm not trying to make you feel guilty. You're building your own life and that's the way it should be."

"Thanks Marge. I miss you too." It was something she had pushed to the back of her emotional closet, but Amy felt the void.

When Tommy and Jessie came through the door everyone yelled, "Happy birthday!" Jessie's little face lit up. Rumble, wearing a cowboy hat, ran around in circles. "He's delivering his present," Marge said.

It took two people to free the hat. "Who tied this mess?" Steve said. "There's more knots than you can shake a stick at!"

Watching a two-year old rip the paper off each gift and delight in the contents was such fun. Jessie only needed one reminder to say, "Thank you." A large quiche, two salads, and fresh baked rolls made a delicious lunch. Amy managed to get a bit of nutrition into Jessie before dessert.

Marge brought the elephant cake she'd prepared to the table. Jason was the only one unimpressed when Jessie blew out the candles by herself. "Geez, will she ever learn to keep her spit in her mouth? Remember last year when—"

"Relax Jason," Steve said. "You were the same at that age. Do you spit now?"

After lunch while Jess played with her new toys, Steve, Tommy, Amy, and Marge visited over coffee. Tommy wore a sullen look and avoided eye contact. He answered questions

From Thorns

directed his way but otherwise didn't participate in the conversation. Marge and Steve were lovely, reminding Amy of their only other dinner together. She had forgotten how nicely Tommy had been treated. It gave her cause to reconsider some now-ingrained assumptions.

Marge expressed concerns to me privately, Amy remembered, but maybe she was just trying to help me think from a different angle. Has Tommy ever given this family a chance? I've seen them reach out to him, but he hasn't reached back.

When Jessie's nap time came, Tommy asked Amy to go out with him for the rest of the afternoon. He didn't thank Marge for her effort or even properly say, "Goodbye." Amy felt embarrassed in spite of voicing her own gratefulness.

Once outside, intending to hold her ground Amy said, "Isn't it great the way we all visited and talked so easily? Especially you and Steve. I can tell he likes you and he's totally into your house. He wants to work with you Tommy, to help you. Isn't that great?"

"You're so naïve! Nobody likes me and Steve doesn't wanna help. They just don't wanna let you go. They see that you're serious about me so they're trying a new approach. If they can convince you they're on our side they've won. They get to keep their claws in you and Jessie."

"That's not true. I know these people. They're loving and honest. I don't think you're giving them a chance. Honestly, I think they were a lot nicer than you were."

Tommy stopped walking and turned her to face him. "How dare you accuse me of not being nice! I agreed to come to this stupid party even though I didn't want to. You forced it on me. And then you expect me to play their game?"

What's wrong with me? Amy wondered. How could I forget

that I imposed this afternoon on him? Why should he have to fake happiness?

"I'm sorry. I didn't think about it that way. I'm sorry, Tommy."

"I can't believe how you stupid you can be. I was planning to ask you to move in with me but maybe that's not such a good idea. You better figure out whose side you're on."

"Of course I'm on your side. If I have to make a choice between them or you, I choose you. But I don't want to be forced to choose."

"Well you might have to."

He's right about Marge, Amy mused. She interferes a lot. We wanted to plan Jessie's birthday ourselves but I let Marge have her way. I let her steal Jessie's birthday celebration.

"I won't put up with them meddling," Tommy said. "I walked away from my own mother because she wouldn't let me be. I'm not going to put up with someone else butting in where they don't belong."

"I thought your parents were dead."

"*Frig*. Why do you have to question everything?" Tommy took a deep breath. "Like I said, my parents were controlling and tried to make me do what they wanted instead of letting me do what I wanted. Eventually I had to put my foot down. It wasn't easy."

"Are your parents still alive?"

"No. My parents died in a car accident just like I told you."

He said he walked away from his *mother*, but *both* his parents were controlling. Is he making up stories? Or am I splitting hairs?

"So what do you think?" Tommy said. "Do you want to move in with me?"

"Yes." Amy nodded enthusiastically. "Thank you for forgiving

From Thorns

my stupid accusation. You can see I'm totally on your side, right?"

When he nodded she closed the space between them, wrapping her arms tightly around him. "I'm so excited. We'll be a proper family."

Amy knew Tommy would be a good provider. Responsible and ambitious, he had ideas for starting his own construction company. Once he had suggested that Amy might be able to run the business end of things while he was at the job site. If that happened she could be home with Jessie and the other children they would have. Even now his income was sufficient to allow Amy to cut back her hours.

This was what I've been dreaming of. A home. A dad for Jessie. More children. A family of my own. Financial independence. Once we've move in with Tommy, Marge will settle down and everything will get back to normal. Tommy will be able to see their genuine love. It's all gonna work out.

"I need some time to get the upstairs in better shape before you and Jess move in." Tommy said. "It won't take long."

"You haven't been together for very long and you've had some problems. These things need to get ironed out before you decide to make such a huge commitment," Marge said through tears. "We don't know anything about him. Have you met his friends? His family?"

"We'd like to know him better so we can fully support you. But he doesn't seem interested in spending time with us," Steve said.

"We're afraid for you. As you've spent more time together, you've lost your confidence and joy."

"You mentioned that he gambles. That's serious. How much

does he spend?"

Amy didn't say much. She knew how it would go. They wouldn't give up until they won.

"We've heard things," Steve said, "including that he's been lying to you. That his parents aren't dead, for example."

"Where did you hear that?" Amy demanded.

"Marge knows his aunt."

Amy stared at Marge. "When did she tell you this?"

"A while back. I didn't say anything because I wanted to give you time to sort through the relationship on your own. If I had told you I worried you would think I was trying to interfere."

"*What?*" Amy spat. "That's kind of a big deal! If you believed it was true you should have told me. If you didn't believe it," Amy turned to look at Steve, "then you shouldn't have said anything now. I don't want to talk about this anymore."

Why can't they just be happy for me? Tommy's successful, hard-working, responsible. Why won't they focus on the good? They obviously don't trust me and I don't deserve that. *Tommy's parents aren't dead*. How dare they!

As she walked away some niggling memories refused to submerge. Like earlier today during the party, Jessie said Daddy took her to his house. Why had he led everyone to think they played at the park? And the time he said he was working late but then let it slip he had a beer with someone? And when he said he couldn't pick them up because of a commitment but it turned out he'd been at the house the whole time.

He lies. You can't trust a liar.

No! she reasoned. These are little things. Everyone lies once in a while.

From Thorns

When she told Tommy about Marge and Steve's reaction he laughed. "See, I told you. They're jealous that you've found someone of your own."

"But they weren't like this with Matt. And they're such nice people. I don't get it."

"Uh-huh. Big surprise. They were okay with Matt but not me. Well, they can shove it!"

Amy spoke softly, just above a whisper. "They said your parents are alive."

"*What?*" Tommy said. "Why are you listening to them? You better figure out what you want and stop letting other people push you around. I want a decision from you *now*. Are you with me or not?"

She didn't want to lose Tommy. "Get me out of there as soon as you can."

From that point on Amy began moving her things to Tommy's, slowly, a few items at a time. And one afternoon when every member of the Raynor family was out, Tommy completed the move.

CHAPTER 25

Marge and Steve walked into the house with bags of groceries. When Amy didn't respond to her name being called and Marge couldn't find a note, she wandered down the stairs to Amy's room.

"Steve!"

She heard his feet pounding across the upper floor and down the stairs. "What's wrong?"

"They're gone."

"What do you mean 'they're gone'?"

"Look around. The closet's empty, the bathroom's clean, all her personal things are gone." With a cry Marge dropped onto the bed.

"How *dare* she! After all we've done for her!" Steve stormed out of the room leaving Marge in a sobbing heap.

When she regained her composure, she picked up the phone. Amy agreed to meet at the café but only if Marge could be supportive.

Over coffee Marge apologized for coming across negatively and critically. "All I ever wanted was for you and Jessie to be happy. I thought it was my responsibility to share my

From Thorns

observations and concerns. I hoped you would be able to see that it was coming from a place of love."

Amy's shoulders relaxed. "You've been so good to me and Jess. All of you. You basically rescued me and I can't thank you enough. But you wouldn't let me make my own decision about Tommy and now you've forced me to choose between you and him."

"No, no, no," Marge said. She reached across the table and took Amy's hands. "You don't have to choose one or the other. We accept your decision and we love you as much as ever. Tommy is now a part of our family. Maybe you can all come for dinner on the weekend."

"Tommy won't go. And he doesn't want me to see you either. I have to prove that I love him by supporting his feelings. I'm sure everything will settle down with time."

Although she arrived at the meeting place determined to be strong, Marge felt a tear spill from one eye. "Remember that I'm just a phone call away if you need to talk. If you need anything at all."

Why can't Amy see that she's closing the door on people who have demonstrated their love for her and Jessie? Has Tommy done anything for her? Aside from things that benefit him. She's choosing a path littered with land mines and plans to walk it with the very person who planted them.

Oh God, please help her. You're all she's got.

CHAPTER 26

"This is so awesome, living together as a family."

Tommy pulled her into a hug. "I'm happy, too."

"Would you be okay if I decorate the bedrooms?" Amy asked.

"If you want to use your savings, sure."

She threw her arms around his neck. "Thank you."

Shopping for sheets, comforters, decorative pillows, window coverings, and framed pictures was every bit as much fun as she'd anticipated. Unfortunately neither the bright pink theme she chose for Jessie's room, nor the beige and yellows she chose for her own, looked great against the grey coloured walls.

"I'll repaint when I have time," Tommy promised.

The only thing he wasn't happy about—Amy insisted her teddy bear sit on a shelf in their bedroom. After she explained how important he was, Tommy shook his head and rolled his eyes but muttered, "Fine," on his way out the door.

She gave up the pharmacy position in favour of the office job. Amy felt that would give her better experience for any future career. Plus it meant no more evening shifts.

"That wasn't very smart," Tommy said. "The church can't give you more than fifteen hours per week. What if we need

From Thorns

you to work more?"

She wished Tommy had spoken up before she gave her notice instead of telling her to make the decision and then criticizing her choice. In hindsight though, she agreed with his thinking.

She made childcare arrangements with a stay-at-home mom from the church. Emily kept Jessie for the two days Amy worked and then Amy looked after Emily's son, Caleb, for two days. The children played well together, but Jessie wasn't herself.

"When can Gamma come to visit?"

"Why can't we live with Gamma?"

"I like Gamma's house better."

No one besides Amy could love Jessie the way Marge had. Not even Tommy. Or maybe he just didn't show it the way she expected. He didn't make much time for Jess and he didn't like interruptions. When she strolled, chattering, into his space he called, "Amy, why aren't you watching her?" He never broke away from his tasks.

I guess it's hard getting used to a toddler intruding, Amy thought. He'll adapt with time. But he continued to be rough, becoming more easily agitated by interruptions and chaos instead of acclimatizing. Eventually Jessie learned not to bother Daddy.

However, when Tommy wasn't working on a project he played with Jess and laughter filled the house. She loved it when her daddy took her to the park or dragged her around on the toboggan. One winter day when he brought her in from the yard she enthusiastically said, "Daddy made me a fort."

"Should I come to see it?"

"Yeah!" Vibrating with excitement, Jessie stood at the door waiting for Amy to get her winter clothes on. Outside they crawled into the structure and a few minutes later Tommy joined them with a dish of cookies in hand.

He was a good father.

Developing a routine came easily. Thankfully Tommy had a clear sense of who should do which household chores, so Amy knew exactly what she had to get done. Every day she appreciated all she'd learned from Marge.

Occasionally when she needed Tommy's assistance she asked, and he usually helped. Of course when occupied with the renovation work he sometimes snapped, "Seriously? You can't manage that on your own?" Or "Can't you see I'm busy? Do it yourself." Amy learned when it was acceptable to ask for help and when she should leave Tommy alone.

Eventually Kate got in touch. For some reason Tommy hated the phone so when he answered Amy's, he made remarks like, "Don't be long; you've got things to do." Or, "This isn't a good time; Jessie needs your attention." Like a sponge Amy absorbed his perspective and before long, even when Tommy wasn't around, she resisted talking on the phone. So Kate dropped by occasionally, always during Tommy's work hours. But given her heavy course load, her visits became fewer and farther between.

Marge never tried to contact Amy at home but frequently stopped by the church office. She spent time chatting with the other ladies before wandering over to Amy's desk. They talked mostly about Jessie but also about life in general.

"It's all good," Amy proudly reported. "Tommy's a great dad."

She felt guilty for stripping Marge of all opportunity to see Jessie. Tommy was firm though, neither Marge nor Steve was welcome in his home. Amy had considered inviting them over when Tommy was at work but that held too much risk. She

From Thorns

thought about taking Jessie to see Marge, meeting somewhere neutral. But Tommy was deeply hurt by what they had said, and Amy knew he would be angry if he learned of any contact. So it had to be this way. For a while. When her mind drifted to the reason for the alienation she eased into that effortless place of assigning blame.

If Marge and Steve had been supportive I wouldn't have been forced to take sides.

And the guilt diminished.

The best part of living with Tommy—reduced work hours and more time with Jessie.

I let Marge have too much of her, Amy realized. She should be closer to me than Marge and now that can happen.

The elimination of travel back and forth between residences made life easier. Less stressful. When Tommy was home Amy used the car and bussing became the exception. She had time to experiment with new recipes in her own kitchen. She planned the herb garden she would build and where the tomato plants would fit in amongst the flowers. She had enjoyed working in Marge's gardens and now she would have her own. She also dreamed of decorating and did some designing in a journal, hoping Tommy would be willing to consider her thoughts.

Having a kitchen to herself was a dream come true. She dove into reorganizing the cupboards, moving the everyday things she needed onto the lower shelves. When Tommy discovered the rearranging, he told her to put everything back.

"But I'll be the one working in here and it'll be better if I can reach things."

"No," he said. "You worked here just fine before we lived

together. I'll put a stool beside the fridge."

Oh well, it was his house after all. She could understand him not wanting everything shuffled around. On top of that, she knew he had a hard time with change. So she put everything back and reorganized slowly, a few things at a time.

Occasionally Tommy bristled. "Where's the kettle? What're ya doin' around here? I can't find anything."

Since *anything* was just the kettle, he calmed down as soon she got it for him.

Sadly, he often returned from work feeling upset. "I showed Ahmad how to fix something and he told me to 'buzz off.' They're so stupid. They don't know what they're doing and they won't listen." Having dinner ready when he got home helped ease his tension but that was impossible on the days Amy worked. So she rearranged her office hours to arrive home a little earlier and then took Jessie into work for the few hours that spilled onto a third day.

She overheard one of her colleagues explain why they accommodated her request. "It won't ever be a problem. We asked Marge to come in to help when Jessie's here. And we've come up with a few tasks that can be done with a child." Sure enough, Marge showed up every time Amy brought Jessie into the office. It did Amy's heart good to see the two of them together. She didn't realize how much guilt she still carried until it began to melt away.

When Tommy found out, only because Jessie said something, his face hardened. "What kinda games are you playing?"

Amy had a rationale prepared. "If Marge doesn't look after her, I'll have to stick to a two-day schedule which means I won't be able to have the house organized and dinner ready when you

From Thorns

get home. It's totally up to you."

Tommy acquiesced after he delivered a lecture about loyalty, reminding Amy where hers lay.

She wondered how Tommy would react if he knew what happened the previous week.

Amy had arrived early. She heard her name coming from the pastor's office. She tiptoed closer.

"I don't see how we can let her keep the job when she doesn't even attend anymore," Sheila said, her voice just above a whisper. "And she's living with someone out of wedlock. People will talk. And complain. I mean, the congregation has been tolerant but—"

"Okay. Enough." Pastor Mike said.

Amy released a long, slow breath.

"Sheila, do you have a problem with Amy working here?"

"Not me. No."

"This job provides us an opportunity to stay connected with Amy and Jessie," Pastor Mike continued. "We want her to know she's loved and I don't think firing her would accomplish that goal."

How would Tommy have reacted if she'd lost the job? She shuddered. He didn't adapt well. When Amy fell behind or did things in a way that made no sense to Tommy or if she made an incorrect assumption, he rolled his eyes, sighed, or shook his head as he walked off sometimes muttering, "You're not the brightest," under his breath. She worked at trying to read him better, to determine what he wanted so she could do things the way he liked and enjoy his praise. But criticism flowed easily, not praise. Losing her job would have proved too much.

Something Amy found hard to accept was Tommy's financial

management. He demanded her pay be deposited into a joint account that he controlled. She had to ask permission to spend, even on groceries. Perhaps this is how it worked in all relationships but Amy didn't like it. After all, she did earn some of the income.

"Of course you can get new clothes," he said. "I have to know how much you need so I can plan. It's expensive to run a house and support a family." But whenever she asked, an interrogation ensued. Why did she need to buy that? Couldn't she find something less expensive? Didn't she just buy something like that last month? "I can't print money."

Whether moodiness, money management, or expectations, she tried to put herself in his shoes to understand his perspective and find a way to accept what she couldn't change.

But as she gradually relaxed into the relationship she began to see her value. She realized she'd been feeling like a beggar who'd been rescued. She didn't earn as much money but she looked after the house, their daughter, and all the daily affairs—that should count for something. As this transition matured, she thought she should be allowed to discuss some of his irritating behaviours since he felt free to criticize her. Initially she'd been upset with herself for even feeling irritated, but as her thoughts resonated she realized it should work both ways. She gathered enough courage to speak with him about one issue—tossing his worn clothing on the floor. The conversation went well and he agreed to stop. When nothing changed, she raised the issue again.

"You're lucky to be living in this house," he blasted. "I don't know where you get off telling *me* how *I* should live in *my* house!" And that was the end of that.

From Thorns

She learned that Tommy wasn't open to compromising; she had to find a way to genuinely accept the things that bothered her. For the most part she was able to adapt. There remained a nagging irritation though, one she was barely conscious of like the itch of a dry scalp. It was unfair that she worked so hard to accept everything about him. Why couldn't he do the same for her? And why didn't he show more appreciation for the good things she brought to his life?

One day after work while collecting Jessie from Emily, Amy brought up the topic of husbands. "Sometimes I feel like Tommy doesn't appreciate what I do for him. Do you ever feel like that?"

Emily nodded. "All the time. They don't know how hard it is to listen to a whining child. They don't know what it's like having a screaming kid who won't sit still in the grocery cart while the whole store is staring at you like you're the worst parent on the face of the earth. Fathers just don't get it."

Amy felt awful as she drove home with Jessie.

Tommy's completely normal. I've been stewing over nothing. And Caleb sounds way more difficult than my Jess.

Although the first year of living together held challenges, Amy felt content. Happy. She enjoyed the house. She enjoyed having her own family. She enjoyed the freedom and independence.

Thank goodness she hadn't allowed Marge or Steve to interfere with her decision.

CHAPTER 27

As the Christmas season descended, exhaustion consumed her. She didn't have enough energy to maintain her routine along with the extra seasonal tasks. She asked Tommy for help.

"Don't start pushing your responsibilities onto me," he said. "If you're too tired to shop then don't. Jessie doesn't need anything. And we certainly don't have money to waste."

But Amy wanted a Christmas just like the one she had organized the previous year. Like the ones she had experienced with the Raynors. What he suggested sounded like her childhood, and her daughter deserved better. Besides, he had enjoyed last year's celebration and would likely complain if she didn't do something similar. So she pushed hard to get through the season and included Jessie in baking, shopping, and decorating.

Christmas day turned out exactly as she had hoped. Jess, now three, could barely contain herself. "I can hardly see any floor under all the bits of wrapping paper," Tommy said. "Clean up is going to be a challenge." He pushed some of the mess aside and got on the floor with Jessie to check out her new toys. He played with her all day, both inside and outside. Amy had the

From Thorns

afternoon in the kitchen which she relished. By dinnertime a magnificent snowman decorated the front yard.

After turkey supper, Jessie returned to her toys. "You've already stayed up too late," Amy said. "The toys will be waiting for you tomorrow when you wake up." She dragged a whining child to her room.

"Thank you for the delicious dinner and for all you did to get ready for today," Tommy said. "You made it wonderful for our daughter, and I had fun too."

Early in the new year Amy confirmed the pregnancy she had suspected in December. Tommy was thrilled. "Yes! It'll be a boy this time. I'm gonna make a crib."

Her fatigue continued to build. Although the folks at work understood, Tommy didn't. He couldn't comprehend why pregnancy would cause her to feel so tired and he believed she made it up as an excuse to push her responsibilities onto him. He laid it out clearly—he brought in the wages which provided for the house and all their needs and he was doing renovation work in his spare time. It was her job to look after Jessie and take care of the daily tasks of running the house since she only worked part-time. It was obvious he had the heavier load and she was being selfish to expect him to do more.

Amy wondered aloud, "Could the renovations be postponed until after the baby's born?"

"Postpone renovations? Meanwhile, you're nagging me to get those bedrooms repainted. You should've got bedspreads that matched the paint on the walls instead of creating more work for me." He turned away, walked to the other side of the room and punched a hole in the wall, fracturing all sense of safety. A minute later the front door slammed.

Memories of Amy's father crashed like ocean waves dragging her to the depths of fear.

When Tommy returned, he took her hand and walked her to the room he had stormed out of earlier. He pointed to the hole and said, "I really didn't need this extra work." He took her by the shoulders. "Look, I'm sorry for getting angry. It's just, well everything I'm doing around here is for you and Jessie. I need to get the work finished before the baby comes so I'll have more time to spend with you."

Through tears Amy apologized and promised to carry her share. "Thank you for working so hard to make a nice house for us. I appreciate everything you're doing."

He kissed the top of her head before heading to the basement. As Tommy walked away she remembered her father apologizing to her mother. Whether he hurled insults, dragged her down the hall by her hair, or punched her in the face, she always forgave him. But nothing ever changed. Maybe she hadn't tried hard enough to please him.

Amy would work harder at pleasing Tommy.

Coworkers helped out. It bothered her knowing that others were picking up some of her workload but she was too tired to refuse. Some offered to fill in if she needed a day off but Tommy's budget counted on her income.

She felt like a vehicle out of gas that was still expected to cover the miles.

"Tommy," Amy yelled doubled over in pain. He burst through the bedroom door. She breathed, "Take me to emergency."

After the miscarriage he took a few days off to care for her.

From Thorns

He prepared food, entertained Jessie, ran errands, and held Amy in his arms as they cried together. This strengthened her faith in their relationship. She didn't completely understand him. His values and priorities were different from hers but she experienced his true love during this awful ordeal.

However, when Amy recovered his aggression charged at her.

"You didn't want this baby, did you?"

"Why didn't you look after yourself properly? I mean, you had no problem with Jessie."

"You wanted to punish me for not being there when Jessie was born."

"You wouldn't take the risk it might be a boy. You just didn't want to give me what I wanted."

Amy wanted to call Marge but knew that was impossible. Although they often spoke in the office, their conversations lacked substance.

Because Tommy remained angry with Marge and Steve, she had allowed each day to roll into the next without working toward a reconciliation. Several times Marge had asked her to go for coffee but she always declined. In fact, she had wanted to repair the relationship but Tommy sucked her into his vortex of control. She should have maintained contact whether Tommy liked it or not. But it was too late now. If she couldn't call Marge, then who?

She hadn't made any new friends because she felt guilty about doing anything outside of her job or housework. Even spending time with Jessie felt like a chore. She knew she had to account to Tommy for her day, to list all she had accomplished.

Unfortunately she'd stopped attending church because Tommy wanted her home on Sunday mornings. She didn't understand why since he rarely spent time with her or Jessie. Instead, he worked on the house and was consistently annoyed at being disturbed. She hadn't really cared about missing the morning services but now she felt too ashamed to reach out to any of the young mothers she had known. Surely they all hated her for essentially dumping them.

She would talk to Emily again.

While fetching Jessie the following day after work, Amy asked if they could chat about marriage as they had done once before.

Emily hesitated.

"Please. I don't have anyone else to talk with." She expressed her unhappiness while Emily picked at her nails muttering, "Uh-huh."

A few minutes in, Emily lurched from the couch and rushed to the window. "Rob's home. You have to go. Sorry I couldn't help. You should talk to the pastor."

"I don't go to the church anymore. You haven't noticed?"

Rob greeted Amy in a friendly fashion as she and Jessie headed through the door.

What's wrong? she wondered. Partway home, the clouds dissipated.

How could I have been so blind?

She'd seen bruises on Emily's arms yet thought nothing of it. After all, she had her own bruises from bumping into things. But now she remembered what her mother's arms had looked like.

Once again she was left with a sense that her own situation was pretty good.

Was there any way she could help Emily?

The following day Amy called. "Can you come by for coffee?

From Thorns

With Caleb."

"I'm really busy today. And unfortunately I'm not going to be able to look after Jessie anymore. Rob prefers that I focus on Caleb without other children to distract my attention. I'm sorry not to give you more notice."

"Don't worry about me," Amy replied. "If you ever need a friend, you know how to find me."

"Well isn't that just freaking fantastic," Tommy said after being told that childcare would have to be found if he wanted Amy to continue working. A couple of days later, he came home with a name. Together they went to meet the wife of one of his work colleagues. Pardeep stayed home with her two young children and looked after one other child. She and her husband, Shane, were friendly and welcoming. The rambunctious children showed no signs of oppression. Jessie easily joined into their play.

The only hitch—Pardeep ran a daycare business and there would be a cost for keeping Jessie.

While driving home Amy asked Jessie if she would like to go back to play with Daj and Sam.

"Yeah."

She would break the news about Caleb when Jessie asked.

"We can't start paying for a babysitter. This is temporary until you find someone you can swap with like you did with Emily." Tommy stared at Amy while the traffic light remained red. "Hello!" he barked.

"I know," Amy said. "It's not as easy as you make it sound. If I knew someone else who wanted to look after each other's kids, I would have said so already."

"You'll find someone. It can't be that hard," Tommy said.

"Unless you want me to sell more drugs."

"*What?*" Amy blurted. "What are you talking about?"

Tommy grinned. "How do you think I afforded the house?"

Without looking at her he continued, "Relax. I stopped dealing after you moved in."

Her coworkers didn't know of anyone looking for a child-sharing partner so Amy asked if she could be given more hours.

No.

Tommy's anger grew with the extra financial burden. He routinely fired off rounds of insults. If Amy had cared, she wouldn't have lost the pregnancy. If Amy had cared, she would have found a better job that paid more and offered better hours. If Amy had cared, she wouldn't have created the problem that led Emily to end their arrangement.

Tommy didn't mention drug dealing again, and she never asked.

CHAPTER 28

The way travel along a highway leaves the starting point further behind, so time created an ever-widening distance between Amy and Tommy.

The relationship became simply a matter of fulfilling the role Tommy defined for her. They conversed about things related to the house or Jessie not concerning themselves with the personal details of each other's lives. They hardly ever argued. For the most part there was peace in their home. Tommy seemed content with this. Amy was not—her relationship was void of depth or meaning. She had experienced Marge and Steve and she didn't want to accept less.

Depression moved in. She entertained thoughts of suicide. But she would never leave Jessie.

On one of the days Amy worked, Matt walked in, glanced her way, and nodded as he continued to the pastor's office. She left before he reappeared, with her stomach in knots.

It took the rest of the day and a night of interrupted sleep before her nerves stopped firing shockwaves of anxiety. As the days rolled into weeks, slowly and subtly thoughts of Matt progressed in her mind. She knew she should push these thoughts away but the memories of their times together, and daydreams of what her life could have been like, brought feelings of happiness. So she allowed herself to pretend.

As the second anniversary of living with Tommy approached Amy determined to try again, resolving to put fantasy aside to work on reality. Five months of imagining and wishing had created more distance, not solutions.

She took Jessie shopping for groceries and bristol board—one red sheet and two white. Amy cut the red one into the shape of a heart and wrote "November 16" diagonally across in black marker while Jessie drew designs on the white sheets. Then Amy wrote simple poems on each:

> *Roses are red*
> *Remember when we said*
> *We'll be together forever*
> *Like Barney and Fred?*

> *Violets are blue*
> *Hearts are true*
> *Let's start again*
> *And make everything new.*

After taping them to the wall she began work on a celebratory meal featuring Tommy's favourite: T-bone steak with roasted rosemary potatoes, corn on the cob, and Caesar salad. And for dessert, chocolate caramel cheesecake. Jessie sat at the table with the lettuce and instructions on how to tear it. She remained focussed on her task with the promise of caramel to come.

When Tommy came through the door, Jessie ran to greet

From Thorns

him with a single red rose.

"What's this for?"

"Mommy has a surprise for your annibersary."

"Anni-v-v-versary," Amy called. "Try again."

"Anniversary?" Tommy said. "I didn't know it was our anniversary."

Tommy and Jessie moved to the kitchen where Amy stood holding a glass of red wine.

"I'm sorry, I didn't know we had an official anniversary date since we never actually got married."

She smiled and offered a hug as she transferred the wine to Tommy. "You're right, and we didn't celebrate last year, but I felt like doing this. I hope it's okay."

After a fun evening Tommy expressed his appreciation, even acknowledging the emotional distance that had settled into their relationship. "Let's make this the first day of the rest of our lives. Let's turn things around, spend more time together, have some fun."

Proud of herself for rising above her feelings, Amy was glad she'd made the effort. With hope for an overhaul to the engine of their relationship she drifted off to sleep with renewed anticipation of good things to come.

Tommy talked more, complained less, offered to get Jessie from the sitter, and participated in bedtime routine. But gradually, over the weeks leading to Christmas, he returned to his previous habits. Amy decided to go deeper and let him know how some of his behaviour made her feel. Her coping strength was weakening. Her ability to adapt and absorb was waning. On a

Saturday evening, after a good meal and after Jessie fell asleep, she donned her courage like a soldier heading into battle.

She provided examples of ways he treated her that hurt and reactions that frightened Jessie.

Tommy retained eye contact but said nothing except, "Please don't stop; I need to hear all of it." When she couldn't think of anything else she asked, "What are you thinking?"

He pushed back his chair and stood, placing his palms firmly on the table, looking down at her. His facial expression shouted the rage suppressed in his voice. "I don't know what you expect of me. All the work I do around here and at my job, providing for you, making a nice house for you, putting up with your pathetic little job that barely covers any of our expenses, allowing you to basically stay home. Guess what? I'd like to stay home and play all day. But I take responsibility. I go to a job I don't even like because I know the bills have to get paid. You don't worry about any of that. Must be nice. I can't believe how ungrateful you are. If you think you can do better somewhere else, then go. But you're not taking Jessie."

He stormed out of the room. Through tears Amy called, "Please don't go. I didn't mean to upset you. I was just trying to tell you how I feel."

She followed him to the front door. "I wasn't trying to criticize. I *am* grateful for everything you do. Please Tommy, please let's talk some more."

When she grabbed his arm, he shoved her to the wall and stormed from the house without closing the door.

She crumpled into a sobbing mass on the floor.

That night Tommy didn't come home.

From Thorns

On Sunday evening when he reappeared, he pushed past her and went straight to the bedroom slamming the door. She followed and quietly opened the door.

"Get out!"

She slept on the couch. In the morning, hearing Tommy in the kitchen, she rolled inward careful to stay quiet. Only when she heard the front door close did she head to her room. A mess of stuffing littered the bedroom floor. What on earth?

And then she froze. Slowly she moved her eyes to the spot where her teddy bear resided, his place of honour on her bookshelf. He was gone. Ripped to bits and strewn all over the room. She dropped to her knees and wailed.

She felt Jessie's arms around her neck. "What's wrong, Mommy?"

Sometime during that week Tommy returned to his old self.

What should I do? Amy wondered. I don't want to go back to the way things were. But if I say anything he'll just explode again. Should I be happy to have peace? He doesn't hit me and he takes care of the house and pays the bills. Sure some things bother me, but every relationship has problems. I should try harder.

For awhile, Amy worked at embracing everything about Tommy. Why was she having such a hard time accepting what she had accepted in the past? Had she always been unhappy deep down? Was her tolerance just wearing out?

Depression settled in. She couldn't go on this way. If only she could talk to Kate who she barely saw due to a busy university schedule. But Kate would tell Marge and Amy didn't want to hear Marge say, "See. I told you."

She swallowed her pride and reached out to some of the

young mothers from the church, the very friendships she'd abandoned. She anticipated rejection but couldn't think of anywhere else to go.

No one answered their phone.

"Hi. This is Amy. Do you remember me from the church? I wanted to talk to you about something. My number is . . ."

Everyone returned the call and each woman assured they held no resentment. Of course Amy didn't believe that, but she expressed gratitude and meet-up arrangements were made. Did they want to gloat over her failure? Amy dreaded seeing them but desperation sent her to the meetings.

Surprisingly, everyone said they were happy to see her again. They all listened attentively and responded as though they cared.

When Amy finished drawing the picture of her marriage, she asked for advice.

Two women told her she was lucky to have such a good provider. Such a hard worker. "Some men just sit around watching sports and drinking." But they also acknowledged the difficulties and made suggestions.

"A holiday would definitely help," one said. "You'd relax and you could make up and start fresh. Do you do date nights? You know, forget about Jessie for the evening and focus on each other. We find that super helpful. And there's always counselling."

The second woman had a different perspective. "Just ignore him and spend time with girlfriends. Don't throw away a good thing. You could do a lot worse than Tommy. As long as the bills are paid, go enjoy yourself. He wants you in his life so he'll let you be. You'll see."

The other three women told her she needed to leave. That the relationship was unhealthy. That it would likely get worse,

From Thorns

not better. "You've done everything you can and he doesn't want to budge. He's showing that he doesn't care about you. Why would you stay?"

Amy didn't want to abandon ship.

She knew Tommy wouldn't be willing to spend money on dates or trips.

She wasn't interested in choosing girlfriends over a proper relationship—she wanted what Marge and Steve had.

But counselling? When she lived with the Raynors she had brief counselling from the pastor and her doctor, and it helped. Would Tommy be open to advice from a counsellor?

When she mentioned it, he responded with shock. "I thought everything was going well. Why would we need counselling? Are you unhappy *again*?" Shaking his head, he walked away mumbling something about her being impossible to please.

Over the next few months her unhappiness grew. Occasionally she found the courage to tell Tommy she felt she was never good enough even though she was doing her best. She felt he didn't really like her, and she certainly didn't feel loved.

He repeatedly told her she had no grounding in reality. That she was idealistic, chasing impossible dreams, believing Hollywood's rendition of family life. That she would never be happy—it was impossible for a person like her. He even suggested she enjoyed being unhappy.

Recently his criticisms had extended beyond her, also being thrown at Jessie. Whenever Amy was within earshot she intercepted, caught the remark, and threw it back.

"Jess isn't lazy. She's young. You expect too much."

"Jess isn't stupid. She's four. She'll do that easily when she's older."

"She's not a brat. She's normal."

"She's not bad, she broke it by accident."

Although she didn't know how to stand up for herself, when it came to Jessie Amy had no fear.

She looked to alcohol for comfort assigning blame with every gulp. She continued to contemplate suicide but she knew she would never act on her ideations.

Tommy gambled more, losing too much. "This is your fault. All your complaining is driving me nuts. And when are you going to get a better job?"

Already pushing too hard with work, caring for Jessie, and trying to maintain an acceptable standard at home, all within a seemingly permanent state of sadness and fatigue, she promised to search for a full-time position, but not until Jessie started school in September.

CHAPTER 29

The first day of kindergarten saw many upset children. Parents moved into the classroom and suddenly Jessie's confidence disappeared. "No Mommy, don't leave me," she cried hanging on to her mother's arm. Amy didn't have the heart to push her away.

When Tommy learned she stayed at the school, he was outraged. "I don't care if other mothers are staying. When I was a kid no one catered to me like that. You're spoiling her. I want you to stop it and do what you promised. Find a full-time job!"

Around the time parents stopped attending, viruses invaded. Jessie brought home every bug, generously sharing each one. Amy remained in a continual state of poor health. The office staff didn't want her bringing her germs into work so she had to miss days.

Tommy's anger escalated. One evening he didn't show up for dinner. When he came home that night she pulled a plate from the oven. He ignored it, showered, and went to bed without saying a word.

There were more nights like this and her despair grew. But nothing prepared her for what happened next.

Alie Cardet

Hearing a loud bang from the basement, Amy thought it wise to get Jessie out of Tommy's way. At the bottom of the stairs, she froze.

With big eyes and teeth clenched, he stood behind Jessie, holding her twisted arm behind her back obviously yanking upward. Balancing on her tippy toes with tears running from her eyes, Jessie released a muffled cry. Why was she holding it in?

"What happened?" Amy yelled.

Tommy turned and went back into his work area. Amy saw tools spilled onto the floor, but Jessie couldn't have dumped that heavy load. She scooped her daughter and ran upstairs filled with an anger she'd never experienced before. Memories of her own childhood surrounded her, closing in, suffocating.

In the living room she yanked Jessie's shirt over her head and checked her body for marks.

"Mommy, stop!"

Amy pulled off the jeans, examining Jessie's legs and buttocks.

Jessie pushed at her mother, crying harder, begging for it to end.

Amy looked into Jessie's frightened, tear-filled eyes. "I'm sorry," she said pulling her small naked child into her arms. "Mommy's so sorry." She pulled a blanket around Jessie. They rocked, crying together, until Jessie fell asleep.

Amy's mind raced with questions as she faced a new reality—Tommy's assaults had progressed from purely verbal.

How long has this been going on?
What else is he doing?
Why hasn't Jessie told me?
Where should I go for help?
Gradually she calmed.

From Thorns

Am I overreacting?
There aren't any bruises or cuts.
Maybe this just happened once.
Obviously it's not like what happened to me.

After ruminating for several days her mind found a place that made sense. Some things were right. Some things were wrong. *This* was wrong.

Amy confronted Tommy.

"How dare you suggest something so ridiculous! This is a scheme you've come up with to have my daughter taken away from me. I knew it all along—that you'd pull some underhanded stunt like this. You're having an affair, aren't you? You're using this absurd accusation to conveniently get rid of me and move on." He stormed out of the room.

She knew Tommy's system. When he didn't like what he heard, he started with denial. When that didn't work, he played the victim. And when that didn't get him the desired result, he exploded. She always responded in fear, removing the problem from Tommy's satchel and dropping it into her own.

Well not this time. Oh, she would feign compliance. She wouldn't raise the subject again. But she would make sure Tommy was never alone with her daughter.

Although she felt sure Jessie was safe now, she continued to replay that one scene over and over. Again she tried to rationalize. She told herself it couldn't be his fault. There had to be a reason. She searched for possibilities and explanations.

He isn't a bad person. He just doesn't realize he hurt Jess. I need to be understanding. I need to love him more. He probably snapped because of all the pressure I put on him.

CHAPTER 30

What is love? Marge spoke of it often. But Amy couldn't pull the pieces into a completed puzzle.

She considered the stories of Christ. He gave up everything—his rights, his pride, his reputation, his life—so people might be forgiven and have access to God. The pastor called it sacrificial love. Selfless love. Since she was sure the portrayal of Jesus was supposed to demonstrate true love, and she had promised to love Tommy, she supposed that meant she had to give up everything that mattered to her. She would love Tommy the way he needed and stop selfishly focusing on herself.

For a while she felt better. Her life had taken on new purpose—to rescue Tommy.

Yet she continued to wonder, was it supposed to be this way? Marge and Steve had fun together. Neither one of them appeared to have given up everything.

Amy had felt loved by Matt. Was that because they were just dating?

Tommy said he loved her.

Easy words.

As Amy lived her new purpose, Tommy seemed happier. But

From Thorns

no matter how much she accomplished, no matter how much she gave, she couldn't do enough.

"The dust is pretty thick. What did ya do all day?"

"Geez, Jessie's toys are everywhere. Why haven't ya taught her to pick up?"

"You overcooked the meat. It's tough."

Eventually she gave up. And their relationship spiralled back down.

The voices of her parents resounded in her mind. Worthless. Stupid. Lazy. Although she tried to fight against the accusations, they were buried too deep in her psyche to conquer. Tommy's disapproval just reinforced the messages.

Her misery consumed her and she seriously contemplated suicide. But when she realized Jess couldn't be left alone with her father, that Jess would have to die too, Amy knew something had to change.

She didn't want to leave. Tommy was Jessie's dad and that was important. Commitment was important. Even her own parents, in their miserable excuse of a marriage, had stayed together.

If she left, Marge and Steve and all the others who sat on their side of the fence would be proven right.

No, she wouldn't leave but neither would she continue with the status quo.

Amy thought back to her meetings with the young women from the church. One of them had told her to look after herself and ignore Tommy. So she decided to stop caring about his reactions. She stopped complying with instructions and made demands of her own. She donned a sullen demeanor. This led to more criticism. She practiced ignoring him and soon she became hardened to his opinions, not concerning herself with what he felt or thought. She ignored the angry outbursts, the smashing of dishes, and his storming out of the house.

Strangely, this brought about change.

"Hey, do ya want me to take care of the dishes tonight?"

"Thanks."

"I'm heading to the hardware store. Can I pick up any groceries on the way back?"

"Sure."

"Would you like me to pick up Jessie on my way home?"

"No."

She removed the pressure and he returned to coldness and oppression.

She had identified a pattern. When she withdrew her love, he demonstrated caring. If she returned to loving, he became a dictator again.

So, like fully inflated tires Amy maintained a hardness. With that came freedom. Her opinions were acknowledged. She executed some of her own decisions, worked the hours she wanted, cooked what she felt like, and did housework on her own agenda.

She enjoyed this outcome but it wasn't the way she wanted to achieve it. She didn't want to control Tommy. She wanted to be his friend and his lover. She wanted to care for him and be cared for by him. She wanted them to be able to enjoy each other and together enjoy their daughter. The way it was with Matt. The way she remembered Marge and Steve.

With Tommy it felt like she and Jessie were nothing more than possessions.

Was commitment more important than anything else? Was it right to continue living with someone who didn't seem to even

From Thorns

like her? Was it right for her to become hard and uncaring? Was it good for Jessie to be with both parents when the environment was cold and manipulative?

She considered separation but that would mean Tommy had Jessie to himself for periods of time. No. She could never let that happen!

Amy simmered in confusion.

"Are you awake, Mommy?" Jessie whispered into her ear.

"Good morning. You're up early."

"Happy birthday Mommy! I made you a present. Get up."

Amy swung her legs over the side of the bed and pushed her feet into slippers. She smelled the delicious aroma of coffee. "Is Daddy still here?"

"Uh-huh and he has a present for you. C'mon Mommy, hurry up!"

A bouquet of flowers adorned the table. A platter of fresh fruit, sliced cheese, and muffins sat next to them. Tommy wore an apron and a big smile. He walked toward her with a mug of steaming coffee.

"Happy birthday." He leaned in and kissed her cheek.

"This is lovely. Thank you."

Jessie crawled under the table and brought out an envelope tied with a blue ribbon. She helped open it and described the various items she had drawn.

"Thank you, Jess. I'm going to hang these beside my bed. You're such a great artist!"

Jessie scampered under the table again, this time coming up with a beautifully wrapped box. Amy looked at Tommy, feeling awkward. She didn't want a gift. After opening the box and pulling back the tissue paper, she gasped. "Oh my gosh. How did you know?"

"Jessie and I went shopping and she told me about your not-so-subtle hint."

"I often go into the gift shop with Jess," Amy said. "It never crossed my mind that she would tell you about the ornament. And if that's what you think I don't want it."

"Of course you want it and I want you to have it. I wouldn't have bought it for you otherwise. But next time you drop a non-hint maybe it can be for something less expensive." He grinned.

"That's not fair. I wasn't dropping hints. And I don't want you spending this much. I know we can't afford it."

"It's okay. I wouldn't buy something I couldn't afford. Granted, we could afford a lot more nice things if you had a better job." He paused. "I'm sorry, I shouldn't have said that. Don't worry about the cost; I wanted to get it for you. The money isn't a problem."

Amy wondered where this would lead. Was he setting her up? This extravagance would likely be rubbed in her face.

No, she wasn't going to play the game Tommy's way.

But what if he was sincere? What if this was from the heart, an honest desire on his part to reach out and express love?

Too late! Any trust she'd shown in the past had backfired. Any reduction in her defences had led to renewed attacks. No, she wasn't going to believe him this time or ever again.

"I appreciate your generosity," she said in as gentle a voice as she could muster, "but this isn't the time. You're right; I need to get a better job so we can afford nice things. I'm gonna return it."

Tommy looked at the floor. When he looked up there were tears. "I tried so hard to make your birthday nice."

Here we go, Amy thought. The game begins.

From Thorns

"I appreciate the thought, I really do. But right now we just can't afford this kind of luxury."

His face hardened. "Do you know how much effort I put into getting this morning organized? I can't believe what an ungrateful b---- you are. There's no pleasing you, is there?" He stormed out of the room and the front door banged against the wall.

It was only in the silence that Amy remembered Jessie. Her tender-hearted little girl stood in a corner with a red, tear-stained face.

"Oh Jessie, Mommy's sorry."

"Why don't you want Daddy's present?" Jessie sobbed. Through her own tears Amy tried to explain in a way a child might understand.

A morning that should have been enjoyed was instead painfully endured. After lunch, while Jess watched a movie, Amy took Tommy's gift to the couch.

A blue jay sat on a branch, looking at her nest. It held three blue sapphire eggs. Amy loved birds. She ran her fingers over the beautiful smooth gems.

When she'd admired this ornament in the shop, she wished she had an allowance to save for special things. But now that the ornament was hers, it spoke of mistrust and manipulation. Something beautiful had become ugly. Amy closed her eyes and let her head fall back against the couch. She visualized a blue jay perched on a branch and a story formed in her mind:

> *The sun was shining,*
> *the air was clear,*
> *the smell of flowers*

filled the atmosphere.
What a perfect day to play.

The blue jay flew into the park to a tall, leafy tree. She flew in among the branches and playfully explored. What good fortune—there were no other nests in this tree. Thick with leaves, the branches offered ideal protection from weather and predators; the perfect place to build a home for her chicks.

Mother-bird gathered twigs, grass, and other bits and pieces of useful material, working diligently until the nest was complete. As the blue jay waited for her eggs to hatch, she reflected on the brilliance of her wise decision to select this tree. The wind didn't disrupt the nest, the rain barely came through, and when the sun's rays beat down, the leaves still provided an excellent amount of shade. And she hadn't so much as seen a cat.

Gradually the tree began to change.

As the chicks pecked out of their shells, tiny flowers blossomed. Sharp thorns grew with them. An almost undetectable wind now created fear. Mother-bird didn't want to leave the tree in case a thorn wounded a chick, but she had to get food. Every trip was dangerous.

While out of the nest the blue jay looked around. Several nests, all safely positioned in different types of trees, were visible. If only she had known. It wasn't fair that her babies were stuck in such a dangerous place. But her chicks couldn't fly so there was no choice. She had to wait.

She returned to the tree looking forward to the day when her babies would be strong enough to fly so they could all leave, never to return to such a harmful place again.

From Thorns

Amy straightened and opened her eyes. The blue jay had to stay in the tree, but Amy didn't have to stay in this home. Tommy had hurt both her and Jessie. His flowers always hid thorns. Any apparent change didn't last. Game playing—nothing real. He couldn't be trusted and she had allowed herself to become someone she didn't like in order to survive. This wasn't the family home Jessie should have modelled.

Amy stood, hands on her hips, and slowly turned focusing on the various aspects of décor she had brought to the room.

"I'm going to miss this house," she mumbled audibly, "but I'm done."

She packed clothes into a duffle bag and snacks into a backpack. Books, colouring books, and crayons went into Jessie's small backpack. She hid everything in the basement.

The next morning when Tommy left for work, Amy and Jessie left for the bus station.

CHAPTER 31

"Two tickets to Vancouver please."

One of Amy's high school projects involved a town on Vancouver Island. The beauty of the ocean and the mountains combined with the need to be thousands of miles from Tommy, motivated her choice.

There would be four days of travel on busses, terminal transfers, and a ferry ride. With planning behind her she moved forward with the only tool she had left—hope. While hope sat in one pocket, fear occupied the other.

She called the school claiming a family emergency. Jess would miss the last four weeks of kindergarten.

When boarding began, Jessie maneuvered her way through the bodies in the aisle. Amy called to her as she placed the backpack on a seat.

No sign of Jessie. Amy called again, louder.

People stared.

Great. Just what I *don't* need.

One helpful type engaged, her voice ringing in a sing-song tone. "Jessie, your mommy's looking for you."

"I wanna sit at the back," Jessie yelled. "The big kids always

From Thorns

get to sit at the back."

Amy grabbed her backpack. Head down she moved toward the seat furthest back where her daughter was happily bouncing.

Once organized into their seats, after explaining to Jessie that "Mommy needs to sit at the front because sitting at the back makes her feel sick," Amy tried to relax. But without any impending tasks to keep her mind busy, worry broke the lock and charged out of its stall.

How would she find a place to live?

How would she afford it?

How quickly could she find employment?

Would they be able to escape Tommy's search party?

How would she explain all of this to Jessie?

The first leg of travel took five hours. While Jessie got into a colouring book Amy reflected on her own childhood, her pregnancy, the generous support she'd received from the entire Raynor family, and the happiness she'd found with them.

Stupid Tommy.

Why couldn't he have just left us alone?

Why did I fall for his act?

What harm has he done to Jessie?

Why didn't I see through his lies and do something sooner?

Why didn't I listen to Marge?

As the end of Tommy's workday approached, anxiety built to a crescendo. When would he realize they weren't coming home? How quickly would he call the police?

She'd been smart enough to buy the bus tickets with cash, but thanks to Jessie several people had noticed them.

She imagined his reaction. *Who does she think she is? She thinks she's better than me, that she knows better than me? Well*

Alie Cardet

I've got news for her. She's a total loser. Running off with my kid. Hiding like a coward. She's probably with Marge. As if I wouldn't figure that out. If Marge has half a brain, she'll send them to one of her loser church friends. Well I know people. I've got contacts. And when I find her, I'll make sure she knows who's boss. She won't pull a stunt like this ever again. No sir. Time for her to learn a lesson. With profanity injected throughout of course.

On the second bus they settled in for a long ride—twenty-four hours to the next destination with several terminal breaks built in. Jessie made friends with children who were happy to share her seat and snacks while sharing their technology in return. The mothers seemed happy enough to have more space. It didn't bother Amy to squish up against the window. Children departed; others boarded. Occasionally they jumped into the aisle to sing and dance to *The Wheels On The Bus Go Round And Round*.

Amy recognized how the wheels on their bus were tossing the miles back into the dust, continually putting more distance between them and Tommy.

Early in the evening panic attacked. She told Jessie to sit still while she paced in the aisle, trying to talk herself down.

You're on your way; you can't turn back; it'll work out.

But what if it doesn't?

What if I can't find a place to live?

How long will it take to find work?

What if there's no work?

What if I'm caught and they take Jessie away?

Should I use a fake name? No, I'll never get Jess to maintain that charade.

From Thorns

Jessie's head hung in the aisle, eyes tuned on her mother.

Amy stole another minute to stand at the back and breathe deeply, slowly, deliberately. After packaging up the distress and giving herself permission to take it out and stress again in an hour, she returned to her seat.

"What were you doing, Mommy?"

"I was just tired of sitting for so long. Sometimes you dance in the aisle, right?"

"Uh-huh."

"Mommies walk in the aisle instead. Let's read a story."

While Jessie rifled through books, Amy set her mind to pictures of their destination—the ocean, the beaches, the cottages, the friendly-looking people. She forced herself to think optimistically, remembering how lost and alone she felt the night she said goodbye to her family home six years earlier. Things had worked out then and they would again.

Yet fear attacked each thought.

While the bus travelled through the night, Jessie slept. Amy closed her eyes and dozed. During times when the anxiety peaked, she paced.

After more bus transfers and *way* too much time sitting, the Vancouver depot was announced. Exhaustion left Jessie cranky and Amy short on patience.

She dragged Jessie to purchase tickets to the ferry terminal, ignoring the whining while dealing with the agent, and then made the somewhat difficult decision not to lock Jessie in the bathroom and leave without her. They loaded onto the bus as the complaining droned on. When seated with backpacks crammed at their feet, Amy calmly explained that the trip was almost over and it would be better for everyone if Jessie would stop fussing. The whining continued with squirming layered in. Amy looked across the aisle at the buildings, the people, the views of the mountains, and began counting to one hundred. That half-hour bus ride felt like the longest part of the trip.

At Horseshoe Bay, they moved to a platform that looked onto the ferry dock. The scene revived Jessie.

"How can a boat be strong enough to hold cars?"

With eyes closed Amy sighed. "I don't know but it can." The warm sun felt good on her back. Resting her elbows on the railing and breathing deeply, she enjoyed the smell of the ocean.

"How many cars can that boat hold?"

"That's a good question. Maybe we can find out after we board."

"There's so many cars going on. Will there be room for us?"

"We won't be getting on that ferry. But there will definitely be room. We don't need space for a car."

"Look at those ropes. Mommy, have you ever seen a big rope like that?"

"Wow. They're huge," Amy replied. The stunning scenery in front of them featured mountains and trees surrounding a harbour filled with water glistening from the sun. A busy docking area with smaller boats, and ferries, and lines of cars, contrasted with the peaceful harbour.

She pointed to the ferry sailing into the harbour. "Hey look, that one might be ours."

"What if it can't stop?" Jessie's voice rose. "It might crash."

Amy pulled Jessie into her arms. "The captain knows how to steer the ferry."

They set course for the passenger loading zone.

From Thorns

Standing at the front of the ferry as it pulled away from shore, they no longer saw a big ferry in a small harbour. They viewed a big ocean from a small watercraft.

"Where does the lake end?"

"This isn't a lake. It's called an ocean, remember? And it goes for a long way. When we get to a beach you can taste the water—it's salty."

"Why is it salty?"

"I can't remember. We'll ask Google."

As the island's shore approached, the butterflies in Amy's gut kicked it up a notch. She kept telling herself it would work out, pushing back at the annoying voice that told her there was no valid reason to believe anything would work.

CHAPTER 32

After the last bus ride post-ferry, they arrived at a place Amy knew only from photos. With backpacks shouldered, she leaned in and took Jessie's hands.

"We're starting our new adventure now. The busses and ferry were part of it but the real adventure begins here, in this town. We're going to find a place to stay tonight and tomorrow we'll do some exploring. Are you ready?"

Jessie nodded. Only once had she asked why her father didn't come and she accepted the answer—that he had to work.

With travel behind them, Amy's plan consisted of walking until she figured out what to do next.

Before long they spotted a church. In the office, a friendly teen greeted them. "How can I help?"

"I need to speak with someone about a place to stay." She was pleased with the confident sound of her voice.

A couple of minutes passed before an older woman came through the door. "Hi, I'm Sandy. I understand you're looking for somewhere to stay. Any specifics?"

"Somewhere inexpensive. I have to look for a job."

After discussing options, they settled on a nearby hostel.

From Thorns

Sandy offered to drive them. "It's on my way home." Along the way she delivered the bad news that there wasn't much work available. "After all, this is a small town." She asked where they had come from.

Amy had a story prepared.

Sandy stayed with the two of them during check-in and continued chatting with the man behind the desk as Amy and Jessie headed to their room.

Too tired to for anything more, Amy pulled nuts and crackers from the backpack. When they were finished snacking, Jessie settled into a bed and Amy dropped onto the next bed over. The massive stress she'd been carrying for days fell to the floor as sleep overtook her.

Jessie woke far too early. She was enraptured with the 'big house' and wanted to explore. "Mommy, there's someone else living with us!"

After showering and dressing in fresh clothes, Amy asked for a breakfast spot recommendation at the check-in desk. Jake handed her a package.

Muffins, orange slices, and apple juice. She pulled out a note.

> Dear Amy,
>
> After I dropped you off last night, I realized you wouldn't have anything for breakfast. I hope you like the little picnic I prepared. I made some calls last evening and have some good news. Please ask Jake to call me when you're ready to be picked up. ~Sandy

"Oh my gosh, how thoughtful!"

But Amy's internal voice countered—has she found out about us and called the cops?

Before her thoughts had time to wander further, Sandy walked into the kitchen. "Jake called to tell me you were up. How did you sleep?"

"Very well, but not long enough." Amy glanced at Jessie. Sandy nodded and smiled.

"Thank you for breakfast. I can't believe how thoughtful you are."

"You're welcome," Sandy said. "Well, I have some good news. After I dropped you off last night I called a friend and it turns out he's looking for a waitress. I also found someone who does daycare. I've already talked to her and she wants to meet you. When you're ready we'll get started."

"You don't have to drive us around. You've been so helpful and kind—"

"Nonsense. You don't know the area."

Have I met another Marge? Amy wondered. Two in one lifetime?

She would know the truth soon enough.

CHAPTER 33

Not much taller than Amy and just a little overweight, Sandy wore a navy suit with high heels. Her shoulder-length dishevelled blonde hair was inconsistent with the rest of her tailored appearance.

At the restaurant, a pleasant-looking man with greying hair came out from the kitchen wiping his hands with a towel as he walked. "Hi Sandy. How are ya this morning?" He wore blue jeans that looked one size too big with a food-stained, loose-fitting, yellow t-shirt. The shirt was tucked in, revealing a good size belly.

"I'm Warren. Sandy tells me you're looking for work."

"I am."

"Start of tourist season," Warren said. "Nancy," he motioned toward the waitress on the other side of the restaurant, "works my breakfast and lunch shifts, and Donna works dinner. Now that it's busier, Nancy'll start doing some dinner shifts with Donna. I'll need you to take breakfast and lunch, and I'll bring in a student when it's too much for one person to handle. Nancy'll train you. You have to be here at 6:30 a.m. You might have to work some nights when Nancy or Donna can't make it in."

Warren looked down at Jessie. "You can't bring her with you." After a pause he asked, "Well, do you want the job?"

"Yes! Thank you!"

He looked at Sandy. "Have you found someone to look after the kid?"

"We're going over to meet Laura. I don't know if she'll be able to keep her through the evening though."

Warren looked back at Amy. "Well you definitely can't bring her. So go see what you can work out and come back afterwards to let me know. I need you to start right away."

That was weird, Amy thought. He didn't even ask if I have experience.

But I got a job!

As soon as they were out the door Jessie chimed, "I don't like him Mommy. I don't want you to work there. Why can't you keep working at the church?"

"This new job is part of the adventure." Amy felt perspiration on her forehead. "I think Warren is actually very nice. He was just being efficient with his words. Do you know what *efficient* means?"

"I don't like him. I wanna go home!"

"How about we give this a try before we decide Warren isn't nice?"

Frowning, Jessie crossed her arms. "I wanna go home!"

Amy turned to Sandy. "I'm sorry. She's such a good child. She's just nervous being in a new place."

Sandy nodded and with a smirk said, "I understand."

But Amy had a feeling she didn't understand at all.

As they loaded into the car Jessie asked, "Where are we going now?"

From Thorns

"We're going to meet a nice lady who you might be able to stay with while Mommy works."

"No!" Jessie started crying. "I don't wanna go somewhere. I wanna stay with you."

Heat crawled up Amy's neck to her face. "I know, Sweetie, and we'll have lots of fun times together. Mommy needs to work to pay for groceries, and you'll make some new friends. Just like when you played with Caleb and then you made new friends with Raj and Sam. Remember how much fun you had?"

"I wanna go home Mommy. I want you to work at the church. I wanna be with Daddy."

While Jessie wailed, Amy looked at Sandy and said, "Like I said yesterday, her father died but I guess she's too young to realize he's never coming back."

"Don't worry, dear. I know what children are like. I texted Laura to let her know we're coming."

Why is she doing so much for us? Amy wondered.

After introductions Laura took Jessie's hands. "I'm so glad to meet you. There's a snack waiting outside. Would you and your mom like to come?"

Jessie stopped whimpering.

Thank God for the warmth of Laura!

On one side of the spacious yard three fruit trees provided the structure for a fort constructed with blankets. Voices sounded from behind the blankets while other children played with the variety of toys decorating the lawn.

Laura had seven children of her own. She pointed out her two and four-year-old who were engrossed in play. Laura asked if Jessie would like to stay to meet her daughter, five-year-old

Kenzie, when she got home from school.

"No."

A girl who was Jessie's size ran toward them. "Wanna play in the fort?"

Jessie accompanied her while keeping an eye on Amy, who used the opportunity to discuss childcare. The only thing Laura wasn't willing to commit to—the occasional evening shift.

One step at a time.

Jessie agreed to stay and play while Amy returned to the restaurant, provided she promise to come right back. With Smarties. "A big bag."

Back at the restaurant Sandy and Warren chatted in low voices before Warren said to Amy, "It's not good that Laura can't take your girl for late shifts, but Sandy will talk to her again. I don't know anyone else looking for work right now so I'll give you a chance. I need you here tomorrow morning at 6:30."

Things couldn't have gone any better and it was all thanks to Sandy. Whatever her motivation, Amy was grateful.

The only thing left to do—avoid arrest.

Jessie and Amy hiked a short trail to the beach and walked barefoot in the cold ocean inlet. Jessie tasted the saltwater which led to a discussion about the difference between lake and ocean water, the thirst-quenching properties of the one but not the other, different freezing points, and density. Amy wondered where Jessie's intelligence came from.

Following dinner, after Jessie settled into bed and Amy completed a few chores, she crawled under the covers hoping for another night of deep sleep. But worry made too much noise.

This was the first of many nights to come. Amy developed

From Thorns

night terror because the night held silence and silence released the lid on her hard-boiling fear. Fighting the fear took a lot of energy.

When the alarm sounded at 5:15 a.m. Amy bolted upright. It took a few seconds for her to remember where she was and why she'd set an alarm.

She carried what felt like a bag of cement to Laura's house, thankful it was a short walk. A better method of transport would have to be found.

Laura's husband answered the door. "C'mon in." The smell of coffee roused Amy's desire for the morning tradition.

"Good morning," Laura said as she entered the room. "Let's settle her on the couch. The kids will be up in an hour. Now you head to work and don't worry. We're going to enjoy having her with us."

Amy sat on the edge of the couch stroking Jessie's hair until her eyes stayed closed. How would she react when she realized she'd been deserted? Although Amy felt guilty, she was glad Laura would be dealing with it.

The restaurant, a rustic log house, came into view.

Nancy opened the front door when Amy knocked. "We'll have to get you a key. Did Warren tell you to get here this early?"

"No, he said 6:30 but I wanted to make sure I wasn't late."

"Lucky for you I'm in early. If you arrive by 6:40, that's enough time. Help yourself to coffee—it's actually pretty good. I'll go get a uniform for you." She shrugged. "Warren insists."

The log walls and the bar with its overhanging wooden counter and wooden stools created a warm, inviting atmosphere. Blue and white gingham cloths covered tables in the dining area. Large windows allowed the sun to spill across tables and onto the floor.

Nancy talked non-stop. Amy learned she'd timed her arrival perfectly. The previous summer, Warren had to bring his wife in for the month before high school let out. "She helps out if someone is sick or has an appointment and that works fine. But last summer was too much togetherness." Nancy winked.

She described the typical breakfast, lunch, and dinner times, and the various tasks Amy would be expected to complete. "And you'll probably have to clean the bathroom before you leave. Can you handle it?"

"No problem."

Diners began drifting in shortly after the restaurant opened. The friendly patrons offered advice like, "Joyce, over at that table, the one with the curly hair, she likes her water glass topped up. She won't tell you but she complains if you don't do it." Amy noticed Nancy roll her eyes as customers relayed their thoughts.

Several asked personal questions. They wanted to know all about Jessie after learning Amy had a daughter. They wanted to know everything about both of them it seemed. But it didn't feel like prying.

Most customers were generous. And clear. "This is for Nancy and this is for you."

Amy handed her tips to Nancy when it slowed. "You're doing all the work."

"Don't be silly," Nancy said. "I got my regular tips. They want to encourage you. Or make you like them. Whichever, I'm sure you can use the money."

The lunch shift wrapped up with everything cleaned and tidied at 3:00. Amy jogged to Laura's house hoping Jessie's day

From Thorns

had been as successful as her own.

Laura led her quietly into a large playroom. Jessie sat right in the thick of things as though she had been a part of this group forever. But she burst into tears at the sight of her mother. "You *left* me this morning. You didn't say goodbye. You just left me!"

Laura brought Jessie out of the group and Amy tried to explain.

"I wanna go home!" Even after she settled, Jessie's mind was made up. She wasn't going back to Laura's.

They returned to the hostel, inspecting bugs, watching birds, and stopping to greet dogs along the way.

While preparing dinner, Amy broached the delicate subject of childcare. "If you don't go to Laura's house you'll have to come to work with me. And you'll probably have to help Warren in the kitchen."

"You're not allowed to bring me to work. He said so."

"People say lots of things, but if you don't go to Laura's you'll be coming with me and Warren will put you to work."

By the end of the evening, Jessie decided she would go back to Laura's on the condition her mother woke her to say goodbye before leaving.

A couple of weeks in, Warren hired a student from the local high school and Nancy worked evenings. Jasmine was confident and easygoing. "I worked here at Christmas. Not a lot of hours, but enough to know how things work. I hate cleaning the bathroom." She scrunched up her nose. "Any chance you'd be willing to do that job? I'll owe you big time!"

Amy laughed. "No problem. There will be times I'll probably need to rearrange my hours around Jessie, if she has an appointment or whatever, so if I can count on you to fill in..."

Before long Jessie and Laura's daughter, Kenzie, developed a friendship and Jessie slept over when Amy worked a dinner shift. The increased tips more than covered the extra cost of childcare. She worked as many shifts as she could, and watched her bank account grow. When sufficient funds accumulated, she and Jessie shopped for badly needed clothes. The freedom felt better than she could have imagined.

And the oppression she'd endured with Tommy came into better focus. As her anger simmered, the lid lifted and the contents spilled out. Why had she put up with him for so long? Fuming didn't do her psyche any good but she couldn't push the loathing back into the pot.

Most evenings, once Jessie got to bed, Amy journaled memories and related feelings. She paced, pounded the table, threw her pen across the room, and then continued to write. With time the intensity diminished.

Between her fear and anger, sleep didn't come easily.

CHAPTER 34

Through Laura, Amy got to know several young mothers. They often met at the park in the evenings to let the youngsters burn off energy before bed. The church ran a summer café where she met others in her age bracket, including some who were backpacking for the season. Through her new group of friends, she was introduced to fun activities. Several families invited Amy and Jessie to join them on their sailboats.

People often asked what brought her to the island.

"My husband died in an accident. I felt we needed a fresh start to begin healing. Jessie will say her dad didn't come with us because he had to work—it seems she's too young to fully understand she's not going to see him again." Amy couldn't manage to produce any tears, but she was able to put on a sad face and sniff repeatedly.

"Kenzie saw my picture on T.V.," Jessie casually said as they walked to the hostel one day after work.

Amy froze. "When?"

"After school."

"Were you watching T.V. with her?"

"No. She told me when I came back from the bathroom."

Amy resumed walking.

"What's wrong Mommy?"

"Nothing." She wanted to keep her panic from Jessie's radar. "I'm just disappointed you didn't get to see it. Wouldn't it be fun to see your picture on television?"

Her gut twisted in knots which left her with no appetite. While Jessie devoured chicken fingers and fries, Amy set to thinking.

I need to know what Kenzie saw. I wonder if she saw Jessie alone or did I appear beside her? *Call the number on your screen if you've seen either of these people.*

She searched the internet.

Nothing.

What did Kenzie see?

"Hey Jess, let's sleep in a different room tonight. We won't tell anyone. It'll be our secret."

"I wanna pick the room."

"Okay. Let's clean the ketchup off your face and hands, and we'll go exploring."

Mysteriously and thankfully Jessie's antenna didn't pick up Amy's dread.

As Jessie drifted to sleep in the new room, Amy got into her pyjamas. When she pulled her robe from the end of the bed she reflected on when she'd received it.

There had been a knock on her bedroom door.

Marge's hand appeared holding a mass of green fabric. "Could you use this housecoat?"

"No thanks, I don't need anything."

Marge asked Amy to accompany her to the master bedroom.

From Thorns

Her open closet looked like an overflowing suitcase. "If you don't take this I'll have to find a charity."

"Really? You're definitely giving it away?"

Marge nodded.

"Well okay. If you're sure." Amy paused at the door. "Won't Steve be mad when he sees me wearing your clothes?" The robe hung between her and Marge dangling from an extended arm. "I don't think this is a good idea."

"Steve's the one who asked me to clean out the closet so he has space for his clothes."

"What about Kate? Would she like it?"

"I guarantee she won't. She needs to clean out her own closet."

"I'd feel better if you checked with her first," Amy said.

When Kate returned from basketball practice and wandered into the kitchen looking for a snack, Marge said, "Help yourself to strawberries. And please look at the robe on the chair. It's yours if you'd like it."

Kate's eyes rolled. "When are you gonna learn I'm not interested in your old clothes?" She winked at Amy.

Amy happily took the robe.

Now she wrapped her arms around herself, glad she had thought to bring it.

Such good memories from living with the Raynors. Why didn't she listen to Marge's advice? Why did she believe Tommy? Why did she turn her back on Matt?

She sighed. If only she had a chance to do it over.

Thinking about what might happen if the police came during the night, she decided to leave their belongings where they were.

They'll probably make noise when they find our stuff and we'll have time to hide.

Alie Cardet

The night offered a very poor sleep, but no police.

In the morning Amy peered out the window. Nothing unusual.

When she dropped Jess off, Laura behaved as she always did.

At work Amy watched people's reactions. There were no noticeable "Aha" moments.

What on earth did Kenzie see?

CHAPTER 35

Sandy remained interested in all their comings and goings. So after a month at the hostel, when Amy decided to find an apartment, she approached Sandy who had the perfect place lined up. She insisted on bringing them to meet the landlords.

What's driving her? Amy wondered. Doesn't she have a life of her own? Is she genuine or just a busybody?

"Oh my gosh," she muttered when Sandy stopped the car in front of a large bungalow.

"What's wrong?"

"I wasn't expecting such a beautiful neighbourhood."

"Well let's not worry about that. The Bentleys are waiting to meet you." Sandy turned to Jessie. "You too. C'mon now."

After getting-to-know-each-other conversation, they went through the backdoor to the two-car garage separate from the house with a studio apartment above. The open space contained a fully equipped kitchen nook, a small table, a day bed with a spare mattress tucked underneath, a coffee table, and a couple of chairs. A small balcony overlooked a beautifully landscaped yard.

"Would you mind if I replaced the bed cover?" Amy asked.

"I'll get rid of that dreary bedspread," Mrs. Bentley said. "Feel free to spruce up the place however you'd like."

Until Jessie grew older this space would be perfect. And the rent was less than the monthly rate Amy had negotiated at the hostel.

She wondered aloud why this room had been constructed.

"When our son attended university," Mr. Bentley said, "we felt he needed some space of his own."

Mrs. Bentley laughed. "Yup, we all needed some space."

"Well Amy, what do you think?" Sandy asked.

It was within walking distance of Laura's house and the restaurant. Amy looked at Jessie. "Would you like living here?"

"Uh-huh." Jessie looked at Mrs. Bentley. "Can we come over now?"

"You come whenever you're ready." She took Jessie by the shoulders. "You remind me of my granddaughter who lives too far away."

As they were leaving, Sandy confessed she'd been thinking about a more permanent accommodation from the very beginning. Just as Amy suspected.

She and Jessie enjoyed the apartment and the setting. The expansive yard hosted some fruit trees and several well-manicured gardens that looked like colourful mosaics. Mrs. Bentley welcomed Amy's help. "I've always loved gardening but my knees are bothering me now."

"I'll help out anytime—I love working in the dirt and watching things grow."

"Can I help?" Jessie asked.

"Of course you can," Mrs. Bentley said. And then to Amy,

From Thorns

"I'm so glad you're both here. Having Jessie around makes me feel younger."

When Amy and Jessie were alone with the flowers Amy used the occasions to talk about Tommy. Not a lot—Amy wanted her to forget. But while memories were fresh, she hoped to learn how much he had hurt Jessie and in what ways.

"Do you remember when you went to the basement with Daddy?"

"Uh-huh."

"Did you get hurt very often?"

No reply.

Jessie remained consistently dismissive. Eventually Amy gave up, hoping there wouldn't be any lasting damage, confident that her daughter's experience wasn't anywhere near as bad as her own.

Jessie occasionally asked when they would return home, which boggled Amy's mind. Why would she want to go back and have to see her father? Amy couldn't remember anything good from those years.

One hot sunny afternoon someone new came into the restaurant. He was quite attractive, so when he caught Amy's attention she had to go to the kitchen to wait for the heat to work its way through her neck and face. After settling she walked to his table.

"Just coffee, thanks."

He worked on his laptop through several refills and left a generous tip.

After three more days of the same routine he asked for her name and invited her to sit with him.

"I can't. Not while I'm working."

"But the restaurant's empty."

Since she would be closing in another fifteen minutes, Amy decided Warren wouldn't mind.

"I like this place," Trevor said. "What's the building's story?"

"I just moved here a couple of months ago. I don't know any history."

"What brought you here?" he asked.

"It's a long story. How about you? Is this a holiday or are you here to stay?"

"I've moved here," he said. "My job lets me work from home so I can live anywhere. This seems like a nice place. Do you think I made a good choice?"

Amy agreed to show Trevor the areas she enjoyed when her shift was done.

Very talkative, he made their walk enjoyable. Amy learned he lived with a friend although he planned to get a place of his own. His work had something to do with stocks and other financial stuff. The company he worked for was based in Vancouver and he had to go into the office from time to time. He mentioned several attractions in and around that area.

"I'd love to visit sometime," Amy said.

"Maybe you can join me on one of my trips over and I'll give you a tour."

"Maybe. But right now I have a daughter who needs to be picked up." Looking up at him she smiled. "I'll see you around."

Trevor continued his afternoon coffee visits. "I like the atmosphere. I don't have a lot of space at my friend's place," he explained.

Amy introduced him to her friends and he became a part of the crowd as easily as she had, joining them in sailing, kayaking,

From Thorns

and hiking. Of course she couldn't go as often as she would have liked. "Thanks for asking, but Jessie . . ."

On one sailing outing Amy overheard Trevor say, "I love cooking. I might start a restaurant someday." She quizzed him and learned he played with gourmet cooking and baking.

"Would you like to cook together?" she asked. "Maybe I can get Jessie to bed early." They decided to meet at his place where his closed room would allow Jess to sleep more easily than in Amy's open space. "I'll find out when my roommate will be out."

For their first get-together Jessie sat at the table drawing and eating macaroni while the chefs worked on chopping and measuring. Trevor's sense of humour kept Amy laughing.

"What's so funny," Jessie asked, with a tone that suggested annoyance.

The following day she delved into criticism. "I didn't like what he made me for supper."

"But you love Kraft Dinner."

"He doesn't make it properly," she said with a sulk as she walked off.

Although Trevor tried to engage Jess, it rarely worked. So the adults continued cooking together while ignoring Jessie's moods.

During one of their shared meals, after Jessie fell asleep Trevor said, "You're really pretty."

Amy pushed her chair away from the table and held up her hands. "I can't get into another relationship right now."

"Sorry, I didn't mean to startle you," Trevor said. "I moved here because of a messy breakup so you don't have to worry about me. I'm not looking for a relationship either."

Amy wanted to believe him but she didn't. Afterward she

felt guarded until she saw him with his arm around Sherri a few weeks later. He pulled his arm away when their eyes met. "Hey Amy, ya ready to go?"

What's going on? she wondered. Doesn't matter—I don't care.

She denied her feelings through that afternoon of hiking, reminding herself that she wasn't interested in Trevor and was actually glad to see he had connected with someone. Except she wasn't feeling glad.

As the summer progressed it became obvious that Trevor and Sherri were a couple.

"Are you okay with me 'n Trevor cooking together?" Amy asked Sherri.

"Yup. He told me you're trying to recover from losing your husband." Sherri put on a downcast face and stroked Amy's arm. "Anyway, you're not his type. He grew up nearby; we know each other really well and we're a good match. Besides, he wouldn't be interested in someone who has a kid." She smiled and draped one arm around Amy's shoulder. "I hope that wasn't harsh. Just wanted you to know I'm definitely not worried."

When Amy got over feeling ticked off, she told Trevor about the discussion.

"Hey, I think you're awesome. You told me you only wanted friendship and at the end of the day, Sherri's right. I'm not ready for kids." He shrugged. "But I like hanging out with you."

"Why didn't you tell me you grew up here?" Amy demanded.

"Does it matter?"

It does, she thought. He tried to make me think he was new to this area. But I guess it's not worth wrecking a friendship over.

They continued cooking together until Trevor announced,

From Thorns

"We're gonna have to stop this. Sherri can't handle it." They kept socializing with the same group, careful to maintain distance.

Through the summer Amy watched peoples' reactions. No suspicious looks, no pointing or whispering. She reviewed the news daily and googled *kidnapping*. Nothing. What had Kenzie seen? Tommy *must* have reported them—why wasn't it in the news? Would she ever completely relax? Sure, she lived a normal life, but she had a constant underlying fear. Like a needle without any thread pricking at her mind and emotions. Every night a sense of dread draped over her body fighting against a peaceful descent into sleep.

As summer waned Nancy confided that she wanted to cut her hours or possibly retire, but she didn't want to leave Warren in a bind. Would Amy like to pick up Nancy's hours in September?

"If he agrees, yes!" Amy had already put out feelers hoping someone would know where she should look for work when Warren eventually announced her layoff. But staying on as a waitress would be best. Tips provided enough income that most of her pay cheque went into savings.

Together they discussed the idea with Warren.

He shrugged. "As long as all my shifts are covered. Will Laura keep your girl?"

In September Jessie settled into Grade One.

Toward the end of the month, at Jessie's birthday, Amy took cupcakes for the class and stayed while the children dove in. Seeing Jessie with the others, not hanging back or experiencing rejection, sent Amy's heart soaring.

Alie Cardet

Jessie talked about the new things she learned each day. She prattled on about her teacher's interactions and the activities she enjoyed with her new friends. She brought home drawings and crafts and entertained anyone who would listen with her new songs.

When Amy attended the first meet-the-teacher event and heard the teacher's praise, she knew she'd finally done something right. Being assured of Jessie's confidence allowed her to relinquish the fear she had tucked away—fear that Tommy had done irreversible damage.

Through the early fall as she walked to and from work, Amy wondered if the colours of the leaves were even more brilliant than what she had known in the east. She wasn't sure. But she *was* sure the days were getting shorter and the air had taken on a nasty chill. With the temperature falling and Jessie now asking to play at friends' houses, it was time to get a car.

When she ran the idea past Mr. Bentley, his eyes lit up. "Would you like some help?"

Soon he had a recommendation. "It's time for my friend to go to one car. I know how their Accord was driven. It's older which is why it's such a good deal. You won't find better."

"I'll take it!"

He took her to get the car and before she drove off he said, "Thank you for letting me help."

"It's *me* who needs to thank *you*," Amy replied.

Mr. Bentley smiled. "Well, I had fun, and I couldn't have done *that* without *you*."

CHAPTER 36

Amy tugged her collar tight as she walked into the cold wind that pulled the dried leaves from their branches. "Why am I walking today?" she muttered to herself. "I must be insane." Wanting to enjoy fresh air for as long as possible, she had hoped she would continue walking until winter. But maybe not.

The restaurant was busier than usual with customers wandering among the tables and chatting with each other, making delivery of meals challenging. The high noise level created a party atmosphere. Everyone complimented Amy on her efficiency and left generous tips. Mr. Brown explained, "With the cold weather we'll be spending more time in front of our fireplaces. So, we all came out for a fall get-together. It's gonna slow *waayyy* down."

She wondered what *slow* would look like and how much her tips would decline.

The busy day left her exhausted.

As she prepared to leave Warren called her into the kitchen. He had the cash, the cash register tape, and the deposit slip out on the counter.

"This doesn't add up. There's $300 missing."

Amy froze. "That's impossible. I just counted the money and

everything matched."

"Well it doesn't match now. Are you calling me a liar?"

"No, I'm sorry, I just don't know how this could have happened."

Warren moved closer. "I'm going to let this go and forget it happened." He put one arm around her waist, pulled her in, and cupped the back of her head. His mouth pressed firmly over hers.

She pushed away. "Don't."

He stepped back. "I could fire you on the spot for trying to steal from me. I could call the cops. Do you want that?"

Amy remained silent.

"Of course you don't. I'm showing you how you can thank me." He moved toward her, his face inches from hers. The putrid smell of his garlic breath filled her nostrils. "Where would you be without this job?" he said as he stroked her arm.

Amy jerked her arm free and backed away.

"You're gonna regret this," he spat.

She ran from the kitchen and, without her coat, into the freezing rain. She continued running for two blocks before stopping to catch her breath. The rain mixed with tears dripped from her face. She crouched to the ground, buried her face in her hands, and sobbed.

She had to find someone who could help. Nancy? Donna? Mrs. Bentley?

Cold and stunned, she jogged home looking at the ground so she wouldn't see anyone. So no one would see her.

Inside the apartment she showered, sitting on her heels, her back pressed against the wall, wailing into the water. Eventually her body warmed but she couldn't stop shaking. She continued to cry, even scream, allowing her voice to release the agony

From Thorns

trapped inside.

When there were no tears left she turned off the shower, wrapped herself in a towel, and crawled into bed.

This can't be happening. What am I gonna do?

She pulled herself into a ball. Disgust held her tight until she fell asleep.

The phone woke her. "Hi Amy, it's Laura. Are you okay?"

"Oh my gosh, I'm sorry. I felt sick. Must've fallen asleep. I'll be right over."

"Hey, it's alright. Do you need me to keep Jess longer?"

"I'm fine now. See you in a few minutes."

With every step her anger fueled determination.

I didn't leave Tommy and go through the past five months to be jerked around by some degenerate. I'll find another job and good luck to Warren. He'll probably have to hire his wife.

"I need to talk to you," Amy said.

Laura ushered her to a couch.

"It's time for me to look for another job. Do you know of any openings?"

"Another job? Why? Does Warren know?"

"Yeah, I think Warren knows," Amy said, her eyes narrowing.

"He must have been upset when you told him. How's he going to manage without you? Donna and Nancy can't go back to working every shift."

How is it, Amy wondered, that absolutely everybody knows everyone else's business?

Her anger burned. Warren constantly made her feel like she owed him for his benevolence in giving her a job. Meanwhile, the whole town knew he was desperate for her help. She was sick of being careful. She was a part of this town now and had as much right to respect as anyone else. "I'm going to tell you something. I hope I can trust you."

Amy recounted the incident, her face getting hot as she spoke. When she finished there was silence. Awkward silence.

"I don't know how to react to this," Laura finally said. "I've known Warren my whole life. He's hard-working and generous. He's done a lot for this community. I'm not saying I don't believe you, but I can't imagine Warren doing something like that. Maybe it was a misunderstanding."

How could he have so many people fooled? Surely Amy wasn't the first. "Are you telling me he's *never* been accused of doing this to anyone else? *Ever*?"

Laura looked away.

"Why would I make up such a horrible story?" Amy said. "You've gotten to know me. That's not who I am."

Laura shifted. "I don't know what to do with this information. I think you should leave." She stood and moved toward the door. "C'mon Jessie, your mom's here."

If Laura didn't believe her, maybe no one else would either. Would Laura gossip? What would she say, exactly? This could get out of hand quickly. Amy didn't hear a word of Jessie's chatter on the walk home.

She decided to talk to Mrs. Bentley.

I can trust her.

At least I hope I can trust her.

She rang the doorbell.

Sandy answered.

From Thorns

"I came by to say hello to Mrs. Bentley," Amy said hoping this was a chance visit. "I'll come back later."

Sandy didn't smile. "I think you should come in." She looked down at Jessie. "I brought a movie. Run along to the back room. Mr. Bentley's waiting."

Well, well, Sandy's thought of everything.

Jessie looked at Amy.

"Sounds like fun," Amy said. Jessie didn't move. Amy brought a positive inflection to her voice. "Go check out the movie. I bet there's a snack waiting for you—Mrs. Bentley's famous chocolate chip cookies."

Jessie glanced back at Sandy as she shuffled along.

Mrs. Bentley joined Sandy and Amy in the living room,

"I got a call from Warren," Sandy said. "He's very upset. I don't know how things worked where you came from but in our town we live by a strong moral code. Warren has been happily married for thirty-one years and he isn't interested in some little tramp trying to come between him and his wife. Now he's willing to—"

"*What*? *He* forced himself on *me*."

Sandy shook her head wearing a look of disbelief. "If you won't take responsibility for what you've done there's nothing I can do. You better think hard. No one's going to believe someone who breezed into town with a child and no husband, never telling any of us where you came from or why you *really* came, and now accusing one of the most respected men in our community. You've got some nerve. Warren wanted to give you another chance. You don't deserve it."

Sandy stood. "Good evening, Joan." Then she looked back at Amy with disgust. "If you decide to tell the truth, call me tomorrow. Otherwise it's time for you to leave."

At the sound of the door closing, Mrs. Bentley took Amy's hands into her own. "You're in a lot of trouble. In this town, gossip is all some have to live for. I've never liked that Warren. There have been other stories, but he contributes a lot to the community. So people forget the bad because it serves their interests to forget. And Sandy's a powerful force. I learned a long time ago that to cross her was a mistake. She and Warren's wife are best friends. Sandy came here tonight to tell us that we should send you packing. Well we're not going to do that. But we can't get you out of this mess. You're going to have to apologize to Warren *and* Sandy. And make the best of it."

"*Apologize*? You can't be serious! He's a disgusting animal."

"Be careful. Apologizing isn't the end of the world. Go home and think about it."

Mrs. Bentley stood and called Jessie.

In a trance Amy got Jess into pyjamas, fed her a peanut butter sandwich, and tucked her into bed with some books.

She pressed her hand against her chest trying to will her heart to stop pounding.

I'm not apologizing for something I haven't done, she thought, gritting her teeth.

She wasn't going to assume the guilt that belonged to Warren. Her parents and Tommy had forced her to take the blame for everything. No more! The Raynors had shown her a better way and she was determined to own that now.

CHAPTER 37

The following day after dropping Jessie at school and calling in sick so she couldn't be accused of being irresponsible, Amy drove to the police station.

"I'd like to report a sexual assault."

The report was taken although Amy noticed a smirk on the officer's face.

He better take this seriously, she thought, because I'm not going away.

From there, Amy walked the sidewalks hoping one would lead to a job. She completed a number of applications.

Next stop—the Bentleys.

Mr. Bentley answered the door but disappeared after calling his wife.

"Yesterday you mentioned there were rumours about Warren," Amy said. "I need you to tell me more."

"I'm not getting involved in this," Mrs. Bentley replied. "You need to apologize."

"I'm not asking you to get involved. I just want the names of people who have accused him or maybe implied that he did something inappropriate."

"I don't have names. I just remember hearing a couple of stories. I don't remember from who. You need to drop this and apologize and it will all blow over."

"I've gone to the police."

Mrs. Bentley froze, wide-eyed. "That wasn't wise. There's a strong old boys club here. I can't imagine they'll help you."

"They don't have a choice. I filed a complaint and they have to check it out." Amy frowned. "Don't they?"

"I don't know." Mrs. Bentley stood. "I'm feeling upset. You need to go."

"Okay. Thank you anyway."

Why did I thank her?

Why do I have to pretend I'm grateful when she did nothing?

Because I need her on my side.

But she isn't.

Maybe she'll come around.

In the apartment Amy felt safe until reality barged through the protective walls. She spent the rest of the afternoon crying. When the clock told her to get Jessie from school, she pulled herself together.

On their way to the park Jessie chattered about her day. Watching her daughter easily interact with other kids deposited a few positive notes into her life's awful symphony.

As the sun drifted toward the horizon Amy called, "C'mon, it's time to go." To which Jessie yelled her standard response. "When can we get a dog?"

From Thorns

After they finished supper there was a loud knock on the door. "How dare you involve my wife in your mess," Mr. Bentley said in a raised voice. "You need to find somewhere else to live."

Amy looked toward Jessie whose eyes were rivetted on the open doorway. Amy stepped out and motioned for Mr. Bentley to move to the lawn. "I haven't involved her," she barked. "I asked if she would help me. She said 'no' and I haven't spoken to her since."

"You've got our town in an uproar." Mr. Bentley scowled. "Y'know it wouldn't have been that hard to apologize. You seemed like such a sensible girl. You've got until the end of the week."

"To what? I'm not going to apologise."

"You need to find another place to live."

Shocked, Amy stood speechless for a few moments and then, "How am I supposed to find another place that fast?"

"Oh, you mean without Sandy's help? You should have thought of that before causing trouble." He turned and walked toward the house.

"I'm not causing trouble," Amy shouted. "I reported someone who tried to assault me. *Warren* caused the trouble."

Mr. Bentley shook his head as he continued walking.

Amy took a minute to calm her breathing before returning inside.

"What's wrong?" Jessie asked.

"It was just a misunderstanding."

"Mr. Bentley's not mad at you?"

"No."

After tucking Jessie in she searched the internet. No rentals. She called Trevor. "I'm in a bit of a mess," she said through tears. He already knew. He believed her version of the story. Warren had a reputation of generosity but he gave some the creeps.

"I've got my own place now. You can stay with me until you figure out what to do. I'm not with Sherri anymore so there's no problem."

"Thanks, but I'd rather not. I need to get settled in our own place. Do you know of anything for rent?"

"Hmmm. Let me get back to you."

An hour later Trevor called. "I'd heard of a rental not too long ago but hadn't paid much attention so I had to make some calls. Anyway, here's the deal. You know Jack. He has an aunt who lives in town. She and her husband left a couple of months ago to spend a year in the east with their son. They wanted someone to live in the house but couldn't find anyone. You can have it if you meet with Jack's Mom, Rhonda, and she likes you. I've already given you a seal of approval so it should be easy."

Amy could picture his grin.

She arranged a meeting with Rhonda.

The two-bedroom house suited perfectly.

"My sister will be happy to know there's such a well-behaved little girl living in her home. I bet she's a handful when you have to say 'no.'"

"Not really. She's been asking for a pet and I always answer the same way and she accepts it every time."

"You can't have a pet in this house. Will that be an issue?"

Amy laughed. "Not a chance."

The school office had provided three names of stay-at-home moms who offered before-and-after-school childcare. Amy started with the individual closest to her new home. Friendly and warm, Lindsay had three children of her own. Although she wasn't willing to keep Jessie past six in the evening, Amy was

From Thorns

too tired to meet with anyone else. She hoped Lindsay would change her mind as Laura had done.

A place to live. Check.

Childcare organized. Check.

A friend on my side. Check.

No harassment from Warren or Sandy. Phew!

Hopefully her nerves would settle so she could start eating again. If she lost anymore more weight she'd have to shop for new clothes, which she couldn't afford.

She packed the car and drove away from a place that had generated good memories until it all turned sour.

What a horrible bunch of people. I wonder if the Bentley's will bother mentioning to Sandy that I left the place cleaner than I found it.

Amy picked Jessie up at the school, returned to the new house, and watched her place her books and toys on the shelves in her new room. "Are you happy to have your own bedroom?"

Jessie ran to her mom and delivered a hug.

They flopped in front of the television before dinner. Tuned out, Amy rested her head against the back of the sofa until Jess called, "Mommy look, I'm on T.V."

Amy straightened. "It's a commercial."

Jessie ran to the screen and pointed.

"She does look a lot like you," Amy said. "Cool!"

Thank you, God, she thought, feeling a load of tension release. Although nothing had happened since Kenzie believed she saw Jess on TV, Amy had remained watchful and worried.

"She looks *exactly* like me. I gonna tell Kenzie it's me."

"You have to tell the truth. She'll never believe anything else you say if she finds out you lied."

If we ever see Kenzie again, Amy thought with sadness.

During the night a panic attack woke her. She'd experienced anxiety in the past but nothing this severe. It felt scary. After spending forty-five minutes pacing and self-talking she managed to settle enough to return to bed.

The police will charge Warren and everyone will see I was falsely accused.

Hopefully.

Even if he gets away with it, we've moved and started over. There's no reason to panic.

Sleep eluded her as the anxiety simmered.

She spent the rest of the week completing applications and revisiting shops where an application had already been delivered. A grocery store and a hardware store indicated they could likely offer part-time work and that she should check again next week.

Two part-time jobs wouldn't provide the income of waitressing. What if the hours clashed? Most of her savings had gone into the car—there was only enough left to carry them for another month or so.

The following week she returned to the two stores. She was greeted abruptly and both delivered the same bad news. "Sorry, we don't have any openings."

"Do you think there might be something later? In a couple of weeks maybe?"

"No. We're not hiring."

What am I gonna do if there's no work? Amy fretted.

Later in the evening Trevor called. "I have bad news."

Word was out all over town. No one was brave enough to stand against Warren or Sandy. Amy wasn't going to get work.

From Thorns

Furthermore, she couldn't stay in the house. Rhonda had called Jack who called Trevor.

"I'm so sorry. You and Jessie can stay with me until you figure out what you're gonna do. But no one can take on Warren and win. I'd lay odds that the police told him about your claim and they all had a beer and laughed. I had hoped you'd triumph but none of this surprises me."

Amy cried audibly through Trevor's delivery.

"I'm coming over," he said.

Tell the truth, do the right thing, and it'll all work out. Warren does the wrong thing, lies about it, and he wins.

With a red, tear stained face, she answered the door and led Trevor to the living room.

"Don't the police work for everyone?" Amy spat. "Aren't they supposed to look for truth? Protect the innocent? Why would they turn a blind eye if there's even a small possibility that Warren molested someone? And why is everyone so afraid of Sandy?"

Trevor held her while she sobbed.

"What am I going to do?"

"This is horrible, Amy. You didn't deserve it."

"I have to move. Jessie's gonna freak. She loves school. She was so upset when I told her she wouldn't be going to Laura's anymore. She keeps asking to play with Kenzie. And now I have to tell her we're moving *again*. That she has to change schools *again*. Make new friends *again*."

They talked into the early morning hours.

"I'm gonna miss you," Trevor said on his way out the door. "Remember, if you want to stay and tackle this I've got space."

But I'd have no income, Amy thought, and no hope of winning.

She found her map of the island. There were many other island destinations where residents wouldn't know Warren. Or Sandy. But could she be sure? What about all the other people who turned against her. What if they had family or friends in any of those places?

She had to get off the island. They had to go to a big city, a place where they could get lost among all the people. A place where everyone didn't know everything about everybody.

Amy tucked into bed with the hope of getting a couple of hour's sleep. Tomorrow she would research jobs and accommodation in Vancouver.

After spending some time on the internet, she learned she couldn't afford Vancouver rent.

What about Calgary? Nope.

Winnipeg? Apartments were available within her price range. And there were job opportunities. Perfect. Winnipeg it would be.

She loaded their possessions into duffle bags.

Seems I'm getting good at this. A skill I shouldn't need.

And when there was nothing more to do, depression moved in to take up the space. She fell to the floor, sobbing. Banging her hands on the carpet, she shouted, "No! No! No! This isn't fair!"

It's a bad dream. I'm going to wake up any minute. She closed her eyes. When she opened them, the stuffed duffle bags sat in front of her.

From Thorns

Cursing, she moved to the couch with ice on her eyes. When the ice melted she tossed the cloth onto the floor and paced, pounding the sofa at every pass.

Stop feeling sorry for yourself. It's time to move forward. We have a car. We have enough cash to get us to Winnipeg and set up. We won't have to ask anyone for help.

She set off to get Jessie from school.

After running through the door on the way to her bedroom, Jessie stopped to inquire about the duffle bags.

"We're going on an adventure," Amy said with excitement.

"Where are we going?" Jessie asked, hesitantly.

"It's a surprise."

"When will we come back?"

Amy cupped Jessie's cheeks. "We can't come back."

Jessie pushed her mother's hands away. "Why not?!"

"There are some bad people here who want to hurt Mommy. We're going to move to another place where there won't be people who want to hurt us."

Jessie ran to her room and slammed the door.

Amy followed her, sat on the edge of the bed, and rubbed Jessie's back until the crying subsided.

"I don't wanna go anywhere else. I like my teacher and my new friends and my new room."

"Remember when we moved here?" Amy said. "How much you hated it at first? But we met nice people. When we move, you'll meet more nice people and you'll make new friends. It'll be fun."

"I don't wanna go!" The crying resumed.

"I understand. I'll come back to check on you soon."

Amy returned to the couch, dropped her head into her hands,

and allowed herself to cry in sync with her daughter.

How am I going to get Jessie into the car? Maybe she'll resign herself by morning. But what if she doesn't?

Such horrible people, making me do this to a child!

The doorbell rang. Rhonda. "Here's your rent. I expect you're packing up to be on your way by the end of the week."

Amy glared as she took the envelope. "I need you to sign my lease agreement showing we no longer rent here." *Void* was written across in bold letters.

"I've given you all your rent back. You should be grateful."

"*Grateful*? You've got to be kidding."

With the cancelled agreement in hand Amy slammed the door.

She felt like punching a hole in the wall or smashing the dishes. But they'd likely hunt her down and demand compensation.

CHAPTER 38

On the road early, anger drove Amy.

At the ferry terminal an hour before departure, Jessie woke. "Where are we?"

Amy took a deep breath. "Remember yesterday when I told you about a new adventure?"

She waited. Nothing.

Phew!

The backdoor opened. Amy turned to see Jessie hop out. "What are you doing?"

"I'm not going with you."

"I see. Are you planning to stay by yourself?"

Jessie folded her arms across her chest and burst into tears. "I don't wanna go."

"I understand but you don't have a choice. Please get in the car."

Jessie stepped back into the car and turned her face away while Amy fastened the seat belt.

One argument after another ensued.

I hope she's not going to keep this up for the whole trip. I might kill her . . .

Once on the ferry Amy moved to the backseat. "I'm sorry. I don't want to go either."

"Then why are you making me leave all my friends?"

"Because you were right about Warren. He's a very bad man."

"But you said we moved away from him."

I'm trying to reason with a six-year-old who wants what she wants.

Amy kissed the top of Jessie's head. "Would you like to go upstairs?"

"No!"

The child was a rock, immovable, securely embedded in her position.

"I hate this road."

"I hate those trees."

"I hate this book."

"I hate these nuts."

And when they took breaks, "I hate this park."

No amount of storytelling, singing, or coaxing had any effect. Jess wouldn't even play with her mother's cell phone. Amy lost count of the number of times she stopped the car for a short run around a parking lot, hoping to release enough tension to keep from lashing out at the belligerent child in the backseat.

After three days of driving with two nights in the car, they pulled into a motel on the outskirts of Winnipeg. Following check-in, Amy found a list of fast-food restaurants and suggested Jessie choose where they would eat.

"I'm not hungry," Jessie moaned.

Amy closed her eyes and took a slow deep breath. "Fine, I'll decide."

From Thorns

The woman at the front desk suggested the restaurant on site. "The food is simple but delicious—everything's home-cooked and inexpensive." She looked at Jessie. "What's wrong?"

Jessie stared at the floor.

The woman winked at Amy who forced a smile.

After three days of eating from the backpack, Amy savoured the taste of her hot turkey sandwich. Jessie took a bite of macaroni and spit it out. "I *hate* the food here."

"I've had it!" Amy slammed her hand on the table. "You've been miserable this whole trip. Whining and complaining. It ends now! Pick up your fork!"

Jessie pushed the food around before taking a small bite. She managed to get some consumed by the time Amy finished. She looked at her mother with mournful, droopy eyes. "I'm full Mommy."

Guilt pushed Amy's anger out of the way.

She moved to sit beside her daughter, choking on suppressed tears. "I'm sorry. I didn't want to move either. But we had to." Jessie, now crying, said nothing. Amy pulled her into a hug and held her until she settled while ignoring the stares from the other tables.

Back at the room Jessie fell asleep before Amy finished reading a story. She sat on the edge of the bed for a few minutes watching her daughter sleep.

Out in the parking lot under a clear sky filled with stars she screamed, "I can't do this." She pounded the air while continuing to chant, "I can't do this." As the fight drained she dropped to her knees, sobbing.

I promised Jessie a good life. I don't know where we'll live or where she'll go to school or whether she'll settle in. I probably only have enough money to get us through the month.

How fast will I find a job?

If this doesn't work, what'll we do?

How would another failure affect Jess?

In the morning, equipped with a cellphone they drove into the city. *Apartment for Rent* signs stood on several properties.

"Are any of the units furnished?" Amy asked at the first apartment viewing.

"No."

An internet search yielded a list of furnished units from which she chose one of the least expensive. It was a small dark basement, but it would do. "We'll take it."

"Last month's rent and the remainder of this month comes to—"

"Last month's?"

"You have to pay the last month upfront. Haven't you ever rented before?"

"I don't have enough. But I'm going to get a job and then I'll be able to pay the full amount," Amy pleaded.

"You said you were a waitress. I won't rent to someone who's unemployed. And I also won't rent to someone who can't pay the final month's deposit. Neither will anyone else by the way."

Standing on the front step of a place she couldn't afford Amy muttered, "I don't know what we're going to do." She and Jessie walked to the car holding hands while tears dribbled down their cheeks.

She found the hostels online. As she began making a list of the ones to check out, a separate list of potential problems fired at her.

From Thorns

Jess will have to start school in the area. She'll probably have to change schools when we can afford to move. I'll have to get hired immediately before all our money's gone. What about childcare? I'll never find someone who's willing to keep her during waitressing hours. Or cashier. Or salesperson.

Maybe I should sell the car.

Amy stared through the window at nothing.

I don't have enough money for the time it's going to take to figure everything out.

Jessie's been through enough without another pile of changes.

I have to go home.

Marge will help us.

Maybe.

Probably not.

Worse comes to worst, I'm sure the church would let us stay there for a while.

It's gonna be hard. I'll have to deal with Tommy. But what other option is there?

A vision of her mother's hate-filled face intruded. *You're so stupid. You'll never make anything of yourself. You're a born loser.*

Amy trembled.

And then she spoke to the messages. No! I'm *not* a loser. I *didn't* fail. My choice failed because of dishonest, unethical people. Now I'm going to fix it and do what's best for my daughter!

Although she didn't entirely believe the words, she clung to them, continuing to speak against the accusations as they hurtled at her.

CHAPTER 39

"Okay Jessie, we're going home to see Gramma."

"Can we stay with her?"

"Yup," Amy said feeling guilty for speaking with certainty when she had no idea where they would land.

"Do we have to move somewhere else after?"

"No. We're going to stay there. No more moving."

"Yay!" Jessie threw her arms around Amy's neck.

"Whoa. You're choking me."

"Can I ride in the front seat with you?"

Amy wished she could feel any degree of excitement. Showing up with her tail between her legs facing people she'd turned her back on, with no money, looking for help . . .

Hoping a strategy for re-entry would surface, she set her compass in the direction of home.

"Will I be in the same class as my friends from kindergarten?" Jessie asked.

"Will you do your old job again?"

"Will we live in our old house?"

"Will we stay with Daddy? Or will we stay with Gramma?"

"We'll have to wait and see," became Amy's standard response

From Thorns

to the never-ending interrogation. She had plenty to figure out.

Knowing a long trip lay ahead and wanting to get a good rest before departing, they checked into a motel.

Jessie's demeanour changed after they got to the room. She became quiet and glum.

"What's wrong, honey?"

Lying on the bed, Jessie said nothing and stared at the quilt.

"Are you thinking about the friends we left behind?"

"No."

"School? Your teacher?"

"No. Can we read a story?"

Hmmm. She's probably tired.

While Jessie slept, Amy mapped out the route. Could they do it in three days? It would probably take four. Should she contact Marge now or later? Or would it be best to go straight to Pastor Mike without notifying anyone ahead of time?

How had everything gone so wrong? How could she face anyone back home? How would she muster the courage to approach Marge? And what about Tommy? Six months had lessened her fear but how would she keep him away from Jessie? If she got arrested Tommy would get custody. Could Marge stop that? Would Marge even be willing to get involved?

Returning home was a bad idea but where else could they go with no money? Maybe a small town along the way would work. That would give her time to figure out a better plan. But how would she explain it to Jessie?

Back on the road before sunrise, Amy asked questions to see what Jessie remembered. She needed reminding about Grampa, Auntie Kate, and Uncle Jason. She thought she remembered Rumble though.

When Amy had enough of talking, Jessie looked at books.
"What are you reading?" Amy asked.
"*The Wonky Donkey.*"
"That's such a fun book. How about you read to me?"
"I'm tired of reading." She tossed the book on the floor and got a colouring book from the backpack. After dropping that to the floor, Jessie stared out the window occasionally turning her head to look at her mother. Amy watched from the corner of her eye.
"Do you like this highway?" she asked.
"I don't know."
Normally Jessie would remark on the scenery and whatever else popped into her creative mind.
"Are you tired?"
"No."
She was beyond quiet to the point of being withdrawn, reminiscent of the previous evening.
"What are you thinking about?"
"Nothing."
Shortly thereafter Jessie fell asleep.
Ah, she's overtired.
Amy inserted a left earbud to listen to a favourite playlist as her mind drifted to her unresolved endgame.
Did Marge know that Amy sometimes brought Jessie to the office after kindergarten for no other reason except to see Marge? That the visits were arranged through Sheila? Marge must have known. But what if she didn't?
What Marge definitely did know was that Amy had taken Jess and disappeared, never explaining why, never making contact.
Even if Marge *was* willing to help, how would Amy make it

From Thorns

happen without getting herself arrested?

What if Tommy showed up and demanded custody?

Steve would call the lawyer, like before. That would give her time to take Jessie to a shelter. If she wasn't in jail. But she didn't want Jessie at a shelter. They weren't returning home to live in hiding.

She would tell the police what Tommy did. No, that wouldn't be enough. And what if Tommy had friends at the police department, like Warren had?

With each mile travelled, the foolishness of her plan came into clearer focus.

We have to stop somewhere along the way and I'll get a job and Jessie'll have to accept it, Amy thought. But Jessie desperately needs normalcy. If it weren't for Jessie I would've made a go of it in Winnipeg. And anyway, I've had enough of small towns.

She saw movement in the passenger seat. "Are you awake?" she asked removing her earbud.

"He said I couldn't tell you."

After a moment of stunned silence Amy asked, "Who said that?"

"Daddy."

She couldn't breathe. Heat consumed her. She pulled the car onto the shoulder and looked at Jessie. "What did Daddy say you couldn't tell me?"

"Sometimes he hurt me."

"Like when he twisted your arm?"

Jessie nodded.

"Was there another time he hurt you?"

Jessie looked away.

"This is important Jess. You need to tell me."

Amy waited.

Nothing.

She put her hand over Jessie's. "It's okay sweetie. You can tell me later. Do you want to listen to *Jungle Jam*?" Marge had given her a tape player along with the tapes. Although Amy enjoyed the series, she didn't hear a word. She could barely focus on the road.

It wasn't long before Jessie mumbled something. Amy turned the audio off. "I didn't hear you—what did you say?"

"When I cried, he said I was being a baby."

While pulling the car onto the shoulder *again*, Amy said, "When I get hurt, I cry. Do you think Mommy's a baby?"

"No," Jessie said.

Amy wanted to get out of the car and smash something, anything. She silently counted—I'll kill him, I'll kill him, I'll kill him, I'll kill him, I'll kill him—to five.

"Can you tell me about a time when Daddy hurt you and you cried?"

Jessie stared at her lap.

"Jessie, please. I need to know what happened."

Silence.

How would she get Jessie to talk?

"Are you hungry?"

"No."

"Tell me when you're hungry. Maybe we can talk about Daddy when we're having a snack later."

After pulling back onto the road she drove too fast. She shook with rage. Her fingers ached from her grip on the steering wheel.

She stopped earlier than planned. Money spent on another motel room would be well worth it if Jessie would talk. Amy

From Thorns

told stories about Rumble, told silly jokes, and laughed. Jessie asked the occasional question and smiled from time to time, but she didn't tell stories of her own. Totally out of character. While they were eating Amy dove in.

"Are you ready to talk about Daddy?"

Silence.

Amy tried gentle persuasion, pleading, creation of possible scenarios.

Silence.

She demanded answers, allowing her voice and facial expression to display anger.

Jessie wouldn't talk. And now she wouldn't eat either.

The next day Jess remained aloof.

They drove into the night, stopping at a random parking lot long after Jessie fell asleep. Before Amy dosed off a police cruiser pulled alongside and instructed her to move the vehicle.

Why does everything have to be a problem?

She moved to a motel parking lot. After a few hours of fitful sleep, while Jessie remained unconscious in the back, Amy returned to the highway.

Her thinking ran in circles. Three of them.

One, how will I get Jessie to talk?

Two, is it my fault? Should I have supervised her more closely? Should I have known what was happening in my own home?

And three, I can't let Tommy get near her. So we definitely can't go home.

But there's no money to go anywhere else. And I can't keep dragging Jessie around the country.

Marge will step up. She'll figure it out. But she's not bigger than the law.

Best case scenario, Tommy'll have her for weekends.

And I'll probably go to jail. Then he'll get sole custody.

Maybe I can find a way to avoid arrest. Steve's lawyer can help. As if Steve's gonna help me!

No, I can't let Tommy get near her—we can't go home.

But where else can we go?

Around and around the analyzing travelled until she was dizzy and still without a plan.

CHAPTER 40

As they approached their destination, Amy gave up the pipe dream of finding another feasible option.

She burrowed into hope. Hope in Marge. Hope in a benevolent God. Hope in the system. Hope that Tommy wouldn't want the bother of a child after experiencing freedom.

Fifteen minutes from the bus station, she took Jessie's hand.

"Mommy has to go away for a little while to find a job. It won't be for long and you'll stay with Gramma and Rumble."

A wail shattered the stillness. "No Mommy, you can't leave me."

Amy was determined to remain stoic through her daughter's sobbing and begging. But when she pulled into the parking lot she could barely breathe. What she was doing to Jessie felt worse than anything she'd ever known. But she couldn't give in so she lied. "How about if I live with Gramma and Grampa too? Would that be okay?"

"Yes Mommy. I don't care where we go as long as I'm with you."

Inside the station Amy explained exactly what was going to happen. She couldn't come with Jessie tonight but would see her tomorrow, and then they would all live together.

Tears cascaded down Jessie's cheeks. "No Mommy, you promised I could stay with you. I won't be bad anymore. I promise."

"My beautiful Jessica, you're never bad." Amy didn't know how she was still coherent. Her insides convulsed. Her limbs felt weak. "We had some hard times in the car and Mommy got upset, but you weren't bad. I just need you to go by yourself for one night."

"No!"

Taking Jessie by the shoulders Amy said firmly, "Enough! You have to do what I say."

Choking on her tears Jessie sputtered, "But Mommy, you promised."

"Look at me Jess. I can't go with you tonight. Don't make Mommy angry. Now you're going to do what we talked about."

She dialled.

Marge answered.

"Jessie's abandoned at the bus terminal. She's sitting against the west wall. Please pick her up. I hope you'll look after her."

Click.

She pulled her little girl into her arms and held her tight. "I love you," she sputtered through sobs. "You're the most special girl in the whole wide world. Never, ever forget that. I'm so proud of you."

"Why do I have to live with them?" Jessie wailed. "I just wanna be with you."

People stared.

Amy swallowed hard, got some control and said, "I already explained. I know you don't like this. Neither do I, but it's just for

From Thorns

tonight. We'll be together in our hearts. It'll be okay, I promise."

"No Mommy, you said you would stay with me." She sucked in a breath. "You have to come too."

The police could arrive any minute. Amy straightened and spoke firmly. "Okay Jessie, don't be scared. I'll come as soon as I can. Maybe even tonight. Now you remember what we talked about. You need to be a big girl and stay here on your own. I'll be watching until I see you're with Gramma."

She walked backwards.

Jessie slid off the bench and ran toward her. "Mommy! No!"

Her eyes, burrowed in a red, swollen, wet face, with snot dripping from her nose, burned a hole through Amy's heart. But she couldn't allow herself to break. Not now. Through gritted teeth she spat, "Stop it!" She wiped Jessie's nose with her sleeve and marched her back to the bench.

So many people stopped and stared.

She stepped away. Jessie didn't move. She didn't call out again. Resignation? Defeat? Was a part of Jessie dying?

All of Amy's dreams came crashing down as she pulled away and moved into the crowd. She ran and hid behind a pillar. Her body spasmed. Someone touched her shoulder. She jerked away, eyes locked on Jessie, barely able to focus her vision through her tears as she watched her daughter cry.

A woman knelt in front of Jessie. She continued to wail and stare in Amy's direction. When the woman put her hands on Jessie's knee she squirmed and jumped from the bench, making a move toward her mother.

But then she stopped and looked to her right.

From behind the pillar Amy saw Marge and Steve approach. Jessie pointed in the direction Amy had gone. Steve scanned the area while Marge rested her hands on her thighs and leaned toward Jessie. After a few minutes they all moved toward the exit with Jess bawling and heaving against Marge's shoulder.

Amy choked on the anguish caught in her throat. She dropped to the floor, weeping. A woman asked, "Are you okay?" Amy stood and ran to the washroom. Her throat released the pain and she sobbed until dry heaving took over. This was worse than any hurt her parents had bestowed over the years.

How had things gone so wrong? Were her parents right all along? That she was incapable of doing anything right?

She splashed her face with cold water and went to the car. While pulling a blanket over her body, she dropped her face into the pillow and resumed crying and moaning and screaming until there was nothing left.

Where was Jessie now? Had she fallen asleep? Or was she still crying? Was she alone, feeling abandoned, suffering in isolation?

After what felt like an hour, Amy drove to a Tim Hortons. When she placed her order the girl behind the counter asked if she needed help. The washroom mirror explained—the swelling wouldn't likely disappear soon. Her stomach couldn't handle the coffee so she tossed it and left.

She drove to the shelter the church had sent supplies to. After speaking to Sarah through the intercom, the door unlocked. Once inside Amy relayed details, frequently descending into uncontrollable grief. Sarah provided the occasional word of encouragement. When Amy finished talking Sarah spoke in a gentle, confident tone. "This is our emergency shelter where women stay for a night. Normally we would move you into another one of our houses where you could stay longer, but I'm not sure what's best in your

From Thorns

case. Tomorrow you can meet with a counsellor."

"What do you mean *in my case*?"

"You suggested you may be guilty of kidnapping," Sarah said. "And you had good reason!" she quickly added. "There are organizations that can help with the legal process. Now let's get some sleep, and tomorrow you can meet with one of my colleagues. Okay?"

CHAPTER 41

The bed felt safe, closing out the rest of the world. A pillow muffled her crying. Amy drifted into a restless sleep, always to wake abruptly and resume crying.

Eventually she moved to the common area. The minutes crawled by. As morning light pierced the blinds, movement began and the smell of food wafted through the open space. Someone wandered into the room. "How about you get some breakfast?" Amy shook her head.

The counsellor arrived mid-morning. After a brief chat she said, "I'll leave you with some information and we'll talk again tomorrow."

"Tomorrow? But. No!" Amy sputtered.

"What's happening?"

"I've deserted my daughter. I can't wait 'til tomorrow. We have to sort this out today. *Now.*"

"This is going to take time," the counsellor said, her lips pursed. "Your daughter's safe, right? You trust the people you left her with?"

"Yes," Amy muttered. "But I lied to make her go. I can't leave her like that. And I can't go to the house 'cause they won't want

From Thorns

anything to do with me. And if I call to say I won't be coming today or anytime soon, that'll just make it worse for Jessie." She leaned forward, elbows resting on her knees, and dug her nails into her scalp until the pain was too much. She looked up. "I'm a fugitive. I can't get in touch with my daughter until this whole mess is sorted out."

"We can probably make arrangements for your daughter to be brought here."

"No, I don't want her to be in a shelter."

"We have other children here and we offer programs for them, as well as childcare."

Amy didn't respond.

"You're going to get help, I promise."

The confident tone of the counsellor did little to alleviate Amy's despair.

She tried to read through the paperwork but couldn't focus. Jessie. What have I done?

Maybe I should call. Maybe Marge'll let me explain. Maybe she'll let me talk to Jess. But then? What's the point in talking to Jessie if I can't be with her? Just another reminder of broken promises. I can't spend months going through the process of getting help from who knows where. And what chance do I have of anything actually working in my favour?

Leaving the paperwork behind, Amy walked the streets except for when crying stole her breath. Thinking, analyzing, hoping for a miracle. But nothing came.

I've broken Jessie's spirit. I'm the reason she'll never trust anyone. Everything I've done for her is a big nothing now. She's probably waiting at the door, expecting. When will she stop crying? Another day of hurt. Another night. And then another and another . . .

And the agony dug in its talons.

She stopped to rest on a bench. No solutions showed up. The thought that had made its way to the forefront of her mind was all she had left.

When I'm gone, Jessie will be devastated for a while but she'll have closure. No more hoping, waiting. She'll settle in with the Raynors. They all love her. Marge will make sure she gets everything she needs. She'll be way better off than she could ever be with me. She'll never have to move again. She'll live in a nice house. She'll have every opportunity. Just like Kate and Jason. She's young. Eventually she'll forget about me. Steve and Marge will make sure Tommy doesn't hurt her. They'll keep her safe.

I can make a new start on my own. With time maybe I'll be able to see her and explain. Maybe she'll understand and forgive me.

That won't happen. She'll never understand. No one's going to forgive me.

I can't go on without my Jess. And now she's living with the agony of knowing I left her, like I didn't care.

The thought of Jessie's pain, knowing she was the cause, circled and tightened until she could barely breathe. Her sobs pierced the silence but she didn't care. Nothing mattered anymore.

The way a racehorse goes from the starting gate to galloping within seconds, Amy made a decision.

She dragged herself to the nearest coffee shop. "Do you have wifi?"

"Are you okay?" the barista asked. "Do you need help?"

From Thorns

"I just need wifi."

From the corner of her eye, Amy saw the barista watching. She began her research while keeping an eye on him.

Aspirin. It's available over the counter. It would be a horrible death, but she wanted to suffer. She deserved pain. Her parents were right. She brought a child into the world and couldn't figure out how to make anything work.

She went to the closest pharmacy to purchase one bottle and walked to another store for the second bottle.

She knew where she wanted to die. The spot would take time to get to which meant more time for painful ruminating. But if she didn't hide, she could end up in the hospital in a coma or some other terrible state. No, she would go to the woods where she wouldn't be found until it was too late. And then it would be over for everyone. Jessie would adapt like every other kid does.

Nothing worked for me. My parents, Tommy, Warren. The whole town. Bunch of cowards. The police should have helped me, but what happened?

As soon as I trust someone, they turn against me.

"I hate you, God! Jessie's all I had. What kind of horrible monster are you?"

The tears poured onto her cheeks.

"I love her so much."

Amy found a secluded spot not far off the path where the sun cast long shadows over fallen, rotting leaves. She would die here where the smell of autumn death hung in the air.

While emptying the first bottle of aspirin into her hand, she heard voices. Crouching to hide, she watched a woman with two little girls.

"Grandma, no fair! Lucy has more."

The woman laughed. "I gave you the same amount."

"Lucy has more red ones."

Smarties or M&Ms. Jessie always wanted red ones too.

When she was a couple of weeks into Grade One she announced, "I wanna be a teacher when I grow up."

Amy tore open a bag of Smarties. "Let's think about all the things you could do." She picked one of each colour and gave a handful to Jessie.

While arranging the candies in a circle Amy explained, "Each colour is a different job. Your first choice is teaching?"

With a mouthful of chocolate, Jessie nodded and Amy pulled the red one from the circle.

"What's next?"

"Gardener."

Amy pulled the yellow one. "Next?"

"Artist.

"Hairdresser.

"Astronaut.

"Elephant doctor."

Amy poured all the remaining Smarties on top of the original six and said, "This is how many things you could do. Always remember, you're clever enough to do anything you want."

As she reflected on that scene she smiled even as her lip quivered.

I wonder what Jessie will do and where she'll end up?

Damn Tommy!

None of it matters now. Like Marge said, there's nothing we can do about the past and we can't know about tomorrow. All we have is now.

From Thorns

She thought about that saying while studying the aspirin in her hand.

All *I* have is now.

I'm making a decision that won't change the past, but how will it affect tomorrow?

Suicide lets me escape the pain of knowing Jessie's hurt.

It lets me escape jail.

I won't have to face people who'll judge me.

It frees me from seeing what happens with Tommy.

Suicide forces Jess to give up hope of ever seeing me again and will allow her to move forward in a new life.

But...

She'll move forward knowing her mother deliberately abandoned her. What affect will that have? I'm sending the message she wasn't worth fighting for.

And she's not going to forget about me—she'll be scarred for life.

I can't do this to Jess.

But...

To be in jail and watch her go to Tommy? Even if I'm not in jail, to send her off to Tommy on weekends?

No! I can't! I don't have that kind of strength.

Amy downed the fistful of aspirin.

Jess needs to understand how hard I fought through life. I had it way worse than she did. My mother never rescued me. She didn't even care.

Well I care about Jess and I stepped in to get her away from Tommy. And now I'm leaving her with good people who will care for her and give her more than I ever could.

But...

Will Jess ever know this? Will she understand how much I loved her? How much I did for her? How hard I tried?

What if she ends up with Tommy full-time? If she could live with me most of the time it'd be better than full-time with that monster.

But...

If I'm in jail, I can't do anything except watch what happens to her.

And I couldn't handle that.

She downed the second bottle of aspirin.

A gunshot cracked her thinking. Amy jumped.

Someone's hunting too close, she thought.

Poor deer. They do everything they're supposed to in order to stay safe and then some hunter sneaks up in camouflage and shoots. It's not fair for someone to steal such a beautiful life.

At least I'm choosing to end mine. Nature doesn't work that way. Animals aren't afraid of what their future holds.

Amy stared up at the clear sky while listening to the moving water.

I'm a coward. I'm choosing to be a coward. Choosing to be weaker than the smallest of creatures. They would fight 'til their last breath.

I've never let fear stop me before. The risks were high when I kidnapped Jess in the first place.

Amy dropped her head into her hands and wailed, allowing her tears to flow freely.

I *have* to keep fighting no matter what.

She shoved her fingers down her throat and vomited up as much as she could.

CHAPTER 42

Her eyes opened slowly. "Marge?" And her eyes closed.
The next time they opened, she felt awake in a groggy sort of way. Her eyes fixed on Marge who said, "How are you feeling?"

"How did you find me?" Amy asked while looking at the tube inserted in her arm.

"The hospital called."

Amy's brow furrowed.

"You stumbled into Emergency and then passed out so they admitted you. Fortunately you had ID and I'm the only emergency contact on file."

A police officer poked his head into the room. "You're awake."

As the officer walked toward her Amy's eyes widened. "You're here to arrest me!"

"I'm here to see what you remember."

Amy stared.

"You overdosed," he said. "How did that happen?"

Her explanation ran in circles.

He left for a while. When he returned he said, "There's no report of any kidnapping on file. Your daughter's safe with Mrs.

Raynor, correct?" Amy nodded. "Someone from Psychiatry will be in to see you and we'll try to get to the bottom of what you're remembering."

"There *must* be a report," Amy said after the officer left. "I mean, Tommy came after Jessie. He demanded joint custody. Why would he just let her go?"

"He probably knows he'd be in a world of trouble if you had a chance to confront his charges," Marge said.

"But Tommy would never admit to being wrong. Everything was always someone else's fault."

"You need some rest. We'll talk about this later."

Amy nodded. "Is Jessie okay?"

"She needs you. Is it alright if I bring her in to visit?"

"Here?"

Marge called for the nurse who explained to Amy that she would be meeting with a psychiatrist and would not be leaving the hospital that day.

Jessie ran to Amy's bedside the following morning. She burst into tears and punched at her mother's arm. Marge pulled her away as Jessie yelled, "You left me! You just left me!"

Amy slid off the bed and held Jessie in a tight hug until she relaxed and the crying subsided. "I love you so much," she whispered.

"I love you too Mommy."

When the hospital released her, Marge and Jessie were waiting. "Let's get you home."

"Home?" Amy frowned. "I appreciate your willingness to look after Jessie, but she needs to be with me. We'll figure out

From Thorns

what to do."

"It's up to you of course. I had hoped you would stay with us for a little while."

Amy was prepared to take responsibility for her crime, but she wasn't prepared for this. "Why? You don't owe me anything."

Marge frowned. "We love you."

"You don't know the whole story."

"Does it matter?"

After Amy delivered a few more arguments Marge shrugged. "If you'd rather go somewhere else, that's fine."

Amy sighed. "I don't know where else to go. I just feel uncomfortable staying with you after everything that's happened."

"Let's go get your car," Marge said.

"I'm driving with Mommy."

When they arrived at the house Kate pulled her into an embrace. "I've missed you."

Jessie wrapped her arms around Amy's waist. "You're not leaving again, are you?"

"Never."

Rumble bounded across the floor with his tail wagging fiercely. Amy leaned toward him and scratched his ears. "Hey boy, I'm happy to see you too." She straightened with Jessie still attached, looked around and asked, "Where's Jason?"

"He's at university," Marge said. "He'll be home at Christmas. That'll give him a few weeks to process his feelings about you being back."

"Oh, I see," Amy said. "Thanks for letting me know. How's Steve feeling?"

Marge looked at Jessie and said, "We're all happy you're back." Then she looked at Amy with raised eyebrows and whispered, "Later."

After greeting Steve and getting a cool response, Amy excused herself.

Jessie grabbed her arm. "I wanna stay with you."

Steve rolled his eyes. "I'm going to get changed," he said.

Amy looked at Marge with tears welling. "Steve hates me. I can't stay."

"Jess, can you look for the book we started reading this morning?" Marge said.

Jessie didn't move. "What's wrong, Mommy?"

"I'm just tired. Please go get the book so we can read together."

Moving slowly toward the stairs, Jessie kept her eyes on her mother. When she stopped at the top step, Amy said, "Please get the book. I want to read with you but I'm tired and I don't have the energy to search for it." With that Jessie disappeared.

"Steve most certainly does *not* hate you. Men don't handle," Marge waved her arms around, "these sorts of things very well. But I promise he's glad you're back. Let's talk about it tomorrow."

When she awoke, Jessie was gone. Amy checked the clock. Steve must have left for work by now. The smell of coffee called her to the kitchen.

"Good morning," Marge said. She nodded toward the window onto the yard where Jessie and Rumble were playing. "He's getting old, but you'd never know it watching him play with Jess."

"While she's outside, can we talk about Steve?" Amy asked as she poured coffee into a mug.

They got comfortable in the living room before Marge spoke. "When you left it felt like we meant nothing to you. Jason's hurt

From Thorns

quickly turned to anger. Steve wouldn't talk about his feelings but I could sense anger." She looked into Amy's eyes. "Honestly, even I experienced a range of emotions including anger."

Amy nodded.

"I know my husband is relieved and glad to see you," Marge said with conviction. "Still, he's going to need time to work through his feelings."

"It's super uncomfortable to be in the same house with someone who hates me. Even though I don't blame him."

"He. Does. Not. Hate. You. It wouldn't be any different if it were Kate. Surely you don't think he would hate Kate! But he's been hurt, and men often deal with hurt by putting up a defensive wall which can look like anger. That doesn't mean he loves you any less. Do you understand?"

"I guess." Amy shrugged. "I should be able to get a job quickly and we'll move out. Or we could go to the shelter right away."

"I'm not going to tell you what to do. But you may need someone to help with Jessie when you start working. I think it would be a lot easier if you stayed with us. For now."

"I'm not going to ask you to look after Jessie!"

"Please think about what's best for your daughter."

"Okay," Amy said. "I better go check on her."

"Look at the jacket she's wearing. I had fun going through the box of clothes Kate wore at that age."

Amy took the day to get organized. She decided to stay until she had a secure job and enough funds to get her own place. Unless Steve made it too uncomfortable.

She agreed with Marge that Jessie didn't have to start school right away. "She's only in Grade One and she's as sharp as my sewing needles," Marge had said. "She won't have any trouble catching up. It makes sense to wait until you know where you want to live."

After accepting Marge's offer to keep Jessie, she delivered applications and attended interviews.

"I want to pay you for looking after Jess."

Marge crossed her arms and cocked her head to one side. "With what? I'm assuming you didn't bring a treasure chest of cash with you. Now stop worrying and go be productive."

"How's Steve gonna feel about this?"

"Steve's fine. We both want to help you get back on your feet."

Steve just wants me out of his house, Amy thought.

It wasn't just Steve who was different. Marge spoke in a matter-of-fact manner. Still kind and helpful, but distant. Hopefully, their relationship would repair with time.

Being close to the Christmas holiday, businesses required extra staff. Amy accepted a cashier job at a local grocery store, and soon after secured a waitressing position that worked around her store hours. She hoped the jobs would extend beyond the holiday season but regardless, it was a start and would generate much-needed income.

A couple of weeks after Amy started working, Steve came around. Probably because he knew she would move out soon. Not that it mattered, Amy was just grateful for a comfortable place to sleep. And help with Jessie.

CHAPTER 43

"Do you know anything about Tommy?" Amy asked one afternoon while Jessie watched T.V.

"I heard he got married," Marge said.

Amy's eyes widened. "You're kidding!"

"It's what I heard from Tommy's aunt. But she's not in touch with him directly."

"You know Tommy's aunt?"

"I do. She introduced me to Tommy's father after you two moved in together."

Amy dropped her head into her hands. "So you were right. His parents are alive."

"I wanted to learn as much as I could about the person you decided to live with," Marge continued. "It's not a pretty picture."

"Tell me."

"Bruce believes Tommy was sexually abused by his mother. Emotionally abused, probably physically as well. He thinks it started when Tommy was very young and likely didn't stop until he moved out. Bruce said Tommy's mother acted like she owned him from the moment she gave birth. He was *her* son, not *their* son. She never left Tommy with his father or anyone else. There were no playgroups or swimming lessons or anything like that. When Tommy got into school, she wouldn't allow him to play with other kids outside of school hours. It was like he was her only friend, her servant, her counsellor, her toy."

Marge locked eyes with Amy. "Tommy and his mother shared a bedroom."

"That's disgusting! Why didn't his father do something?" Amy demanded. "Even kidnap his child like I did."

"Why indeed. I could tell he wasn't proud of his actions. But he said he couldn't break through the wall his wife built around herself and Tommy. It was like a prison cell that only she had the key to. She locked Tommy in and everyone else out.

"Also, she came from money," Marge continued. "Her family could afford the best lawyers so no one could win against them. Bruce didn't see the point in even trying.

"He hung in for twelve years before leaving. He gave up any chance at a relationship with his son in exchange for no alimony or child support. He married someone else, started a new family, and never looked back."

Amy spoke just above a whisper. "That's really sad."

"Yeah. I imagine Tommy's pretty messed up."

Marge's tone changed. "But he's not stupid. He knows why you left and he knows he's responsible."

"You don't think he'll come after Jessie?"

"Who knows." Marge shrugged. "Maybe he wants to start over. New wife. New children. And no baggage from his past."

"That poor woman," Amy said, shaking her head. "I feel sorry for Tommy now, but he's not someone any woman should have to live with."

From Thorns

She met with the lawyer who had seen her through Tommy's initial entry into Jessie's life. He couldn't offer any reassurance. Amy would have to wait for Tommy to reassert himself but even then, with no reports of abusive behaviour combined with her taking their child without permission, it was unlikely the law would be on her side.

Children's Aid responded with more empathy and pointed to various organizations that could help if and when Tommy showed up.

Amy told Jess that Daddy had moved away—it seemed like the most expedient way to handle things, for now.

Perhaps she and Jessie would ultimately end up in a shelter hiding from Tommy and working with helpful agencies. But at least they weren't running anymore.

It only took a couple of weeks for Amy to feel confident in her work. "I've done it all before," she told Marge. "There's no challenge, but for now I like it that way."

On one of her days off, while Steve was at work and Jessie was occupied, she plopped into a chair in the living room.

Marge looked up from her book. "What's up?"

"I catch myself dreaming of happiness and it scares me. Every time I've hoped, I've fallen into a cesspool."

"Of course you should hope for happiness," Marge said. "Past mistakes don't have to define your future. God wants to pour his blessings into your life beyond anything you could ever imagine. So go ahead and dream."

"If there is a God, I'm quite sure he doesn't love me," Amy said. "How could a caring God sit back and watch a child be hurt over and over again by cruel parents?" She felt heat rise in her cheeks.

Abruptly she stood, turned her back to Marge, and yanked her sweater over her head. "Look what they did to me."

Marge gasped.

As she grabbed her sweater from the floor Amy continued spitting words. "My father beat me, cut me, and used my flesh to extinguish his cigarettes, always telling me not to let anyone see or they would know what a bad girl I was. Don't tell me God loves me." She stormed out of the room.

Why did Marge have to make everything about God? Geez! Amy felt like an elastic band stretched to the limit, about to snap.

If I get kicked out I don't care.

In her room she grabbed a crossword puzzle. Working through them helped her relax.

When she heard Jessie laughing, she wandered upstairs and found her up on her knees, elbows on the table, playing cards with Marge.

"Hi Mommy!" Jessie said. "I'm winning."

Amy smiled at Marge. "Sounds like you've got some tough competition."

"Know what?" Jessie said. "April has a new puppy. Can we get a dog? Please?"

"Rumble would be very lonely if you started playing with a new dog," Marge said.

Amy mouthed, "Thank you."

"I would still play with Rumble," Jessie assured as she scouted the area. "I think he would like to have a friend."

Amy took Jessie's face into her hands. "I promise we'll get a dog. But not right now."

With a pout Jessie went to find Rumble.

"I guess that's the end of Go Fish," Marge said. And then,

From Thorns

"I'm so sorry for what you've been through. Please forgive me for talking about God. If I had known..."

"It's okay. I just wanted you to understand why it's so hard to believe God loves me." Amy shrugged. "You'll be happy to know though, I've thought a lot about something you told me before Jess was born."

"Oh?"

"You said you thought God brought me to this family so you could look after me. I definitely felt loved when I lived with you."

Marge nodded. "I've had a few related thoughts along the way, but let's move on."

"I'm curious. Tell me."

Marge studied her face.

"I promise I won't blow up." Amy pulled out a chair and sat.

"When Matt came along I felt sure that God brought him into your life. When Tommy conned you into a relationship I think God tried to look after you, to keep you from the tragedy you've experienced." Marge sighed. "But you were determined to do it your own way." Her face flushed. "I'm sorry—I'm not accusing. Every one of us has to walk our own road and we make lots of mistakes along the way."

"How did God try to look after me? After allowing that creep to find me in the first place?"

"God gives us the freedom to make our own choices. Tommy chose to go after Jessie. You initially met with him for Jessie's sake but then it started to grow. Soon after you got involved his true colours painted a distressing picture." Marge shrugged. "You chose to ignore the evidence. You rationalized your way into believing him."

"And ignoring you," Amy said shaking her head. "I've sure

regretted that. But where was God when Warren and that whole town of cowards turned on me?"

"I think God used that mess to bring you home."

"I never thought of that. So you think God wanted me to live here, not out west. Why would He care?"

"Good question," Marge said. "I think it's important for you to be back here to mend broken relationships. But I'm not God so I don't know the answer."

When Jason arrived home for the holiday, Amy was surprised to see the boy replaced by a young man whose voice was deep and whose feet were huge. Bitterness oozed from the wound she had inflicted. She overheard him speaking to Marge in a loud voice. "She chose Tommy over us and she had no right to come back. Why are you taking her side?"

"I'm not taking anyone's side," Marge replied.

Jason stomped off.

"Should I leave to restore a peaceful family atmosphere?" Amy asked.

Marge and Steve saw this as an opportunity for Jason to grow. His life had always been comfortable and easy. "It's time for him to deal with a challenging situation," Steve said. "And the way he handles it will show what he's made of." Marge talked about how effortless it is to be nice when everything is smooth sailing. "It's only in rough waters that we test our ability to deal with the storms of life. Jason's stuck in a storm."

Although Marge said it was unnecessary, Amy took Jess to a hotel on Christmas Eve. It cost too much but alleviated Jessie's disappointment at leaving the tree and a mountain of gifts behind and allowed for a cheerful atmosphere at the house.

From Thorns

Jessie chose pizza for dinner and then had a blast at the pool with the fun slides.

In the morning she woke to loads of presents. The day filled with happiness and laughter—skating, tobogganing, and then back to the pool and hot tub. The fun concluded with a fantastic turkey dinner in the hotel dining room.

Before he returned to school Jason approached Amy. "Mom says I should give you a chance to explain."

Amy tried.

"Yeah, Mom told me that already. It's no excuse for what you did." He allowed his thoughts to spill with an angry intensity.

She resigned herself to this consequence of her choices and she hoped someday Jason could understand. But for now it was her job to do the understanding.

Later in the day she heard him talking to Marge. "Maybe love forgives but Jason doesn't!"

Amy smiled remembering all the times Marge said 'love is' something-or-other. Patient, kind, forgiving...

Once she decided where they would live, when she could afford to move into her own place, Jessie registered at the neighbourhood school. She easily settled in and quickly made friends. Amy kept a watchful eye on her, looking for signs of lingering trauma. She knew it would be years before she would stop worrying.

They remained with the Raynors into the new year as they adapted to their new routines.

Gradually Amy felt ready to move forward in life, this time with more caution and wisdom packed in her arsenal.

PART 2

CHAPTER 44

Just four months after being hired at the grocery store, Amy received a promotion to full-time supervisor. She continued to waitress one evening per week. When she'd saved enough to afford her own place, she sold the car to reduce expenses.

Marge offered to help paint the two-bedroom apartment. "If Jessie wants to assist, then I better come too."

A couple of hours into the task, when Jessie was supposed to be working on a craft, she called, "Mommy, come see what I did." A blue handprint decorated her newly painted yellow wall.

"You've got quite the artistic eye," Amy said, with raised eyebrows. "And not enough restraint!" Neither Amy nor Marge knew much about painting, but they knew about colour and found ways to turn their mistakes into good memories. With a lot of supervision and layers of sheets on the floor, Jessie finished decorating her bedroom with handprints.

"That looks great," Amy said. "You might want to think about interior decorating as a career."

"What's interior decorating?" Jessie asked.

"I'll explain while we're cleaning you up. To the bathroom please, and don't touch anything along the way. I mean it!

It won't be funny if I find a handprint anywhere outside of your bedroom."

Through Marge's contacts, Amy purchased used furniture, a vacuum, dishes, and small kitchen appliances. On move-in day, the apartment had everything she needed.

"Now, no more running off!" Marge said.

Isn't it funny how we always want more?

Less than a year earlier all that mattered was survival, Jessie's safety, and not getting caught.

But now, back home with the support of trustworthy people, a vastly diminished fear of Tommy, a secure job, and a place to live without worry of eviction, Amy's mind drifted to Matt. She told herself to stop being silly. The only reason for these thoughts was the lack of a suitable distraction. Hadn't things been good with Tommy at first? Until they lived together. It would likely have been the same with Matt, or any other man.

Occasionally Kate suggested a double-date but Amy wouldn't take the risk.

The *only* thing I care about is Tommy never returning, Amy thought. Hoping for anything more will only lead to disappointment. And Jessie doesn't need some father figure forced into her life.

In between the self-talks, Amy continued to think about Matt. The warm, comforting memories felt safe and delivered feelings of happiness. She could get lost in her thoughts while not having to deal with the reality of a relationship. At the end of each day after Jessie fell asleep, she wrote notes.

Matt, I miss you, and I feel sad.

From Thorns

> I wish I could see you to tell you how bad
> I feel about pushing you out of my life
> so abruptly and harshly—did it cut like a knife
> when I said "goodbye"?
>
> I wish I could see you to tell you the story
> of what came next, certainly no glory.
> In my foolish decision to return to the man
> who cared not enough for the things that matter,
> but was selfish instead and it all fell in shatters.
>
> I ran away, Matt, ran from all that I knew,
> in hopes I could find a place safe and removed
> from the hurt and disaster, a chance to start anew.
> But my plan failed, and more trouble ensued.
>
> Life's come full circle. I'm doing well now,
> but I miss you; I only wish that somehow
> I could turn back the clock, wipe out the past
> and have you back in my life at last.

But she didn't really want him back in her life. She only wanted the idea of him. Her past held so much failure that she found herself looking for things to go wrong, expecting something bad to happen. Marge said God wanted her to be positive, and negative thoughts were destructive. Amy worked at being optimistic and discovered that when she actively looked for the positives, there were lots to be found.

CHAPTER 45

"Can I start you off with something to drink?"

Tommy looked up from his menu into Amy's eyes. "Yes. We're looking at the beer selection. Come back in a few minutes."

Amy rushed to the kitchen and leaned against the wall, feeling the room spin around her. Breathing deeply, she closed her eyes, willing her heart to stop pounding.

"Are you okay?" Megs asked, balancing plates.

"I need a favour. Deliver your meals and come back."

A few minutes later, Megs returned. "What happened?"

"My ex is at table four. I can't serve him. Can you take the table? I'll take one of yours."

Megs fetched the manager.

"You're shaking," Šhuka said. "You need to take the night off. Can you look after your tables until I get someone to replace you? I'll take care of table four until then."

At home, after paying the sitter Amy called Marge.

"Oh, dear..." Marge listened while Amy listed every potential disastrous outcome. "Let's remember that he never formally accused you of kidnapping. So the worst that happens is a joint

269

From Thorns

custody demand."

"I don't want him near her ever again!"

The next day Shuka texted. "He left a note for you. Do you want it? Or should I shred it?"

When her grocery store shift ended, Amy bussed to the restaurant with her stomach in knots. She took the envelope to the washroom.

> You got a lot of nerve coming back here. I don't want you butting into my life. So you don't know me. Got it? If you ever see me you'll walk away. If you cause trouble I'm going to the police and you'll get arrested and I'll take Jess.

Sobbing, Amy called Marge. "It's one thing for *me* to ignore him. What if Jessie recognizes him and says something?"

Marge waited until Amy stopped crying and finished blowing her nose. "You said he's got a beard now and shorter hair. Jessie hasn't seen him for almost a year—she probably wouldn't recognise him. And you can be sure he'll be avoiding you, so she won't likely even have a chance to see him."

"This is terrible," Amy said. "I have to move."

"Whoa. You're not going anywhere. You have a right to live here and feel safe."

"But we're not safe!"

"There's a reason Tommy didn't chase after you when you left. Now that you're back, he's found you for one purpose—to tell you he wants nothing to do with you. He's afraid you might cause trouble for *him* in *his* new life: he's not interested in yours."

"But—"

"I know there's no guarantees. However, the evidence screams in your favour. Time has passed, he's moved on, and let's not forget his abusive behaviour during your time together. You've got *that* against *him*."

Neither spoke for a few moments, and then Marge continued.

"If worse comes to worst we'll help you deal with whatever he throws your way, but I really don't think he's going to take the risk of heading down another road with you."

"Okay, thanks Marge. I'm gonna think about everything you said and I'm going to write all my thoughts and I'm gonna plan what to do if he decides to muscle back into our lives. Like if this marriage fails, which it probably will, he might decide to retrace his steps back to his daughter."

After tucking Jessie into bed, Amy journaled. And fretted. And journaled some more.

Why did I choose to come back here?

For stability for Jess. I can't drag her off somewhere else.

When I decided to continue living, for Jess, I knew Tommy could maneuver his way back into her life. I knew I could go to jail. I didn't know if the Raynors would have anything to do with me. At least now I have their support, even if the rest is unknown.

Marge makes a good case. He obviously wants us out of his life.

If I see him again, what'll I do?

I'll walk right past him, just like he wants.

What if Jessie sees him and says, "Hi, Daddy?"

I'll apologize and say he looks a lot like her father.

What if he changes his mind and comes after her?

I'll go to the Children's Aid Society. I'll hire a lawyer. And if

From Thorns

it looks like he's going to win, we'll go to a shelter. I better find out how that would work.

This is going to be hard. Will I have to look over my shoulder for the rest of my life? I can't live every day not knowing.

At times, Amy thought she saw Tommy at a distance. Or was her mind playing tricks? With each passing week the fear lessened, but the nagging anxiety hung on like a sliver embedded too deep to remove.

CHAPTER 46

After being home for several months, she decided to attend a Sunday church service. She'd put it off for fear of the looks she anticipated receiving. She arrived just as the service began and sat at the back with Jessie. In the middle of speaking from the pulpit, the pastor made eye contact. And right there in front of the whole church he said, "Is that you, Amy?"

When she nodded, he came off the platform and down the aisle with all eyes following him. He took her hands. "It's wonderful to see you. We'll talk after service, okay?"

From the corner of her eye, she saw Sheila waving. If only she could melt into the seat.

After service, when she apologized for leaving the church and abandoning everyone Pastor Mike said, "We never stopped praying for you and Jess. When you left, we knew we'd let you down. After all, if you'd known you were loved you would have come to us for help."

She would never understand the perspective of these people.

With Jessie approaching the age to join some of the programs, Amy dove back into youth ministries. She knew some of the

From Thorns

volunteers from her previous time with the group. But instead of welcoming her they avoided her and looked away when she approached, offering cool replies when questioned.

She spoke with the pastor. "They obviously don't want my involvement. Honestly, I don't blame them; I know I deserve a cold shoulder."

"Deserve? Do you seriously believe you deserve disapproval?"

Amy smiled. "No, but not everyone has walked my road."

"Okay, I think we need to confront this head-on. You're not doing anyone any favours by quietly bowing out. We need to give everyone a chance to see they're judging and we need to give them a chance to stop."

"You've gotta be kidding."

Pastor Mike called a meeting following the next youth event.

After the group gathered, he turned it over to Amy and sat down.

"I want to apologize for abandoning the church and running away. I should have had more courage and stood up to Tommy. At least I should have trusted everyone enough to explain what was going on. But by then I was too confused."

She looked at the pastor.

"Anyone want to respond?" he asked.

After a few moments of silence, Becky said, "We're just wondering if we can trust you to stick around this time."

"Hold on, we don't know her story," Jeff said.

Becky's face turned a bright shade of red. "I'm not criticizing. But her coming and going left us scrambling."

"Amy, how are you feeling?" Pastor Mike asked.

"Uncomfortable. I'm wondering how many people are talking behind my back. Maybe I should find another church."

"I'm sorry," Becky said. "Everyone's happy you're back. No one's judging. But some are worried about whether we can count on you this time."

"Becky," Pastor Mike said, "thank you for having the courage to speak honestly."

"I feel like the bad guy."

"Well, you're not," Pastor Mike assured. "We know you're not the only one who's concerned."

Arms crossed, Amy said, "I've lived through my own little form of hell. Now I've come back to my church and people are talking. Believe me, I would have rather lived any of your lives than—"

"Okay, I think we understand where she's coming from," Pastor Mike said. "She takes responsibility for her actions and she'd like all of us to bring our concerns to her directly."

Becky looked at Amy. "I'll talk with you later. I can help put this to bed."

"Sunday?"

"Sounds good."

"If anyone here has brewed coffee using a percolator," Pastor Mike said, "you know that over brewing ruins the coffee. So let's not continue brewing these negative thoughts. Hopefully we can all see how important honesty is. Burying our feelings only serves to damage relationships."

On Sunday after the service, Amy met with Becky.

"I feel terrible," Becky said. "I worried about your commitment but I never even asked what happened—why you disappeared."

"Don't worry about it," Amy said. "I appreciate your courage

From Thorns

to speak up. Now you're going to help me sort this out, right?"

"Yeah."

Following their meeting, as Amy packed up, she heard Pastor Mike's voice from the hall. "She sure has come a long way. You should have seen her at a meeting we had after Adventure Club. I won't get into detail—can't break confidence—but I can tell you that she broached a difficult topic with tremendous courage. I can't imagine many her age being able to handle themselves as well as she did."

"Yes, she's matured."

Marge's voice.

"When she returned we weren't sure what we'd be facing. But she's acknowledged the hurt she caused, she understands there are consequences to her actions, and she's taking responsibility. She's grown."

"She's been through a lot," Pastor Mike said. "That tends to make one grow up real fast."

It felt so good to hear these positive words. They countered the accusations that continued to assault her when all was quiet.

Once the voices faded, Amy retrieved Jessie. "Thanks for staying behind to watch her."

"You're welcome," Paige said. "I'm sorry for how you were treated around here. It's funny how we only see things from our own perspective. It's hard to squeeze into someone else's shoes, if you know what I mean."

Amy smiled. "Yeah, I get it."

CHAPTER 47

As the weekend of the church's youth retreat approached, although she still teetered on the edge of discomfort, there's no way she'd back out of the commitment she made.

The group involved teens between the ages of thirteen and sixteen.

"Why can't I come?" Jessie whined.

"When you get older it'll be your turn."

The tears started. "No. You might not come back."

It was approaching a year since their return home and that horrible separation at the train station. Was Jessie working a manipulation or was she genuinely afraid?

Marge stepped in. "Mommy's not leaving you at the train station. She's not hiding. That's never going to happen again. But if you feel afraid while Mommy's away, I'll take you to see her. Okay?"

Marge's love. A pillar to lean on.

Friday evening, the cars were packed, a headcount was taken, and they headed off. Following dinner at a fast food place, they went straight to the hosting church where they were directed to two large rooms—one for the girls, another for the boys. The

From Thorns

adults set up while the teens expended their pent-up energy in the gym. Eventually the young people settled, allowing the adults to enjoy a cup of tea and a bit of conversation before crawling into their own sleeping bags.

The smell of bacon woke them at 7:00. A couple of families from the host church served breakfast before everyone loaded into vehicles. They arrived at the retreat meeting centre, a neighbourhood school, in time for the 8:30 start. As the kids filed into the auditorium, Amy wandered around to familiarize herself with the school's layout, location of washrooms, etcetera.

And that's when it happened.

Her heart lurched. She couldn't breathe. There he was. After all this time. She looked down and pushed through the crowd.

Janney grabbed Amy's arm as she shoved past. "Are you okay?"

"Just a little light-headed. I'm going to get some air."

Her heart raced as she jogged along the hallway and out the door. Bending forward, hands on her thighs, she breathed deeply. Did he remember her? Or had he shoved those memories into a dark dungeon? Or would he remember her, but with anger and resentment?

Back in the large hall filled with hundreds of people, Amy scanned the area. She wanted to see him again, and at the same time she was afraid to see him.

The first speaker was introduced: Matt Argyle, who had started his own company and designed some computer games. The games were listed, the kids cheered, and Amy stood in a daze.

Matt spoke eloquently. The whole room quieted except for the occasional applause or burst of laughter. Amy didn't hear a word. And then he looked right at her. No, it couldn't be. In a room this size? Impossible! But he paused, looking distracted. He turned away and continued speaking, moving his head slowly across the room in the other direction. Then his eyes came back, straight to Amy's. Her stomach did somersaults.

When he finished speaking, the kids headed to various classrooms. Amy helped the teens in her care find their way. She joined one of the groups but couldn't focus so decided to take a walk.

On her way down the hall, there he stood engrossed in conversation. She stopped abruptly and both parties turned to face her. "Hello Amy," Matt said.

"Hi. It's good to see you." She impressed herself at the calm she displayed despite feeling like she was about to collapse. "You spoke well in front of such a large audience."

Matt smiled and looked at his shoes. The man he'd been speaking with said, "We'll catch up later," and walked off.

"Thank you," Matt said to Amy, ignoring his friend. "Honestly, it's really not that tough when you know more about the subject than anyone else in the room."

"Well you impressed me and I have a feeling you're just being modest. You started your own company making computer games? Didn't you major in philosophy?"

Matt nodded. "It's a long story."

"Where are you living now?"

"About an hour away. And you?" Instead of pausing to let her respond, "Are you still with . . .?"

Uncomfortable, she didn't reply.

"Look, I don't want to be intrusive or inappropriate," he continued. "I have no idea what's going on in your life, how Jessie's doing, where you're living. But I'd love to catch up. Would

From Thorns

you be willing to go for coffee tonight? Are you here with a church group?"

Amy, trying to breathe normally, replied, "Yes, I'm with a group but I should be able to get away after 8:30."

"Can I pick you up at 9:00?"

She remained in a daze for the rest of the day.

CHAPTER 48

The dark green sports coup with the black leather interior sure looked impressive. "Nice car," spilled from her lips. She wished she'd said "Hello" first.

"I wondered if you'd like it. I remember you being very practical and I felt concerned you might think my values had gotten messed."

"Oh Matt, I'm hardly sitting here judging you! It's so great to see you again, and I'm looking forward to hearing about your life."

He reached across the front seat and squeezed her hand.

She felt her body fill with heat.

She told herself to settle down. He's probably married with kids; he shouldn't touch her like that.

They made easy small talk during the short drive.

As he pulled into a parking lot he said, "Doesn't this look like a cute place? Wait 'til you see inside—I think it'll appeal to your artistic sensibilities."

Burgundy window coverings accented the beige walls. The tabletops had colourful mosaic inserts which coordinated well with the multicoloured tiffany light fixtures. The warm lighting

From Thorns

created an intimate atmosphere. Varieties of coffees and teas and decadent desserts were available along with wines, soft drinks, and some interesting appetizers for those who didn't want anything hot to drink or sweet to eat. A few people occupied the bar seating with only one of the tables taken. After Matt led the way to a quiet corner table, the server arrived.

The smell of the food—savoury mixed with sweet—was especially appealing after the dinner of chili dogs served at the church. But Amy's knotted stomach wouldn't allow for more than a beverage.

After ordering coffee Matt said, "So, tell me what you've been up to since I last saw you."

You've got to be kidding, Amy thought.

"Wow, that's quite the request. How about I tell you what I'm doing now?" She didn't wait for an answer. "Jessie and I have just moved into an apartment. I'm working at the supermarket close to Marge and Steve's place. Do you remember it?"

"Absolutely. What are you doing there?"

Oh great, Amy mused. He runs his own company, and what do I do?

The conversation continued on an easy track for a while. Amy took the initial plunge into deeper waters. "I'm dying to know if you're married, how many children, pets, house, apartment..."

Matt stared into his coffee for a few moments. "After you and I split, my heart broke." He looked into her eyes. "Did you know how much I loved you?" He looked back into his cup and continued, "I told myself I needed to meet someone else and soon I did. Her name was Suzanne. We had a lot in common and we started to fall in love. I thought she could be the one but we didn't have a chance. She was killed in a car accident ten months after we met."

He sighed, leaned back, and stared at the ceiling. "It was terrible. I lost you and it hurt so much, and then I lost her in such a horrible way. I determined that I wouldn't *ever* get involved with anyone *ever* again. So I went from using someone to get over someone else to wanting nothing to do with anyone. I've been working on healing."

"I don't know what to say."

"It's been awful. But I'm trying to focus on the future now."

He brought his gaze back to Amy. "Now it's your turn. Tell me what's been going on in your life. What happened with Jessie's father? You ended our relationship for him but sounds like you're living on your own now. Is he still in the picture?"

"No."

"What became of him?" Matt asked, with zero intonation.

She began to tell her story. One disclosure led to another until it was all out there like dirty water spilled across the table. She felt small, wishing she hadn't divulged so much, but it was too late now.

That's the trouble with not preparing.

Her eyes remained riveted to her coffee.

Silence.

What was he thinking? She wanted to evaporate.

Matt reached across the table and wrapped his hands around hers. "I can't believe what you've been through. Hoping for a good relationship with the father of your child and you ended up forced to run. Then another disgusting creep tried to take advantage of you. And a town full of backstabbers got thrown into the mix. How have you survived?"

She looked into his eyes. "Listen Matt, I know how kind and

From Thorns

compassionate you are. But let's face reality—there's nothing admirable in any part of my story. I'm ashamed, embarrassed, and I feel humiliated sitting here with you. You did things right with awful results. Terrible things have happened to me because I *didn't* do things right. Please don't praise me. It makes a mockery of everything good."

"At the risk of being told off again, I have to disagree. I see a strong person who's had to fight her way through life just to survive. You didn't give up and you don't feel sorry for yourself. So I hope you can accept that my perception is a perfectly valid one, albeit different from yours." With eyes wide, he cocked his head.

Amy felt heat moving up her neck and onto her face.

Matt looked at his watch and said, "Our time is running out tonight but I'd like to continue our conversation. Any chance we could get together again next week? If you don't want to I'll understand."

How could she *not* want to see him again? This was an impossible dream come true. But right now, the weight of shame and worthlessness made the dream feel like a nightmare.

She heard herself say, "I'd love to." In fact, she had no idea what she wanted, whether she could even process this evening and deal with her embarrassment. But she could always bow out if she changed her mind.

"I'm so glad," Matt said. And then, "Let me get you back to the church before your colleagues think you've been abducted. You're going to need your sleep to manage all those hooligans. It's another early start tomorrow."

After he paid the bill they walked in silence to his car. He helped her in before climbing behind the wheel.

At the church he ushered her to the door, took her hand and held it while he said, "This has been a wonderful evening. Thank you for spending it with me. I'll call you next week."

With electricity firing through her body, she slipped inside the building barely able to breathe.

Her raging thoughts kept her from sleeping soundly. The sleeping bag, twisting around her body every time she turned, didn't help.

She questioned the sanity of another visit with Matt. Seeing him again would stir feelings, and to what end? What if she fell in love with him again but without reciprocation? And what about the other side of the coin—if Matt fell for her but she realized he wasn't the right one? And what if Jessie really loved Matt and Amy had to tell her that he couldn't be in their life just because Mommy says so?

The clock displayed 4:06 the last time she looked at it.

The smell of frying ham woke her far too early. The group managed to leave the church hall in relatively good shape and they got to the conference on time.

During the morning Matt snuck up behind her and whispered, "Hi there." She jumped. He moved around to face her, looking straight into her eyes with a mischievous grin. She melted, her resolve from the night before dripping away like the wax of a burning candle. She caught herself, blew out the flame, and remembered that Jessie was too important to allow any more foolish decisions.

"Hi Matt. You look great this morning. You obviously slept better than I did."

From Thorns

"You couldn't sleep? That's too bad." His grin widened. "I guess I shouldn't tell you that I slept like a baby." The grin disappeared. "I'm being insensitive. Let me try again. I'm sorry to hear you didn't sleep well. I hope you'll be able to get through the day." He cocked his head. "I mean it. I know how tough it is trying to work with a gang of teenagers on little sleep." He paused and the smile returned. "Hey, I need your phone number. I'll give you a call next week."

"Well actually, I thought about that some more and I've decided I would rather we didn't see each other again. I think it might be too hard on Jessie. I hope you can understand."

Matt's playful expression turned serious. "I get it. Jessie needs to be protected." He studied the wall for a few moments. Then he looked back at Amy and said, "I'm wondering if you'd be willing to think about it a little more. Can I call you next week just to talk, to see if you've changed your mind?"

"Probably not a good idea." She ran to catch the group she was assigned to. The day proved to be as busy as the previous one.

Just before leaving, Amy found Matt and handed him a slip of paper with her phone number. "I haven't changed my mind but I guess it would be okay if you wanted to touch base next week."

The played-out teens delivered a quiet return trip, nothing like the rowdy behaviour two evenings earlier.

Back home, she got a ride to her apartment where Marge sat reading while Jessie slept. Amy filled her in on the weekend events including the chance meeting with Matt. She could tell Marge wanted more detail but thankfully didn't ask.

CHAPTER 49

Monday morning sent Jessie to school and Amy to work. Throughout the day, she thought about Matt but her position didn't change. Seeing him again would be a bad idea.

When he called a few days later, Amy relayed her decision. His tone of voice revealed his disappointment but he didn't pressure her. He asked her to take his phone number just in case she changed her mind. He wished her all of life's best. And that was that. A reopened chapter closed.

She returned to writing notes that would stay buried in her journal. It felt safe to pretend.

> Missing you,
>   feeling blue,
>   wanting more,
>   time to explore,
>   the mystery of us.

As though it were possible.

From Thorns

Life is hard, filled with pain and suffering and
    endless challenges.
But along the way there are moments of joy,
Moments of happiness, and times of hope.
Those wondrous moments haven't been plentiful
    for me,
But they have been.
Summed up simply—they are meeting Marge, having
Jessie, and knowing you.

I don't know much about good.
I don't know much about truth.
I don't know much about love.
I don't know much about how it's supposed to be.
But I know what you meant to me.
I know that you are special and good and true.
I remember your touch. Your laugh. Your care
    and understanding.

I miss it.
I miss you.

As though he could hear her words and know her heart.

Why is life so hard?
Why so full of hurt?
Why can't we just be happy?
Like children playing
Without a care,
Without concern

Of what society expects.
I want to let go,
To give in,
To what feels natural and easy.
Let someone else
Bear the burden
Of all the rights and wrongs
Of living life
And looking after
All that we must do.
Why is life so hard?

As though he could help her figure it out.

It took a couple of weeks of feeling depressed before Amy reached out to Marge. After all, she reasoned, if she'd trusted Marge's advice about Tommy she and Jessie could have been spared a lot of pain. Hopefully Marge would have equally good advice now.

She didn't say a word during Amy's long tirade of details. The facts, the feelings, the pros and cons, the potentially disastrous fallout.

"What do you think?" Amy asked after repeating each argument at least once.

"I think you should call him and get together."

"Have you been listening? Have you thought about how this could affect Jessie? Or how it could affect me if it doesn't work out? Or how it could affect Matt?"

Marge smiled. "Yes, there could be a negative outcome. Sometimes life involves risk. Let's weigh the risk of potential

From Thorns

hurt against the risk of lost opportunity."

Amy frowned. "What?"

"If you shut down out of fear you may lose something good. You'll never know if you don't try." Marge paused. "You're a smart girl Amy. You'll make sure Jessie doesn't get too close too quickly. We'd be happy to have her for a sleepover whenever you and Matt get together. You can introduce them if and when you think it wise. I would hate to see you avoid relationships until after Jessie has grown up and left home.

"You know maybe, just maybe, God brought Matt back into your life. And when God is the instigator, it can only be good."

Silence moved in while Amy stared into space.

When she looked back at Marge she said, "Can I call Matt now? I'd rather Jessie not overhear the conversation."

"I've got laundry on the go." Marge headed for the stairs.

The answering machine picked up. "Hi Matt, it's Amy. I know I said we shouldn't see each other again but I actually want to so if you're still open to the idea you've got my number. Unless you threw it out. 969-6523. You know the area code. Hope to hear from you."

Amy cringed after ending the call.

I should have written out what I wanted to say.

CHAPTER 50

Saturday morning, as the sun shone into the kitchen, the phone rang.

"Hello, this is Jessie speaking."

A few moments later, "I don't know. Mommy, are you available?"

Matt and Amy arranged a time to get together the following weekend.

She traded some shifts to make it possible.

It felt like the longest week of her life. Eventually each day did end and finally Saturday arrived. Jessie helped tidy the apartment, even dusting her own room. She wanted to do the vacuuming but the machine was too big for her to mange.

I wonder if she'll be this anxious to help in a few more years, Amy wondered.

When the apartment reached presentation standard, the girls went shopping. Jessie loved to help her mom pick out clothing—a fashion critic in the making.

Together they picked three outfits. Black pants with a three-quarter sleeve silky red top, the same pants with a long-sleeve

From Thorns

magenta top, and a long-sleeve black dress. Amy already had shoes and jewelry. When purchasing accessories of any kind, she made sure they would coordinate with many outfits. And she had several outfits because she shopped the sales, careful to choose only items that would mix and match with things she already owned. On her salary she couldn't afford frivolity.

Jessie preferred the form-fitting dress with a glamorous slit up the side. And Amy agreed. With black stockings and heels, she hoped she would look good enough to feel confident.

With shopping done, they stopped at Marge's to get her opinion. She approved and suggested Amy use one of her necklaces. Stunning, artistically crafted items filled Marge's jewelry box and she had an eye for what went best with what.

Jessie stayed at Gramma's for a sleepover.

Back at home Amy showered, fussed with her hair, filed and polished her nails, applied make-up (something she rarely bothered with) and perfume (a gift Marge had given her that she never expected to use), and finally she got into the dress. The mirror assured her that she'd pulled it together nicely.

Matt was late. She paced, adjusted the towels in the bathroom, wiped a spot off the mirror, smoothed Jessie's quilt, again. She was in the process of reorganizing the kitchen dishes when the doorbell rang.

"Wow, you look beautiful." He presented her with a single red rose but his dazed look continued. "You should be on the cover of . . .

"I don't know . . .

"Some fashion magazine. You look fantastic!"

Amy wondered if she routinely looked like a bum.

Matt must have picked up on her thoughts. "Not that you didn't look great at the retreat, but you weren't dressed up."

Her focus drifted to the scars that lay hidden beneath her clothes and she shuddered before pushing those thoughts away.

"You're looking pretty good yourself," she said. "Would you like to come in and see my little place?"

The tour didn't take long. Matt lingered at Jessie's doorway. "I look forward to seeing her again." He looked at Amy. "When you feel that would be appropriate."

"I have a great picture of her in my room. C'mon, I'll show you."

Matt admired the décor before moving to the picture. "She's beautiful, like her mother."

Ignoring the compliment Amy said, "Everything cost next to nothing. You don't have to offer praise."

"If you decorated this well on a small budget, the praise is higher. It's easy to make a place look great when you've got loads of money. To make it this nice without a lot of cash takes talent. So let me rephrase—I love the way you've decorated and I'm impressed by your ability."

"Okay, you win."

"I've made a reservation at a place close by. We could walk or," he grinned, "I brought that little car you like."

As they walked to the car, Matt's arm brushed lightly against hers. Shivers travelled through her body.

He took her to a quaint seafood restaurant. The smell of garlic frying in butter filled the air. They talked and laughed and even cried. It was only when the waitress told them it was closing time that Amy realized they'd been together for five hours. Five hours without a minute of awkward silence or strained conversation.

From Thorns

"Are you up for a walk before I take you home?" Matt asked as he helped Amy into the car.

At a park they used to frequent he took her hand as they walked. For several minutes no one spoke. Matt broke the silence. "I badly want a second chance with you. I know you're afraid. I don't want to pressure you. I don't want to interfere with your plans. I don't want to get in the way of your relationship with Jessie or Marge or any other friendship. But if you're willing to give this a shot, a bit of time, a chance for us . . ."

Amy pulled Matt to face her. "I never stopped thinking about you. I was so happy to see you at the retreat and to have that one evening. Sure I'm afraid, but I definitely want to spend time with you to see where this goes. I wouldn't have called otherwise. There's so much I need to know about you, about Suzanne, about who you are now, and your goals, and—"

Matt placed his hand gently over her mouth. He smiled. "We have loads of time for that. I look forward to answering every question. And I want to get to know the person you've become. I don't expect you to be the same girl I knew." His eyes locked on hers and he slowly moved his hand away from her mouth, replacing it with his lips. He kissed her gently, tenderly.

She sucked in a deep breath and held it, feeling the sensation of his lips against hers through her entire body.

They continued to walk until the cool night air turned cold. On their way to the car Matt stopped at a large oak tree. "Do you remember?"

Before she could answer he wrapped his arms loosely around her waist. He moved his hands up her back and brought them to rest on the sides of her face. He tilted her head back and looked into her eyes. His fingers softly brushed the hair off her face and weaved into the hair that had fallen down her back. He brought his mouth to hover over hers, just barely moving, scarcely touching her lips. She could feel his breath, his warmth. He drew his head back and pulled her tight into his arms. They stood there, wrapped up and around each other for several moments. When Matt pulled away he pointed to the initials he had carved into the tree several years earlier.

Amy nodded. "Yeah, I remember. I love that you remember too."

He slept in Jessie's room. "My feet will hang off the end but I'll sleep just fine."

In the morning he surprised Amy with pancakes and coffee. He had packed the ingredients, and his expresso machine.

Tears rolled down her cheeks as she waved to the departing car. Tears of sadness at having to part. Tears of joy at the hope of what might lie ahead.

CHAPTER 51

The sweet smell of baking greeted Amy. "Sure smells good in here," she said on her way into the kitchen. Jessie stood on a low stool at the kitchen counter helping Marge scrape batter into muffin tins. Amy helped herself to a cup of coffee.

"We went to the park with another grandma and Jody. Then we had an ice cream sundae with three toppings. And Gramma let me have a bubble bath and I get to keep the rest. And we had pancakes for breakfast." Jessie grinned large. "With chocolate chips!"

"Wow. What are you making now?"

"Muffins with blueberries. I got to crack the eggs. A piece of shell fell in the bowl but Gramma got it out so it's okay. And we get to bring the muffins to our house."

Marge winked.

Imagining the mess that would accompany this baking endeavour, Amy marvelled at Marge's patience. She found baking with Jessie somewhat challenging even though she enjoyed working with food and Jessie was her own child.

"Did you go to church this morning?"

After sucking in a huge breath Jessie said, "We didn't go

because I fell on the way to the car and my knee was bleeding and it really hurt so Gramma thought we should stay home today. Look at the big bandage."

"No need to worry," Marge said. It was a nasty scrape though, and we could all tell it hurt."

She suggested Jessie go watch her new movie while the muffins baked. Jessie delivered a hug to her mom before heading down the stairs with Rumble in tow.

"Thank you for making last evening possible," Amy said.

"You're most welcome. Now, tell me all about it."

She told Marge about the restaurant, the ease of conversation, and the breakfast prepared by Matt. Then she talked about her feelings, both excitement and fear. Finally, she asked for advice.

Marge looked away for a few moments, then said, "How would you advise a friend who was in your position?"

"Oh Marge, I just want you to tell me what to do. If I had listened to you about Tommy . . ." Amy shook her head. "Please don't turn this back to me; just tell me what you think."

"If only it were that easy." Marge laughed. "Unfortunately *you* have to decide what to do. I'll give you my thoughts, don't worry. Now, how would you advise a friend?"

Marge waited while Amy paced.

"I think I would tell my friend to go for it. What's the worst that could happen? If it doesn't work out one or both might get hurt, but if they don't give it a chance they could lose out on something wonderful."

Marge nodded. "And I think that's exactly what I would say to you. Trust yourself. I know you're afraid because of what happened with Tommy, but we need to keep in mind two important differences between then and now.

From Thorns

"One, you've matured.

"Secondly, if I can be honest, I don't think you were using your head in that situation. You chose to believe what you wanted to believe instead of what the evidence showed.

"And that leads to part B of my second point. Matt's not Tommy!"

Amy laughed. "You're right."

She looked away. "Matt's a successful businessman. What could he possibly see in me? At some point he's bound to wake up and realize I'm far beneath his worth."

"Interesting," Marge said. "Did you know that Steve is also a successful businessman? And I bake muffins with children. Are you suggesting I'm far beneath Steve? That he's a fool for loving me?"

"Cute," Amy smiled. "You're twisting this to suit your own purposes. You have a master's degree in Chemistry. I barely finished high school. There's no comparison."

"I'm thinking that degrees don't make a person. You're a marvellous young woman. I knew it from the moment I met you. You're a fighter. You work hard. You give of yourself. You've got tremendous talent. How could any of that compare with a degree?"

"Fine, we'll leave that for now. There's more I'm afraid of. Scared stiff to be more accurate. You've seen my scars."

"If that sends Matt packing then I have seriously misjudged him. You deserve much better than a man who cares about some scarring!"

"It's not *some* scarring. My body's a mess."

"Would you feel better if you talked to Matt about it?"

Amy shrugged. "I guess I should. This'll be over before it

gets started."

"I doubt it," Marge said. "Now, why don't you stay for a while? I know Steve would love to see you when he gets back. He sure loves being a grandpa!"

At the end of the day, after Jessie was tucked into bed and sound asleep, Amy called Matt.

His answering machine picked up. "Hi, it's me. I'll be home all evening and would like to chat if you have time. Thank you for a wonderful evening and breakfast this morning. I'm looking forward to seeing you again. And next time, it's my turn to feed you."

As she hung up she wondered if her message sounded alright. The more she thought about it, the more she decided it was terrible. For the rest of the evening she reflected on what she *should* have said.

Just after settling into bed, the phone rang.

"Hi." Matt's voice. "I'm sorry to be calling this late. We had a dilemma at work and I love problem-solving."

Marge's words of encouragement from earlier in the day suddenly didn't carry any weight. "What was the dilemma?" she asked, immediately regretting the question knowing she wouldn't understand the answer. She also wondered why he worked on Sunday but decided not to ask.

"It had to do with a new feature in a game. I'll spare you the boring details. I'm just sorry I wasn't here when you called. I'd much rather talk to you than be at work."

"Oh Matt, I have to be honest. I'd love to go down this road with you but I don't see how someone like you could be interested in someone like me. You're so intelligent and

From Thorns

accomplished. And I'm not. How could this possibly work?"

"Do you have to go into the store tomorrow?" Matt asked after a few moments of awkward silence.

"No, I took the day off. Dentist appointment. Why?"

"If it's okay with you, I'd like to come over. Sounds like we have some important things to talk about."

"Now? It's midnight."

"I don't have to go into work tomorrow—that's the great thing about running your own business—and I love to drive, so . . ."

He sure has a lot of energy, Amy thought.

"Whaddya say?" he continued. "Can I come?"

"What about Jessie? I don't want her to know about you. Not yet."

"So many options. I could go to a motel. An all-night coffee shop. There's always my car. I don't need much sleep but I guess I shouldn't deprive you."

"I won't sleep at all knowing you could've come. I'll have a bottle of wine waiting."

Amy hoped for a short nap but sleep eluded her. When she heard the knock she sprinted across the room, afraid another knock would wake Jessie.

CHAPTER 52

Holding a bottle of wine and a bag of pretzels, Matt walked through the door. "I know, odd combination but I had a craving."

Amy frowned. "I told you I'd have a bottle waiting."

"Let's save yours. The one I brought goes great with pretzels." Matt pulled her into a hug. "Oh, it's good to see you."

"Yeah, it's been a whole twelve hours."

They moved into the living room.

"I've been thinking about what you said and I'm *still* lost for words," Matt blurted. "And that's not like me. I wanted to come over because I didn't know what to say on the phone. But here I am still struggling." He looked down, shaking his head.

After a few moments of silence he looked up. "You're an amazing person. I knew it back then and even more so now. I see you as strong, determined, intelligent, responsible, caring. I look at what you've been through and how you've come through it. I don't know anyone else like you. On top of that, you're interesting and fun. And, at the risk of sounding quite shallow, you're the most beautiful thing I've ever seen. That's why I asked you to coffee that first evening we met at the church five years ago.

From Thorns

Do you remember? I didn't know you at all but I was awestruck at your beauty."

"Humph," Amy muttered. "Look Matt, you're kind and encouraging. But I'm not at your level. I don't even have an education. Meanwhile you run your own business. You're famous, right?"

He laughed. "Hardly. My company has produced some computer games that are selling, but we're small." He paused. "What I do is not who I am. Same for you. It's about how we think, what we live for, and what we believe in. That means far more than some executive position or a big salary."

"Step into my shoes. If I had accomplished impressive things and you were a clerk in a store, how would you feel?"

"Yeah, I know." He released a muffled laugh. "You know, most women would jump at the chance to be with someone successful, someone who appeared to have money, but not you. You want to run away because you don't think you're good enough. I certainly don't have to worry about you taking advantage of me!" He shook his head. "Please give this time. I'm telling you that I don't care about money or position. The fact that you care makes you more desirable, as if that were even possible. It would be so sad to lose this chance at something great. I don't want to diminish your feelings. They're real and they need to be addressed. But it might take some time. Can you put it aside for a little while, spend time with me, and see where this goes?"

"Okay. But I'm sure I'll need to talk about it more at some point."

Amy pushed off the couch and paced. "I need to tell you something."

"You're making me nervous."

She looked into his eyes. "Have you noticed that I always wear long sleeves and my legs are always covered?"

"I hadn't really thought about it. Why?"

What's coming? Matt wondered.

Amy frowned. "Oh right, when we were together before it was fall and winter. It's fall again. Nothing unusual about long sleeves." She grabbed a cushion from the couch and hugged it.

"I told you about my parents and how they treated me, why I got into the situation that led to my pregnancy, and why I left home. But I didn't tell you everything."

He steeled himself. He felt a rage swell at the mere thought of what she might be about to say.

"They used to punish me with a belt and fire and . . ."

She stared at the floor, ashamed, wondering what he thought of her beauty now. "I have scars, terrible scars. I wouldn't expect any man to accept such ugliness. Tommy didn't care when he was using me. He called me ugly but I already knew so it didn't matter. And when he came back and wanted to live with me, I thought he was okay with it. But he wasn't. He just wanted Jessie. And a nanny. And a servant. Since Tommy, there hasn't been anyone else."

Looking up she said, "I should have told you. I was too scared to speak about it and now here you are telling me I'm beautiful. I should have told you way back but I didn't want to lose you. I'm so sorry."

Matt felt heat consume his body.

"I'm sorry. I'm so sorry," Amy said, as she walked backward.

"Stop!" he said, his eyes dark. "You have nothing to be sorry for." He stood, walked to the wall, and knocked his fist against it. He turned to look at her before continuing. "I can barely contain

From Thorns

myself. How could anyone hurt a child? How could God allow that to happen to you?"

"Are you angry at me?" Amy whispered. "For not telling you sooner?"

"*At you?*" Matt choked on his words. "Why on earth would I be angry at you? Honestly, sometimes your logic escapes me."

He walked to where she had crouched in the corner holding the pillow so tight it had folded in half. He leaned over and unclasped her tight fists. He pulled her to her feet, wrapped his arms around her, and held her.

For a while they stood in silence. Then Matt pulled back, never letting go of Amy as his hands slid from her back down her arms and around her hands. She looked away. He leaned in the direction of her gaze until he was in her range of vision. She moved her eyes to meet his.

"I want you to show me your scars."

"No!"

"I want a relationship with you. A full, complete, intimate relationship. How can that happen if you can't trust me to love you, all of you? We all have beauty and ugliness. I want you to accept all of me, and I need to know and accept all of you."

"You're twisting things. You do *not* have the kind of ugliness I've got all over my body."

"Why do we associate ugliness with something physical? Doesn't God see ugliness *inside* of us? Our deep dark secrets. The lies we've told, the gossip we've repeated without caring who got hurt. That's ugly. Our bodies are just vehicles we move around in."

"You told me, you said it earlier tonight, that you asked me out because you thought I was pretty. Well I'm *not* pretty. I'm a mess of scars." She moved away from him, turned, and pulled up her top.

Matt's mind went crazy. He wondered how this could have been done without killing her. He wondered how no one would have known and intervened. He wondered how she had felt when this was happening. Logic. To escape emotion. Emotion could come later. Right now, Amy needed him to be strong.

Pulling her shirt down, she turned back to face him.

"May I touch a scar?"

"*What*?"

"I want you to trust me. I want you to believe that I can love you, all of you, scars included."

"If that's what you want." Her face and demeanour were flat. Had she completely shut down?

Matt walked toward her looking into her eyes with every step. He never broke eye contact as he reached back and slowly moved his hand up and under her top.

She looked away.

He gently lowered the palm of his hand onto her back and gingerly let his hand roam. Not far, just a few inches.

She didn't move.

"What are you feeling, Amy?"

"I'm waiting for you to run to the bathroom to throw up. I'm waiting for you to tell me you can't do this. Maybe you won't tonight, because you're kind and I know you don't want to hurt me. But you *will* tell me. It's okay, I wouldn't want to be with me either. And that's not all of it. Just the worst of it."

"I'm not going to pretend I have any idea what you've been through or how you feel." His eyes filled with tears. "But I can assure you that I will *not* be going anywhere. The monsters

From Thorns

who called themselves your parents tried to destroy you but they didn't succeed. You're beautiful Amy, the most beautiful woman I know. I have no idea how I'm going to convince you that your scars don't matter. But I *will* convince you. If I have to spend my life doing it, I will."

Amy said nothing.

Matt continued, "I can see how uncomfortable you are and it's late, so I'm going to go. I'll call in the morning. What time does Jessie go to school?"

"I'll be here alone at 9:00."

"I'll call you at 9:05."

Silence.

"Are you alright? Is it okay for me to leave now or would you rather I stay?"

"Please go. If you call in the morning we can talk more then."

"I *will* call!"

Matt held her hand as they walked to the door together. He took her face in his hands, kissed her, and said goodnight.

He ran down the stairs, barely making it out of the building before throwing up. With clenched teeth and a steering wheel grip that turned his fingers white, he drove erratically. While rage drove him, his admiration for Amy took another leap forward. He wondered about the rest of her body. What other scars lay hidden?

Her back is gross, he thought, tears blurring his vision. Scrambled flesh. I have to make her believe it doesn't matter. I have to show her it doesn't bother me, even though it does. I have to find a way for it not to bother me.

He wondered how he would convince her that he still wanted

her. He loved her, and her back didn't change that despite him feeling nauseous at the memory. Playing it cool had seemed like a good idea at the start so he wouldn't scare her off. But now, maybe the direction needed to change.

In his room he yelled at God. "How could you allow this? An innocent, helpless child. You handed her over to a world of evil. How could you?" He let a pillow absorb his anger. Stuffing drifted to the floor.

And then a clear message formed in his mind. God designed people with freedom and freedom comes with risk. Amy's parents used their freedom to hurt and destroy. So God led her to the Raynor family to begin healing.

Now He's led her to me. I can support her as she continues to heal.

Through the night he tossed and turned, seeing her flesh, feeling the horror. Eventually he drifted off to sleep. Before turning out the light he set the alarm for 7:30. It was rare for him to sleep past 5:00 but he wouldn't take any risk of sleeping late. She *would* get her phone call at 9:05. Perhaps he should get to the apartment before Jessie left for school, just in case she decided not to be home when he called.

CHAPTER 53

Amy awoke to the sound of Jessie singing in the bathroom. "Thank you God, for my beautiful daughter. Jessie's enough."

She pulled on her jeans and a t-shirt. She bought the t-shirt a while back thinking how fun it would be to wear something stylish, but it revealed scars. She sometimes wore it to watch T.V. but it never left the apartment. Today she didn't care.

At 9:00 she sat at the kitchen table enjoying the soothing taste of coffee, wondering if Matt had bailed.

The phone rang at 9:05. "I've had breakfast, checked out of the hotel, and I have an idea for today."

Amy's nerves fired electric currents through her gut. Could she do it? Face him and act normal? But what would he do if she refused to see him? "I'll meet you downstairs," she said.

Matt stood leaning against the passenger door of his car, hands in his pockets, looking handsome from head to toe. He opened the door for her but pulled her into a hug before helping her in.

"I need to know what you're thinking," Amy said.

"Last night was tough. I think you are braver and stronger and more amazing than I knew. I think it's time to tell you I love you."

Amy just stared, wide-eyed.

"I loved you five years ago and I never stopped loving you. I tried to get over you. I might have married Suzanne, and I did love her, but I still loved you in a way that a man shouldn't when he's involved with someone else." Matt looked away. "I suppose that makes me a bad person." He turned back to Amy. "But I never expected to have you back in my life so I tried to move on. When I saw you at the retreat my heart skipped a beat. I was afraid to hope. But I *did* hope that you would be willing to see me again. That maybe you could fall in love with me."

"I dreamed of you," Amy admitted. "I wrote little notes that allowed me to feel close to you. I missed you so much."

She looked away, shaking her head. "I don't understand how you're able to forgive me after I left you for Tommy?"

"He's the father of your child." Matt shrugged. "You put Jessie's needs above everything else, as you should have. I don't need to analyze the whole Tommy situation for you. Bottom line—I understood. There's nothing to forgive."

Did I do it for Jessie? Amy wondered. I guess. Somewhat.

"What about my scars. You can't say I'm beautiful. You know better now."

"Actually I *can* say you're beautiful. Because you are. The scars are horrible. Mostly because of what they represent. I can't imagine living the life you endured. *And* I don't see you as any less beautiful. You are, beyond a shadow of a doubt, the most beautiful woman I've ever met."

His assurances made no sense.

"I have a feeling there's nothing I can say to convince you," Matt continued. "So I'm going to toss the ball into your court.

From Thorns

Here's the thing, I want you in my life. Now you have to decide—are you willing to give this a chance? You'll have to trust me enough to continue spending time together. It's up to you."

"Well done." Amy smiled. "You're good. I can see you running a company—you know how to take charge and hand off the problem." She sighed. "Yes, I wanna give this a chance. But I think you're playing a game with yourself and I think you'll wake up one day and realize you're a desirable man who could have any woman he wants. And you'll realize you want someone who isn't covered in scars. But it sounds like you want to continue for now, so," she reached for Matt's hand, "I'm going to try to trust you."

Matt nodded. "Good."

"I'm counting on you to be honest," Amy said. "The minute you decide you don't want to be with someone so damaged you have to tell me. I know you won't want to hurt me but if you aren't honest, only hurt can come out of this."

Matt nodded.

"I need you to promise!"

"I promise. Thank you for giving me your trust. I won't betray it."

They sat quietly until his expression changed from serious to playful. "Now, do you want to hear my idea for today?"

Amy nodded.

"I wanna get a dog. And I'd like your input."

"Oh my gosh, I'd *love* that. I wish Jessie could be with us."

"I remember you and Jessie with Rumble. I'm glad your love of dogs hasn't changed," Matt said. "Part two of my idea—how would you feel about asking Marge to join us for lunch?"

"Sure, I'll give her a call."

Marge invited them for coffee. She served so many snacks

that no one was hungry for lunch and time got away from them.

"Rats!" Amy said. "My dentist appointment is in half an hour."

Matt looked at his watch. "I guess dog shopping will have to wait."

As he pulled away from the dental office he called out the window, "I hope you'll have time to chat this evening. I miss you already..."

The next time they spoke Matt asked, "You okay?"

"Yeah, I'm fine."

"Man, that was a tough conversation on Sunday. I feel like we talked everything through but," Matt paused, "I'm worried about where you're at."

"Honestly, I'm a little on edge—I was hoping it didn't show."

"I'm just wondering how you're feeling about yourself and about us."

"Okay, I'll tell you. Now that you know the truth about me, every time I hear your voice I'm going to expect you to say, 'It's over.'"

"That's what I was afraid of. What can I do to fix this?"

"I think," Amy said, "we should put that heavy topic away for a while. We both know it's there waiting to explode, but if we talk about it every time we get together it'll keep my stress level sky high."

"We definitely don't want that! But if I don't bring it up and ask how you're feeling, I'm afraid you'll think I don't care. Plus I'm worried you'll be stewing about it."

"I promise I won't think you don't care. I'll think you're being respectful and leaving it alone because I asked you to."

"All right then," Matt said, "it's in your court and I'll trust

From Thorns

you to bring it up when you need or want to talk some more."

Of course I'm distressed, Amy thought. Of course it's on the top of my mind. Of course I can't fully relax. I hope he sticks to his word and never brings it up again until he has to, when he stops kidding himself and wants to end this relationship.

CHAPTER 54

The next few weeks carried them like a fast-moving wind. They walked and talked and rediscovered each other. They took in movies followed by analysis over a latte. They agreed on passages of scripture to study privately and then debated their interpretations. Matt explained stock market strategies and Amy did some investing on her own. After losing most of her small savings, she gave it up. Matt suggested cooking together but soon realized his involvement just slowed the process down. They got to know each other for the people they'd become. Their basic values hadn't changed but some of their ideas about life had, and this led to interesting discussions and arguments.

And every time, after they parted, Amy wondered what he was thinking.

I know he's not playing me; he's too good a person. But he's gotta be playing a game with himself. He's pushed his disgust down and tried to bury it but it's not dead. At some point it's going to burst through the surface and he'll have to admit he can't cope with a mess of a body like mine.

Meanwhile, Matt delivered flowers. He complimented her appearance. He admired her ideas. And he listened. He listened

From Thorns

carefully and thoughtfully. He made it hard for her to believe he would change his mind someday.

He ran his hands over her scarring as though she had perfect skin. Slow, tender, gentle. She froze every time, wanting to pull his hands away but knowing she had to let him touch her if she wanted the relationship to continue. "How can you stand the feel of my flesh?"

"You're kidding, right?"

"I understand how you can brush past some of the scars, but my back..."

"I love you," Matt said, emphatically. "All of you."

"I wish I could let it go, but I can't."

"I wish you could let it go, but I understand."

The Christmas season limited their time together. Jason returned from university with a gift of forgiveness. When he had learned Amy was seeing Matt again, he was able to let go of his anger and move on. He accompanied Amy and Jessie in checking out neighbourhood Christmas lights. Amy attended school presentations with Marge and Kate. Jessie helped decorate their apartment and made numerous Christmas drawings for the walls and decorations for the tree. They stayed overnight at the Raynors' on Christmas Eve.

Amy's determination to protect Jessie from more hurt won the battle over desire. Although she and Matt spoke on the phone daily, they didn't see each other much during December.

The excitement of the 25th left Jessie content to stay with her grandparents on Boxing Day while Matt and Amy enjoyed a private Christmas celebration. He flew in after spending the holiday with his family and drove directly to the apartment. "Oh wow, it smells good in here!" he said, as he stepped through the door. He breathed in deeply. "It's the sage."

She served another turkey dinner by candlelight at her small table.

"This is so good," Matt said. "Don't tell my mother but it's better than the meal she served yesterday."

Amy grinned. "You sure know how to pour it on."

"Hey, I'm not lying. This is the best dinner I've ever had."

As soon as Matt opened Amy's gift, he pulled the dark red shirt over his t-shirt and wore it for the rest of the evening. She promised to wear the champagne-coloured cashmere sweater with the coordinating pashmina the next time they went out.

As time passed Amy began to wonder if Marge was right—that Matt could truly accept her scarring. She remained on alert though, wanting to be prepared if he broke it off.

When January took Jessie back to school, Matt suggested Amy stay at his place for a weekend. "What d'ya say?"

"I'd love that."

Matt arrived Saturday morning in his truck. The blustery wind blew snow across the road, reducing visibility.

"I don't know how you're managing to stay out of the ditch," Amy said. "Going forward we need to do our visiting at my place since I don't have a car and can't do my share of the driving back and forth."

"I can fix that. I have an extra vehicle ya know."

"Yeah, that's not gonna happen."

About an hour into their drive Matt asked if she was hungry.

"Don't stop on my account. I had a good breakfast before we left." He didn't need to know that her good breakfast consisted

From Thorns

of a single banana since her nerves had rallied a little chaos in her gut.

"Do you mind if we stop? I didn't plan for anything back at the house. You know I can't really cook."

She smiled. "You make fantastic pancakes."

Matt pulled off at the next road stop. Amy enjoyed a coffee while he devoured a club sandwich. They were back on the road for another hour when he announced, "We're almost there. Bad weather has made it a long drive."

At the end of a short road, Matt pulled onto his driveway.

She felt her nerve ends firing as she stared at the sprawling property ahead of her. "You never told me you lived in a place like this. I never expected..."

"I was afraid to tell you. I didn't want to scare you off. The house looks impressive, but it's just a house."

"Are you kidding? I can't be with someone who has all this."

"That's what I was afraid of. Why can't you be with someone who has all this?"

"Don't you get it Matt? I don't have anything to offer or contribute. I love you, I really do, but this is too much. You deserve way better than me. If you don't see it now, you will. And I don't want to be around when you do."

"I don't even know where to start. What makes you think I'm better than you because I have a big house? We've come a long way. We've gotten over some pretty significant hurdles. You knew I had money; what kind of house were you expecting?"

"The big house, the fancy car, this truck. All a result of what you've accomplished. You're running your own company. You invent stuff. The world looks up to you, and rightly so. I've accomplished nothing."

Matt sighed. "It's cold out here."

Does he want me to drop this and toddle on inside? Amy wondered. Not happening.

"Look at me, Amy. You're wrong. I'm more impressed with what you've accomplished than anyone else I know, least of all me. I don't understand why you can't see it. Look at where you came from and all you've been through. I came from a loving home. My parents encouraged me and put me through school. Even when I changed direction and decided to drop philosophy, they encouraged and supported me. They believed in me. And I agree, I've done well with the opportunities I was given. You, on the other hand, were tortured and abandoned. And look at where you are today. I respect you so much."

"I was pregnant at sixteen," Amy scoffed. "I'm supposed to be proud of that?"

His voice took on an impatient tone. "Yes, you had a child in unfortunate circumstances. You could have abandoned her and given up on life."

"I almost did."

"But in the end, you didn't. How many times have you wanted to plan something with me but you stayed home for Jessie's sake? Let me tell you about some of my colleagues. They also have big houses and cool cars. And they have children. And those kids are being raised by hired help so the parents can earn lots of money and spend their evenings at galas and travel the world. Many of those children are spoiled disobedient brats. Now you tell me—who's successful? You or them? Who should be proud—you or them?"

Silence.

"You know Amy, I don't *deserve* this house. I make a lot of

From Thorns

money because society values what I do and people are willing to pay a lot for my product. But I'm not any more deserving than anyone else."

More silence.

"I want to be able to give to you, to share what I have with you. I don't know how I'm supposed to do that with all this resistance." He opened the car door. "I'd like to show you my house. And I'd like to be able to feel good about it. Are you going to let me?"

"Matthew Argyle! That is *such* a manipulative thing to say. The way I feel is the way I feel. If you can't handle it, that's your issue not mine. Should I apologize for my feelings?"

A sheepish expression swept the annoyance off his face as he closed the car door.

"I wish I could be exactly what you'd like me to be," Amy said, "to feel what you want me to feel. But I'm not, and I don't. I'm uncomfortable with your wealth. Your perspective, generous as it is, cannot simply be applied to me and absorbed like paint on drywall. You've earned this. I haven't. For me, it's as simple as that."

Matt stared into his lap.

She continued, "Look, I appreciate everything you've said. You make me feel good about myself. Nonetheless, I don't have the qualifications to be able to earn a good wage. You earned this and I can't contribute anything. That's reality and I feel undeserving. If you want honesty in our relationship, don't belittle my feelings!"

Matt raised his eyes to hers. "You're right. Once again, you're right. And I might add at this point, that you've come a long way in a short time. That was quite a tongue lashing."

She couldn't suppress a grin.

"Please forgive me and let me try again.

"Although you are uncomfortable, I'm very proud of my home and I'm anxious to show it off. I would like it if you'd be willing to accompany me for the grand tour even though I know you're going to find it hard." He held out his hand toward her. "Was that better?" The genuine expression on his face tore through her defensive wall.

As she got out of the car she felt weak. Matt saw a strength that wasn't real. The knowledge born from all the studying she'd done on healthy communication had not buried itself in her psyche. She hoped she wouldn't fall apart and start apologizing for everything she'd said.

CHAPTER 55

"This house is well planned. I don't see how the layout could be improved. And the colours, the lighting, the furnishings..."

"I'd love to take credit," Matt said, "but an architect and decorator figured it out."

"What about the art? I feel like I'm in a gallery similar to the one Jessie and I visited on the island."

Matt shrugged. "I chose some of it."

The five-bedroom house hosted three bathrooms on the upper level. The master bedroom housed one of them, along with a huge closet. "You're not filling this very well," Amy said.

"I have to leave room for your clothes." He winked.

On the main level, expensive-looking furniture decorated the large living room. A gorgeous bouquet of flowers sat on a coffee table. Amy stuck her nose into the arrangement. "Mmm, lovely."

"Those are going home with you," Matt said.

She cocked her head to one side. "Thank you. You're so good to me."

A table with ten chairs filled the adjacent dining room. Candles, art, and lamps accentuated the furnishings. Amy didn't like the light fixture—the style of the furniture required something more modern—but she kept her thoughts to herself, remembering how Tommy had reacted to her suggestions.

When they moved into the kitchen she said, "Oh my goodness, this is amazing."

"Someone comes in to cook and clean for me." Matt scrunched up his nose. "I'm kinda spoiled."

The kitchen expanded into another seating area with two loveseats.

He opened the door to the yard. Amy pulled the blanket from the loveseat and wrapped it around her shoulders. There was a pool and hot tub, both closed up for the winter. Matt tried to explain where the gardens were located but after a few minutes they decided to wait for spring.

I hope we'll still be together come spring, Amy thought.

An office, powder room, and laundry room occupied the rest of the main floor. The laundry room was the size of Jessie's bedroom. Matt explained a closeted laundry facility had been built upstairs should someone need the ground floor area for a sixth bedroom. Since he didn't need the extra space, and he liked having his laundry area out of the way so he could leave clothes lying around, he had decided to have the room equipped for the washer and dryer.

Amy remembered Tommy's messiness and wondered if all men were the same.

Matt led her down another flight of stairs to his favorite space which included a pool table and a home theatre. His excitement shone during his explanation of various aspects of the construction and the built-in technology.

As the sun made its way toward the horizon, they settled

From Thorns

onto a soft leather sofa in the living room and watched the fire dance. Matt lit the candles on the mantel and hearth and the scent of sweet apples filled the air.

Amy tucked her feet in behind her and reached for one of the large cushions. For some reason being able to hug it tight and hide behind it helped her relax.

"How are you feeling?" Matt asked.

"I'm not overwhelmed anymore. The initial shock of seeing your property has worn off." She smiled. "Thank you for being patient."

He laughed. "I didn't have much choice."

"True enough," Amy said. "Oh Matt, I'm loving our times together and my love for you is growing. I need to tell you that my fear is growing as well. I keep expecting you to wake up one day, give your head a shake, and call this whole thing off."

"Why do you love me?" he asked.

"Well, that's easy. You're kind, considerate, compassionate, easy to talk with, intelligent, funny, honest, and you love God. I had a hard time believing in God but I've gotten there and I wouldn't want to share my life with someone who wasn't on the same page."

"Hmm, you didn't mention my house or my job or my money. Doesn't that matter?"

"Matt! How could you say such a thing? You know that I don't care about any of this." Her arm swept across the room.

"So why am I not allowed to feel the same way as you?"

"What do you mean?"

"You don't care about what I bring to the relationship materially. I don't care what you bring materially. You love me for who I am, for the connection we have. I love you for who you are and the happiness you bring to me." He grinned. "I have to admit, I especially love that you're such a good cook and that you enjoy feeding me. And you know I love your beauty."

"You're very good at making your point but c'mon, wealth and possessions do matter."

"I know. But it matters way more than it should. We don't know what the future holds. Maybe God wants to give you the opportunity to develop your talent, maybe go back to school or open your own business. I could help with that."

"If you have an expectation that I'm going to blossom into a successful businesswoman, we're in serious trouble."

Matt moved across the sofa and pulled her close. "I love you exactly as you are. All I'm saying is that I know you could do anything you set your mind to. You have more talent than any one person could possibly use in their lifetime. So if you decide that you want to take a course to fine-tune a skill or learn something new I'll stand with you and support you in whatever way I can."

She was distracted by the suggestions they were both uttering of being together forever.

"I love you, Amy Peterson. I love you for your compassion and determination. As a successful, well-off businessman, I've had many women show interest in me, but I want you."

A few men had shown interest in her, but not many. "Really, you've had opportunities to be with other women but you weren't interested?"

"Of course! After Suzanne died several women approached me." He arched his eyebrows. "I had realized some success by then."

"But I knew I needed time to heal and I knew I never stopped

From Thorns

loving you. And I wanted a strong independent partner who loved me for *me*, not for my money. You know how my learning disability leads to some inappropriate reactions. I need someone who understands me, accepts me, and is willing to support me when I need it. I found that in you." Matt pushed back and looked into her eyes. "Remember our first few times together at that coffee shop after Adventure Club? What a disaster!"

Amy laughed.

"You helped me in ways you probably aren't aware of. You prepared me to meet the family, and especially Steve, by suggesting things to talk about and subjects to avoid. My learning disability is a huge problem in social situations—who knows how I might have behaved and what crazy things I might have said if you hadn't coached me."

The doorbell rang. "Back in a minute." After a brief conversation, Matt ushered a man and a woman into the kitchen.

"They're fabulous cooks," he whispered upon his return. "Not better than you but I wanted a weekend with no chores or distractions. Wait 'til you see the dessert they brought!"

The living room filled with delicious aromas and soon they were invited into the dining room where the appetizer awaited. "Thank you," Matt said. "Amy, meet Shawn and Siân."

"Really?" Amy said. "You're both named Sean?"

"Yup," Siân replied. "Now please sit and enjoy the meal."

They ate by candlelight, savouring a bottle of Matt's favourite wine with soft music playing in the background.

Following dinner they relaxed in the living room. When a love song played Matt pulled Amy to her feet, wrapped his arms around her, and moved to the music.

Eventually fatigue stole their energy and they headed

upstairs. Amy climbed into the queen size bed with its light blue satin sheets. Knowing Matt was just across the hall filled her with desire. And respect. He could have pulled her into his room but he was willing to continue waiting.

Unless it's my scars, she panicked. Distress got in the way of a peaceful descent into pleasant dreams.

The sun, peeking through an opening in the blinds and landing on Amy's face, woke her. She opened the blinds allowing the sun's brilliance to flood the room. Now she could digest what she had seen only briefly the day before. Beautiful antique furniture against pale blue walls. The rocking chair had a quilt hanging over the back. As she moved toward the chair to examine the quilt she heard footsteps and hopped back into bed.

"Can I come in?" Matt called through the door.

"Sure."

He sat on the edge of the bed. "How did you sleep?"

"Very well. My bed is nowhere near as comfortable. I wish I could take this mattress home with me."

"That can be arranged."

Amy laughed. "I think the bed should stay right here." Her demeanour changed. "Are you ever going to want to sleep with me? I mean, with all scarring."

He walked to the other side of the bed and climbed in. "When I got into bed last night I wanted you bad. But neither of us wants to let the wrong things get in the way of building what's important for a lasting relationship. Right?"

"Yeah. I just worry."

"It's okay. Someday you'll be confident in my love and my desire for every inch of you."

From Thorns

She lifted his arm and placed it around her shoulders. He pulled her close and ran his fingers through her hair as they continued talking.

"Last night I thought about our day together," Matt said, as though they hadn't just talked about something terrifying to Amy. "I'm so impressed at how you stand up for yourself. You're a lot different from the timid girl I met at church a few years back. I was wondering, did something specific happen during our time apart that prompted the change?"

"Did you get some sleep in between all that thinking?"

"I did. Is that your way of dismissing my question?"

"No." Amy looked away.

"On my birthday, before I left Tommy, he gave me an ornament. It was something I'd admired so I should've loved it but I didn't trust him anymore. The ornament led to a story forming in my mind and I realized I was trapped. That I had drawn Jessie into the trap. We were stuck and there was no easy way out. And then I realized I had created the trap and I knew I *had* to break out for Jessie's sake if not my own.

"From that point on I made up my mind to fight harder against the internal voices of my parents and stand up for myself."

"So when I knew you before," Matt said, "you were holding onto those messages?"

"When I lived with the Raynors I started crawling out of that dark pit but I got swept back into the cycle of abuse with Tommy. What's interesting is, although I felt miserable in that relationship I was comfortable there. It's what I knew and understood. With the Raynors I felt like I didn't belong. Like I wasn't good enough. Even though I had made progress and started to think that maybe I was okay after all, in my heart I didn't believe it.

So jumping off a raft I was unsure of and into Tommy's boat was easy."

"Seriously?" Matt whispered.

"There's no way you can understand unless you've been there. Someone who comes from abuse doesn't usually feel comfortable in a healthy relationship even though it's what we want. You remember how I struggled when we were first together?" Amy shrugged. "At the end of the day, although I loved you, I was more comfortable with Tommy."

"Whew," Matt said, "it's a lot to process."

"Please don't hate me."

Matt looked at her with an incredulous expression. "I have so much respect for you! Where would hate even come from? Now, let's get up."

He whipped up an omelette. "I can do breakfast but don't ask me to take on anything else."

"I'd love to prepare all my meals in this amazing kitchen," Amy said.

Matt grinned. "That can be arranged."

Following a second cup of coffee he asked if she would like to meet his brother. "He lives close by. He works for my company and we're good friends and he'd love to meet you. No pressure."

"Are you sure it's a good idea? What if we break up next week?"

"Is there something you need to tell me?"

"No, but what if . . . "

"Anything's possible. What does that have to do with meeting my brother?"

Greg looked like Matt in his facial expressions but their colouring and builds differed. It was obvious they shared a close friendship

From Thorns

in the way they bantered with each other. "He's awesome," Amy reflected after he left.

"I have a feeling he thinks the same about you. Ya know what? My sister, Rachel, is gonna be jealous that he got to meet you before she did."

CHAPTER 56

With less-than-ideal winter driving conditions, they decided not to plan anymore weekends at Matt's until the weather calmed. Instead, they hung out at her place on the evenings Amy didn't work. But after a few weeks Matt said, "I wanna take you to my place on your days off so we can have more time. I know we can't count on weather forecasts but I don't care. I've checked with Marge and she said she's been missing Jessie's sleepovers and loves the idea of having her for longer stays."

"Marge, Marge, Marge." Amy shook her head. "Always giving. I guess she didn't mention that Jess stays overnight every time I do a shift at the restaurant."

"Oh. No, she didn't mention that."

"I'll understand if we spend less time together during the thick of winter. All this driving in blowing snow is too much."

"No way," Matt said. "I can handle the drive."

Time dragged—too many hours between get-togethers. By now it felt like they'd always been a couple. So one day when Matt casually said, "I think I wanna marry you," and Amy replied,

From Thorns

"Are you sure?" lines formed across his forehead. "I can't believe you just said that."

"I love you," she said, "and I dream of spending the rest of our lives together. I guess I still have a hard time believing you really want me. I'm sorry. I guess that's not very trusting, is it?"

"Correct. I need you to know, deep down, through and through, in your head and in your heart, that I love you. You. Only you. I don't want to ever be with anyone else ever again."

"Okay. Got it."

"So I think it's time we brought Jessie into our relationship," Matt said.

"I've been thinking the same thing and I have an idea. Let's arrange a dinner with Marge and Steve. That way Jess is surrounded by people she feels safe with. If she's not comfortable seeing you and me together she can tell Marge who will get her talking, and that should help us sort things out. What do you think?"

"Brilliant!"

When Amy asked Marge she clapped her hands. "Wonderful idea!"

"I miss you Marge. Once Jessie's brought into the picture we'll be able to do things as a family."

"I miss you too my sweet girl, but you need time with Matt to really get to know each other."

"Do you feel like I'm using you like it was with Tommy?"

"Not at all. Steve and I adore Jess. We can't get enough of her—she keeps up entertained.

"I see a good relationship growing. And anyway, love wants what's best for the other person."

Amy laughed. "Another one of your *love is, love wants, love thinks* statements."

Marge smiled. "Really? I didn't know I said that. I must say it without thinking."

Amy called Matt to let him know a plan was in place. "I have an idea that might stack the deck in our favour."

"What is it?"

"Awhile back you mentioned getting a dog. Were you serious?"

"At the time, yes. But I realized he would be alone a lot and that's not fair to the animal."

"Ah, too bad," Amy said. "Jessie loves dogs. If you had one that you could've brought along for the first meeting, I think it would've helped."

Matt didn't respond. After a few moments he said, "I guess I could bring him to work, and if I could bring him to your place when we get together . . ."

"For sure you can bring him."

"I love the idea! Is it okay if I choose him on my own? We don't have a lot of time before the big meeting."

"Of course! I'll look forward to being surprised."

CHAPTER 57

The next time Matt drove to Amy's he brought a dog. "He's a rescue pet. The poor thing was mistreated by his previous owner but the pound has been working with him and they assured me he was ready to go. I've been playing with him for a couple of days—he's great—super gentle and he even listens when I tell him to sit. I was going to get a puppy but it would have taken ages to get one from a breeder. And anyway, there are too many animals waiting for adoption."

Amy froze. "He's adorable," she said, from the floor where she scratched his ears.

"What should we call him?"

Amy shrugged. "He's your dog. You decide."

"Are you okay?"

"Actually, I think you should go."

Silence.

"Because of the dog?" Matt said.

"No. I'm just, well, I need some time."

"I don't understand."

"I need you to give me some space," Amy snapped.

Matt slammed the door on his way out.

She called Marge in tears. "Cancel dinner with Matt. It's over."

"Would you like to talk about it?"

"Not right now."

An hour later there was a knock on the door.

Matt burst in, red-faced, with the dog in tow. "What's the matter with you? The dog was *your* idea! You can't just kick me out without any explanation."

Amy knew her face wore signs of crying but Matt showed no concern. "I just need some time," she said.

"Well you can't have it. I deserve better."

Amy dropped onto the couch and buried her head in her hands. When she looked up Matt stood across the room with his arms crossed.

"I'm feeling concerned about your choice of a *rescue* pet. It makes me wonder if I'm a *rescue* girlfriend."

Matt sank to the floor and pulled the dog into a cuddle, his cheeks a shade redder. "The *last* thing you are is some kind of a rescue project." He shook his head. "Haven't we had enough time together for you to be confident in our relationship? I love you. I want to be with you because I love you. It's as simple and as complex as that. I loved you before I knew anything about your past. I continue to love you as the layers peel away. The dog is *a dog*. No comparison!"

Amy nodded.

"I'm going," Matt said. This time he didn't slam the door.

He called the next day. "Are you okay?"

"Yes. And I'm sorry for how I reacted. You're right; you deserve better."

"I had to sort through my feelings," Matt said. "It hurt. Your

From Thorns

lack of trust shocked me. This is the first time I've wondered about us. If you can't feel my love and trust it I dunno what to say."

"Of course I feel your love. But the inner voices still yell at me. 'You're worthless. You're ugly. Who would want you?' Sure, I push back. But when you brought the dog, the voices won. I wish I could tell you it'll never happen again but I can't."

Silence.

"I've come a long way," she continued.

"I know," Matt said. "But now I have to ask you to do something. I *need* you to communicate better."

After a moment of stunned silence Amy managed, "Geez, Matt. I think I do pretty well."

"I need you to tell me what you're hearing, feeling, and thinking instead of shutting down. If you trusted me, you could have told me what you felt when I said the word *rescue*."

"Okay, now listen," Amy said. Then, "Never mind. This is a bottle of wine conversation."

"Should I come now? Or would you rather wait a few days?"

"If you're up to it, come now. I hate when things are unresolved."

How am I gonna face him? He would never shrink to my level. He has no idea what I feel. There's no way he can relate. I don't care what he says or how much he really does love me, he's gonna see me as a loser.

So I can't let him know how I'm feeling. Yet he just said he wants to know my feelings.

She called Marge to ask for advice.

"Matt needs to know what's happening when it's going to affect your relationship. Like with the dog. You retreated into a cocoon and sent Matt packing. He couldn't handle it so he wants you to tell him what you're feeling. That doesn't mean you have to tell him *every* negative thought or feeling, every fear, every doubt."

Amy thought for a few moments before saying, "I'm confused."

"In my opinion, Matt doesn't need to know you're feeling like a loser. In this situation your reaction had nothing to do with feeling like a loser. He does need to know what led you to shut down because that impacts him directly. Does that make sense?"

Amy sighed. "I think so. Thank you, Marge."

Her gut tied itself into knots while she waited.

When Matt arrived he pulled her into a hug, held her tight, and whispered, "I love you."

That did nothing to relieve the knots but now she knew he hadn't arrived with anger.

While hanging up his jacket and then pouring wine they talked about traffic and weather.

"I'd like to jump right into it if that's okay," Amy said.

Matt reached across the couch, squeezed her hand, and then sat back. "Let's do it."

She took a deep breath. "I understand how I hurt you and I understand how my reaction must have felt unfair, like I didn't trust you. The thing is, when the old messages yell at me sometimes they entrap me. Like a tall wire fence wraps around me and pulls so tight that my flesh is forced through the holes making me bleed. I panic and I can't think."

Matt stared.

"What are you thinking?" Amy asked.

"I'm thinking I don't know what to say." He picked up the wine bottle and studied the label.

From Thorns

"I want to be able to tell you what I'm feeling in those horrible situations," Amy said, "but I don't know if I'll be able to."

"I understand," Matt said.

Amy looked into his eyes. "Seriously? You want me to believe you understand?"

Matt's face reddened. "I'm *trying*! Cut me some slack."

"Sorry." No one spoke for a few minutes.

"I've been thinking about how we should look at this," Amy said, "and a highway image came to mind.

"I think we're at a roadblock but not an impasse. Roadblocks take time and effort to clear. But they do clear. An impasse means you can't go any further. You have to turn back."

"Don't look at me." Matt shrugged. "Roadblocks, impasses?"

"I'll get to the point."

"Good."

"I can't think when the voices get too loud and I shut down. You can't handle when I shut down without explaining. We're at a roadblock.

"If I said something like, 'I'm feeling sick; I need to be alone,' would that clear the road?"

After much discussion they agreed Amy wouldn't be able to think during a panic attack. But in a severe reaction like what happened with the word *rescue*, Matt could ask if panic was happening.

Amy nodded. "Yeah, that would probably work."

They had a place to start.

CHAPTER 58

A couple of days before the scheduled family dinner, Amy began to fret. She tried to remember what it had been like with Tommy before they lived together. How could she know if she was playing a mind game with herself as she had with Tommy? She asked for Marge's opinion. "Do you see similarities between Tommy and Matt?"

"Well, they're both male." Marge studied the ceiling. "That's about it."

Amy laughed. "I'm serious."

"Tommy was secretive, negative, and tried to convince you that your family stood against you. Does Matt?"

"No. But I don't trust myself."

"I remember the times he joined us for meals back before that Tommy creature. We had good times. Matt easily joined our conversations and even helped Steve around the house. Let's see how our dinner goes. Then we can reassess. Okay?"

"Okay." Amy grinned. "Thanks for helping, *Mom*."

"Ohhh . . . I love that. Will you start calling me Mom from now on?"

From Thorns

"Probably not. Jessie would wonder. But we both know that you've become my mother."

Amy waited until the day of the dinner itself to tell Jessie.

"I think I remember him," Jessie said. "He used to play with me and Rumble."

Although highly unlikely that she remembered Matt playing with her as a one-year-old, Amy was glad for the positive response.

"He's still lots of fun," Amy said. "And now he has a dog!"

"What's his name?"

"He doesn't have a name yet. Matt wants *you* to name him."

"Will he bring the dog tonight?"

"Yup. Now go get dressed."

They made their way to Marge's in time for Amy to help with dinner. Jessie bounced in and out of the kitchen asking, "When will he get here?" At the sound of the doorbell, she ran.

"Hi," Matt said. She was entirely focussed on the dog so he stepped around her and closed the door. "Smells wonderful in here. Roast beef?"

"Jessie!" Amy barked. "Say hello to our guest."

"Hi," she said glancing up.

"It's fine," Matt said looking at Amy. Then to Jessie, "I think he likes you."

"What kinda dog is it?"

"He's a mix. Pretty handsome isn't he?"

Jessie grinned. "Yeah. Can I take him to meet Rumble?"

"Have you thought of name for him?"

"I'll decide after I play with him."

Fifteen minutes later when she came into the house with

both dogs she announced, "I'm naming him Ranger."

The evening heard good conversation, laughter, and Matt discussing his business and whatever all else with Steve. Amy felt reassured Matt's relationship with Marge and Steve would be nothing like Tommy's. Although Ranger got his name they hadn't accomplished the evening's intention. Jessie had devoted her attention entirely to the dog (leaving Rumble a little depressed). "Ranger was supposed to provide a positive reinforcement to the visit not completely take over," Amy said.

"Maybe it's for the best. If she associates me with Ranger it can only work in my favour."

After they decided to bring Jessie to Matt's the following weekend, he looked across the table and said, "Why don't you two join us?"

"Oh no, we don't want to intrude."

"You won't be intruding," Matt assured.

"I think it could be helpful to have you with us," Amy said, "in case Jessie has any moments of shyness or discomfort in seeing me with Matt."

Arrangements were made.

"Wow! Do you live here? Mom, could we get a house like this?"

Aren't kids great? No inhibitions. They just say what's on their minds with all their feelings and thoughts on display.

"Yup, that's my house," Matt said. "Do you wanna see inside? Ranger's waiting for you. And by the way, he loves his new name. I don't think he liked it when I called him Dawg." He winked at Amy.

The home theatre and games room called not only Jessie, but also Steve. Marge and Amy took their time preparing dinner on

From Thorns

Friday giving the kids, big and small, lots of time to play video games. Laughter and loud voices frequently interrupted their quiet conversation.

"Dinner's ready," Marge called to the rec room. Then to Amy, "We better keep everything warm until we hear them on the stairs."

"This is amazing," Matt said after his first bite.

"I agree!" Steve said. "I encourage you ladies to cook together more often."

Jessie had one focus. "What are we gonna do after dinner?"

She fell asleep before the movie ended.

Saturday's weather took everyone outside kicking a soccer ball, throwing sticks for Ranger, and hiking a nearby trail. Amy handed a bag to Jessie. "It's your turn to pick up the poop."

"Gross!"

"If you want a dog, you have to take responsibility," Amy said as Jessie ran ahead.

They enjoyed their first barbeque of the season before the sun set, and Jessie got another movie night.

In the morning they attended Matt's church followed by a quick lunch back at the house.

"C'mon Jessie," Amy called when they were ready to leave. "Gramma and Grampa are waiting."

"Why can't I have my own dog?" a teary Jessie said as she came from the kitchen with Ranger on her heels.

"Do ya wanna take him?" Matt whispered in Amy's ear.

"No!"

Looking back to Jessie Amy said, "You'll get your own dog someday."

Jessie scowled. "Someday, someday, that's what you

always say."

Amy sighed and looking at Matt said, "And here I thought the dog was a good idea." She shook her head. "It's more than the dog. You've spoiled her this weekend. She's likely going to expect this much fun every time we visit."

"I'm not sure who had more fun, her or me. Now *that* should give you something to worry about!" He ushered everyone to the car.

Jessie reached out the window to wave. "Bye Ranger!"

The weekend alleviated all concern of any possible similarity between a life with Matt and a life with Tommy. Hopefully that fear could now be swept from the crevices of her mind.

They spent the following weekends together with Jessie. They visited a zoo, went bike riding, and Matt taught her how to skateboard. In between outdoor activities Matt played video games with, and read stories to, Jessie and Ranger.

A visit to Matt's parents introduced Carl and Jan who were as friendly and welcoming as Marge and Steve. Jan served a delicious beef stew after Jessie announced her state of starvation. Over the weekend Amy spent enough time with Matt's sister, Rachel, to know they could be friends if life allowed their paths to connect.

On Easter Friday after Jessie fell asleep, Amy and Matt hid plastic eggs containing chocolate in the park across from Amy's apartment. When Jessie awoke Saturday morning, Matt handed her a list of clues that led her to the park. For the first time she got annoyed with Ranger who destroyed too many eggs before Matt put him on a leash.

"Geez, I never thought about the dumb dog. Chocolate's poison for him. I'm calling the vet." Matt stormed off while

From Thorns

lecturing the dog who didn't look particularly concerned about anything except the chocolate he would miss out on.

At the end of May they celebrated Amy's twenty-fourth birthday at Matt's place. Marge arrived early to get dinner started. Steve, with Jason and his girlfriend, Taylor, were happy to spend the afternoon by the pool. Jason and Taylor met at university and had been together for several months. She flew in for a weekend visit earlier that day. Kate and her new boyfriend, Peter, drove in later with Amy and Jessie. As they walked along the side of the house toward the yard, laughter and loud voices replaced the sound of the birds singing.

The kitchen and dining room doors were open at the edge of the cobblestone patio. Amy popped into the kitchen to drag Marge outside while the others walked straight to the pool.

"Hey Jessie," Matt shouted. "Get your bathing suit on and c'mon in."

"With Ranger?"

"Ranger has his own pool right over there." Matt pointed to the small plastic pool on the patio.

When Peter, Kate, and Jessie peeled off their outer clothing and jumped in, splashing water everywhere, Steve got out. "Time for a beer." Shortly thereafter Matt and Peter joined him at the barbeque and a delicious smell wafted over the pool. "What's for dinner," Jason hollered.

"Why don't you come join us and then you'll see," Steve called back.

"I can't leave Taylor alone with Amy and Kate. Who knows what kind of stories they might tell."

While the men laughed, Kate put her arm around Taylor's

shoulder. "I'm dying to have some time alone with her. We promise not to reveal too much."

Amy grinned. "Moo-ha-ha."

"Don't believe a word they say," Jason said as he climbed out of the pool.

Marge sat at the edge of the pool with Amy, their legs dangling in the water.

After a yummy meal Kate delivered the cake with candles burning. "I made it. I decided I need to learn how to cook."

"This icing. It's *so good*," Amy said. Kate looked at Peter who promptly acknowledged the icing and said the cake was the best he'd ever tasted. Following dessert Amy opened gifts. Matt's was last. "Are they real pearls?" Kate asked.

"You bet," Matt said.

"I'm so happy to see you treating her the way she deserves," Kate said while everyone looked at Amy, nodding. "Let's move on," Amy said with flushed cheeks. When conversation resumed, she leaned into Matt. "Thank you for such a beautiful, generous gift."

After everyone left and Jessie fell asleep, Matt and Amy relaxed on a wicker loveseat facing the fire pit.

"I feel like I haven't had any time alone with you over the past few months," Matt said. "Our time has revolved around activities with Jessie which has been fun, but I'm missing *you*. How about I take you to that seafood restaurant we enjoyed so much on our first official date eight months ago?"

"Wonderful idea!"

CHAPTER 59

She wore the same outfit she'd worn on their first date. He remembered! They walked to the restaurant, enjoying the evening sun.

Out on the patio while sharing a seafood dip they reminisced, remembering the difficult times along with the magical. "I'm sure glad my fear didn't destroy what we've got."

"So am I," Matt said, emphatically.

"I know it was hard on you, tippy-toeing around my issues."

"We've both had our challenges," he said, "and there will be more ahead. But for now let's enjoy the time we have all to ourselves."

The pace of course delivery provided a slow, drawn-out evening. Matt ordered an expensive bottle of wine, insisting it offered the best compliment to their food. "Can you see how it enhances the taste of your salmon?"

"Not really. You know I don't have experience with food and wine pairing."

Matt grinned. "We're gonna fix that."

When their plates were empty they enjoyed the remaining wine, slowly, holding hands and staring into each other's eyes.

A single rose alongside her carrot cake decorated the dessert plate. Amy looked at Matt, puzzled. "That's different."

He smiled, and then moved around the table and got down on one knee.

She felt her face flush as butterflies rushed into her gut.

"Will you marry me?"

She threw her hands over her mouth as tears welled in her eyes. She choked out "Yes," while surrounding patrons cheered.

"It's beautiful!" The platinum ring with a solitary diamond in a setting that looked like a rose, mounted on a band covered in small diamonds, was far too grand for Amy.

"I wanted to buy you a bigger diamond but I knew you'd have a fit."

On a tear stained face, a smile appeared. "I love it."

"August 15th?" Matt asked. "The date is pre-approved by Marge and Steve."

"You told them you were going to propose? How did they react?"

"Actually, I asked Steve for your hand. He didn't hesitate to give the go-ahead." Matt grinned. "I think he likes me."

Amy nodded.

"I know there's a lot to be done in a short amount of time, but this way Jessie can start her year at the new school. I'm sorry we can't live here but I need to be close to my office and I'm pretty sure Jess loves the house with the theatre and the dog. I want you to know I appreciate your willingness—"

"Please stop talking," Amy said. "We can start planning tomorrow. But tonight I want to bask in the moment. I am so in love with you! I can't believe how blessed I am."

"I can't believe how blessed *I am*. Thank you for agreeing

From Thorns

to be my wife."

He pulled her into his arms and kissed her passionately, bringing another round of cheers from the surrounding tables.

"Oh Amy, it's gorgeous!" Marge said. "Were you involved in designing it?"

"No. I had no idea he was going to propose. I mean, I knew that was the direction we were headed but I wasn't expecting it yet. And this ring—it's beautiful but it's too much."

Marge shook her head, "It's *not* too much. God has blessed you with a man who understands your worth. I'm glad he wants to spoil you."

Amy wrapped her arms around Marge. "Thank you for being a wonderful mother, for loving Jessie and me, for giving us a home, and for forgiving an awful lot."

"It's been a privilege to share in your journey. I hope, someday, you'll be able to appreciate the joy you and Jessie brought to our family." Her expression changed from serious to playful. "Now, we have a wedding to plan."

Amy's eyes grew large. "And we have less than three months!"

Kate and Matt's sister, Rachel, eagerly agreed to be bridesmaids. Matt asked his brother, Greg, and Jason to stand with him. Jessie would be the flower girl standing with her mother during the ceremony.

"Can Ranger sit beside me at the front?" Jessie pleaded.

"He can be with you at your wedding but not at mine," Amy replied.

"Please Mom."

"No."

Amy wanted the wedding and reception to take place in Matt's backyard and Marge offered to look after all the arrangements. When Matt's mom, Jan, learned of Marge's role she muttered, "Sounds like you're in good hands."

Amy asked Marge to reach out. "I know she lives too far away to be part of everything. But she can help with some of it."

"Wonderful idea. This will give us a chance to get to know each other."

Marge, Jan, Rachel, and Kate accompanied Amy to bridal shops in search of a dress.

"It needs more lace."

"I liked the last one better."

"You need a different cut to show off your beautiful neck."

"That one makes you look too short."

Eventually Amy went out on her own, found the dress, and invited the committee to a viewing. Everyone agreed that Amy's choice suited her perfectly.

The bridesmaids chose mid-calf sleeveless mauve dresses. Marge had a seamstress friend who turned floral fabric into a dress for Jessie. The leftover fabric became ties for the men.

Kate took Amy lingerie shopping. "I'll never be comfortable on our honeymoon if my back isn't hidden." They found a silky over-jacket that covered Amy's back, arms, and the top of her legs.

"I doubt Matt's going to want you wearing this," Kate said. "But hey, that's yours to deal with."

Invitations went out to family and friends. Suddenly over one hundred people were planning to attend. Thankfully Matt's yard

From Thorns

could accommodate, but how would Marge and Jan manage this many people? Amy called a meeting. "Is it time to bring in a caterer?"

Although disappointed the mothers agreed, but they continued to manage all reception details.

"I'm so glad they're willing," Amy said to Matt. "I could never have juggled it all."

"I'm not sure *willing* is the right word," Matt replied. "They're ecstatic to be in charge."

"Oh Marge, you should see the wedding band Matt bought me. There are diamonds all around the top. And he's already bought me this," Amy said as she raised her ring finger with all its glitter. "But he says he only wants a plain band. I'm sure that's because he doesn't want me trying to afford what he deserves. What should I do?"

"I think you should talk to him."

"I can't do that. He'll just tell me it doesn't matter but that's not right. The least I can do is get him a nice ring but I can't afford what he deserves."

"Honestly, I don't think he cares. Sure he has a big house with all the toys, but I've noticed he doesn't wear jewelry. No watch, no university ring, no chain around his neck. I don't think it's going to matter what his band looks like."

"Well it matters to me."

"Then you need to talk to him."

The following evening after finishing their meal and getting Jessie into bed, Amy took a deep breath. "I need to talk to you about something. This is really hard for me." She started to cry. Dabbing her tears with a tissue, she took another deep breath and looked into his eyes. "We haven't got your wedding band yet and I wanna get you a ring that says *Matt Argyle is the most wonderful man in the world and his wife loves him more than words can say* but I've looked around and I can't afford anything nice and I certainly don't want you to pay for it."

Matt stopped holding his breath. "I thought you were going to tell me you weren't ready for marriage or worse, you've realized I'm not the right man for you. Geez, my heart's pounding."

He stood, pulled her to her feet, and took hold of her shoulders. "I don't care about the band. I just want you. And I expected to pay for both the bands. I never thought you'd want to pick something on your own."

Amy sniffled.

"Can you accept that I don't want anything fancy?" Matt asked. "I would hate anything more than a simple band. I'm not the flashy jewelry type."

No response.

"Right, so I want simple and that's what you can afford. Perfect!"

Continued silence.

Matt pouted. "I feel like you don't believe me."

"I just wanted to be able to spoil you this once the way you spoil me."

Matt laughed. "You're kidding, right? You spoil me every time you make a meal. Every time you make me laugh. Every time you assure me of your love."

Amy shrugged. "I can't help wishing."

The following week they went to the jeweller to get Amy's band sized, and she picked out a ring for him that was plain but classy.

From Thorns

The only part of the wedding Matt insisted on keeping secret was the honeymoon.

"Will we be here for Jessie to start school?" Amy asked.

"I thought of that and yes, we'll be back."

Amy only learned about the two weeks in Hawaii when they got to the airport. It was a place he had never visited so it would be a first for them both, a part of the world they would explore together.

A month before the wedding they met with Pastor Mike to start a brief marriage preparation course.

After the last session Amy asked Marge to go for coffee.

"You know all those times when you said *love is* something or other? Like *love is patient* or *love forgives*? Well last night the pastor read 1 Corinthians 13, the love chapter. He's gonna read it at our wedding. He explained that love has to be about caring enough to forgive and being patient and humble and kind. The evidence of love is in our behaviour. It's not about how we *feel*; it's about how we *act*. So now I finally understand what you meant when you said those things. You were *choosing* to be patient with me, you were *choosing* to be kind, you *chose* to forgive. You may not have felt like it, but you did it for me. That's what love is about, isn't it? It's about choosing to do what's best for the other person even if it's not what you feel like doing."

Marge smiled. "There are different kinds of love. Those feelings you have for Matt are important but yes, you're right, when we choose to do what's best for the other person we're giving them the best of love. It's unselfish, sometimes sacrificial. It isn't about what we want; it's all about the other person. And if you choose that in marriage, where each of you focuses on the other person's needs, you'll have success. I bet that's what Pastor Mike told you."

"That's *exactly* what he said."

"Just remember," Marge warned, "it's not easy. If you ask Steve, he'll tell you I blow it far too often."

CHAPTER 60

"We want your last night as a single woman to be sister-special," Kate said.

"We've got the theatre for the night since Matt's going out with Greg and Jason. Not that he had much choice." Rachel grinned. "His sister knows how to take charge."

"The only question," Kate said, "how late do you want to stay up? That'll determine our start time."

"Since I doubt I'll sleep a wink," Amy said, "it's really more about how much sleep you two need."

The girls met in the theatre at 9:00, in pyjamas, having relaxed with the bath and body products Amy gifted them. With three bathrooms, no one had to rush.

"I love the matching P.J.s you got us," Rachel said when she and Kate descended the stairs to the theatre, "but don't get your hopes set on Matt liking them." Kate and Rachel descended into laughter while Amy just shook her head. "And who's responsible for the new slippers?" The girls looked at each other, puzzled, and then said in unison, "The moms."

"Should we start with *Titanic* or *My Big Fat Greek Wedding*?" Rachel asked. "Kate and I can't agree so you have to decide."

Amy chose *Titanic*. The girls had set up a mimosa table with papaya, pineapple, and orange juices. Before starting the movie, Marge brought in decadent snacks. More than could possibly be consumed. Amy wondered if she'd be able to eat anything since her tummy was doing a gymnastics routine.

At 2:00 in the morning the girls wrapped up.

They had decided to share a room for the night. Once the chatting petered out and Amy heard both girls breathing evenly, she looked to the ceiling and whispered, "Before I walk down that aisle, I want to commit my future to you. All is wonderful now, but life likely has some challenges waiting. Oh God, please remind me to check in with you before taking matters into my own hands. Please give me whatever strength I'm going to need. Thank you for Matt, and please be with us tomorrow and forevermore. Amen."

Early on wedding day, given the sketchy forecast, the caterers set up canopies to provide protection from whatever weather might occur. There would be finger food for everyone to enjoy following the early afternoon ceremony, and later on immediate family would head to a restaurant for dinner. Photos would be taken in the house and yard, weather permitting, during and after the ceremony so the bride and groom wouldn't have to miss any part of the day's festivities.

The women spent their morning getting hair, nails, and makeup done. But Marge and Jan rushed so they could return to supervising set-up activities.

"Please relax," Amy said. "You've worked hard; you've assigned tasks to the men; we know they'll do everything right. I want you to enjoy this time."

From Thorns

Jan and Marge looked at each other. "Sorry Amy, no can do."

At noon the ladies gathered in the master bedroom to get dressed. Marge wanted to stay with Amy until the last minute.

"Geez Mom," Kate said, "the bridesmaids stay with the bride, not the mother."

"Why don't you let Jason usher you to your seat?" Amy encouraged. "I won't run away."

"No, you'll *never* leave us again. In a few minutes you'll belong to Matt, but I know you'll always belong to our family too."

Amy hugged the woman who had become her mother. "I can't believe where I came from, all the terrible mistakes I made along the way, and look at me now. I have a fantastic family, an incredible daughter, and I'm about to marry the most wonderful man in the world. Who would have ever thought?"

"God is good, Amy. God is good."

Kate and Rachel helped the bride make her way down the stairs and to the back of the house.

"Fer the lovapete," Steve said, "what were you girls doing? I thought you were gonna miss the ceremony."

Kate laughed. "Relax Dad. The bride can arrive whenever she wants."

Shortly after the planned start time, Rachel stepped out the door, followed by Kate.

Amy slid her arm through Steve's and they walked along the path, through the shrubbery, and into the open yard where her future husband stood waiting.

Alie Cardet

Coming to the Father, the perfect Father,
Unloading all my burdens at his feet,
I wonder if He cares; is He really listening?
He tells me there's no other love that runs so deep.

I'm scared, I'm hurt, I don't know how to cope.
He tells me to trust Him; He knows what's best;
He wants to end the hurt and make me heal.
But not my way; I have to obey and yield.

I cry out to Him, Lord you don't understand.
You must do something now; I can't take anymore.
Why do you leave me here? Can't you see my pain?
Maybe it's time for me, alone, to fight this war.

Then His gentle voice says, Oh, my precious child,
How long will you fight me? Have I ever let you down?
So much time is wasted in your worry and fear.
Trust me, please trust me, I won't let you drown.

I feel your pain; I hear your cry,
I love you, my child, and I want to lift you high.
So please let me work out my perfect plan,
Which is better than anything you could understand.
It's time to stop groaning and fearing the worst.
Walk with me, lean on me; I won't let you be cursed.

Okay, I'll try, but I might not hear your voice
When I can't see the road or know your planned choice.

Going to the Father, the perfect Father,
It's the only place to find peaceful rest.
He looks after me despite myself.
Thank you God, for taking hold and doing what's best.

ACKNOWLEDGEMENTS

The hard journey of life provided the inspiration for this story. The Word Guild opened a door to the world of writing.

The Ottawa Christian Writers Fellowship offered years of support and enriched my life as a writer. Tim, thank you for trying to teach me long-forgotten grammar. Denyse, Nicole, thank you for giving so much of yourselves.

My Novel Blueprint, a curriculum created by best selling author, Jerry Jenkins, is where I learned the craft of writing. Along with eleven other aspiring writers, I was accepted into Jerry's *Inner Circle* mentoring group where we received coaching and teaching on a variety of topics.

That *Inner Circle* group of twelve, with members from Canada, the United States, and Norway, continues to work together and support each other. I'm grateful for each person and the contributions they've made to my writing.

My husband, John, and family and friends, Joy, Melissa, Andrew, Mary, Donna, Vicki, who read and critiqued along the way provided invaluable feedback.

To our God and Father be glory for ever and ever.
—Philippians 4:20

Printed in Canada